ANOTHER
MOTHERFAKER

WILLOW ASTER

LAURA PAVLOV

To our husbands and kids and dogs for cheering us on the most. We love you so much!

CHAPTER ONE

Caden

I check my reflection in the windows, making sure I'm presentable for my last appointment of the day. The offices of Dubois Designs fill me with a combination of dread and anticipation every time I enter the glass doors and hear the echo of voices bouncing off the marble floor.

But today, something is off.

Susan, the receptionist, runs past me, her silk blouse untucked from her perfectly tailored pants. I've often wondered if there's a dress code to work here because everyone looks like they've stepped out of a movie set.

I hear a screech and see Vivienne Dubois running through, heels in her hand.

"Louie," she yells. Mascara is running down her face.

The hell? Vivienne is the owner of the design company, and when I say I have never seen a hair out of place, I mean the woman's hair wouldn't blow if she was standing next to a helicopter. I look around for Cosette, Vivienne's daughter and the most beautiful woman I've ever seen. Perfection in a petite yet curvy frame, white-blonde hair, violet eyes, and freckles … God, don't get me started on her freckles—

"Louie François Dubois!"

The screech is real and makes every hair on my body stand on end.

Vivienne runs by again, weeping. I think I hear her say something about chocolate, but that can't be right.

"What's happening?" I ask Susan when she stops near her desk to catch her breath. "Who is Louie?"

I'm half expecting a fugitive to dart through the building. A distinguished French cowboy—oh, or maybe French mafia? With that kind of name … the Dubois family has some kind of history with France and they must have a distant cousin who doesn't fit their pristine mold. We all have an unhinged one in the bunch. My brother Gus comes to mind.

I hear wailing and another screech and I'm getting really concerned. I hope Cosette is okay. Clearly, there is a maniac on the loose. I decide to take matters into my own hands since Susan isn't giving me any answers and Vivienne is too distraught.

I walk past the reception desk and tentatively check the conference room. No one is in there. In fact, it seems the office has cleared out. If Vivienne and Cosette let their employees go so they'd be safe, that's really admirable. I look in several of the offices and am to the end of the hall where only Cosette and Vivienne's offices are left.

I'm about to open Cosette's door wider, when out of the corner of my eye, I see something dart past me. I turn and rush through Vivienne's door, and Cosette is inching toward a tiny brown fluff ball.

Too big for a rat. Too small for a dog.

No, wait. I think it *is* a dog.

"Where is Louie? Are you safe?" I move toward her, looking around the spacious office. I check the bathroom, but it's empty, and Cosette is still focused on the dog.

Cosette whispers, "Stay back. He can be violent." She takes a step closer and the dog growls as he digs into whatever he's protecting at all costs. "Louie, it's okay, I'll give you another treat." She makes a little sound with her mouth, trying to coax him away.

I laugh—I can't help it. "*This* is Louie?" I walk up to the dog, ignoring the way he snarls. "Oh, shit, he's eating chocolate. Hold up." I dig in my messenger bag and open my snack for later—a package of beef jerky. I take out a large piece and break it into a few bite-sizes for this little pup, still chuckling. I hold it out toward Louie and he looks up from the chocolate.

When his mouth opens, I choke back my surprise.

Fuck me, he only has three or four teeth at the most. Not sure how violent the little guy can get when he's this tooth-deprived, but I'll take Cosette's word for it. He gives me a snaggletoothed pant, two teeth hanging out of his mostly closed mouth. His tail starts to wag.

"Want this, little guy? It's yours." I carefully hold the jerky out, but far enough that he'll have to move away from the chocolate. He snorts and his little pink tongue lodges between the few teeth he has. He's so pitiful he's cute. He gradually moves toward me and snatches the jerky out of my hand. Cosette moves in and gets the chocolate out of the way, while I give Louie the scoundrel a few more bites of jerky.

A sound at the door makes us all look up, and Vivienne rushes in. I can barely recognize her in there. It's like her long-lost twin, who lived a completely different lifestyle, has arrived and gone H.A.M. on the proper twin. Her shoulders shake as she swoops up the dog. He looks eagerly at me for more treats and tries to squirm out of her arms.

"My poor darling," Vivienne cries. "I don't know if your stomach will take another pumping, but we'll try." She presses her lips together and her eyes close for a second as she gathers her strength.

I look at Cosette for guidance because I'm at a loss here. The most awful sound erupts and Cosette stares at her mother in horror. I turn to look and Louie François Dubois has vomited all over Vivienne's cream linen suit. She's stunned and before she can move him away from her, horrifying things come out the other end of the dog. For a little thing, a lot can certainly come out of him.

The smell is literally gagging.

The Vivienne I've seen—with a confusing accent, more than a little snobby, pretentious, and always, *always* in control—would hand the dog off to Cosette to deal with the mess. But this Vivienne clutches the dog to her, whimpering, "It will be all right, précieux. It will be all right."

And God bless her, she bolts out of there—I guess to rush him to the vet.

It's silent for a few moments after they leave. I'm processing, and Cosette is … looking as gorgeous as ever. She looks at me and smiles, and I ignore the way my heart acts like we're sweating away at a swing dance festival. Not that I can even swing dance, but—

"Sorry for the madness," Cosette interrupts my own madness. Seems to be a common occurrence when I'm around her. She finds a can of Lysol and sprays a few times, wincing. Perhaps the Louie madness is another common occurrence.

I shake my head and make a face. "Are you kidding me? This is the most excitement I've had all day."

She laughs and it's like music. I keep things professional and so does she. We're friends. Tacos come up in our conversations quite often, because who doesn't love tacos? And we've bonded over our love of design. But damn, she's also so fucking pretty. And sweet.

"Do you need to reschedule the meeting? I should've asked that right away. You could've gone with your mom."

She shudders. "*No*. This meeting is a gift. That car ride to the vet is *not* going to be pleasant."

My face curls up along with hers, both revisiting all the disgusting brown spots on Vivienne's cream suit. The smell starting to fade from the room.

Cosette motions for me to sit down and I do, while she turns her computer screen to face us and sits down next to me instead of behind her desk. I catch her faint floral scent and want to stick my nose in her neck and inhale it like I would a bouquet of flowers. I shift uncomfortably in my seat and fiddle with the top of my shirt, needing some air.

Cosette opens up the program she's working on for her designs and I stare at the picture of the boutique hotel my brothers and I have been renovating in New York for months now. It's been a huge undertaking—some would say we've bitten off more than we can chew—but so far, things are going as scheduled and the place is looking fantastic. Our projected unveiling is in three months and we're going to nail that.

Cosette grabs a sketchpad that's sitting on her desk. "My mother would probably have a fit if she knew I was doing this." She clears her throat and looks nervous. "She had another plan for you guys, and it's beautiful. You guys love it and I'm happy with it too—I helped design it, I should love it. But..." She swallows hard and I want to reach out and take her hand to calm her.

"Say it," I encourage her. "You know me well enough by now to know that I'll tell you what I really think."

"Well, I just know it's too late to be coming up with something new, but—" She clutches her neck and I get distracted by the way her pale pink nails look against her black silky shirt. And then she lifts them to tug on her necklace and I imagine her tugging my hair the way she's tugging that chain. Or tugging other things…

Fuck me. I take a deep breath and look at the picture she's holding out.

"Wow, Cosette. This is … this is next level. That is gorgeous."

She's nodding and beaming and looks ecstatic. "It is, isn't it. Inspiration hit me in the middle of the night, and I wasn't even going to show you since we are ready to place orders for everything and have even ordered some things already— which will still totally work with this aesthetic … should you choose to go more in this direction." She shakes her head and closes her eyes. "Not that you would. Please don't feel like you have to, just—"

"Cosette." I reach out and put my hand on her arm and she stills, her lips parting as she stares at me. "This is perfect. I loved the other sketches, but when I look at this, the old one feels too formal. This is alive. It's fresh and it's like I can feel the heartbeat of the room. It. Is. Perfect."

"Ahhhhh. I love you!" she yells. And then looks at me horrified, eyes round and wild. "I did not mean. I mean, I meant it, but not. I mean, you know what I mean."

I laugh so loud that it startles her at first and then she joins in, relieved. "I know what you mean," I assure her. "We have to go this direction. My brothers trust me to make the decisions in this area and I'm telling you, I love it. I really do."

She leans back in her seat, legs stretched out. Her long legs are toned like a dancer and are just the perfect length to—

"My mother will not like this." She sighs. "But I just had to show you anyway."

"I'll insist on using these. They're better." I shrug. "Surely she'll be able to see that."

She shakes her head, sitting upright again. "I'm not so sure about that, but we'll try. Oh, hey…" She reaches out and grabs an envelope that has *The Taylor Family* written on the front. "I've meant to give you this the past two times I've seen you. I hope I'm not too late. I wanted to invite all of you to the opening of my parents' new restaurant this Friday night. Well, my parents and my ex, Jeremy…"

I was tracking until she said ex, Jeremy. And now that's all I got out of that conversation segue. Jeremy, the bastard I met when my brothers, Spence, Gus, and Jesse, and Spence and Jesse's girlfriends, Emma and Mya, and I went to Vegas before we started the hotel renovation. I remember him practically snapping his fingers at Cosette for her to follow and how sad she looked before I went over to talk to her. *Ex.* I like the sound of that. A whole damn lot.

The guy was a real dickshart to Cosette.

"You and Jeremy broke up?" I say like the creep that I am. I can't even inject the slightest bit of sympathy into my voice. I am *thrilled* she dumped that dickloop.

"I actually broke up with him a couple of months ago, but my parents *and* Jeremy can't seem to get it in their heads that I mean it." She smiles again, but this time it's forced.

I get the sense that there is so much she's not saying. Volumes.

"I'll be there and I'll share this with the brothers too."

"Tell them to bring their girlfriends, and you're welcome to bring a date too, of course."

"I will be flying solo," I tell her.

And now I'm distracted by the way her full lips pucker slightly and her icy violet eyes light up.

What a day this has turned out to be.

CHAPTER TWO

Cosette

My head is pounding after a grueling conversation with Jeremy. The man is relentless. For a guy who wasn't faithful, he sure isn't taking the breakup well. I've encouraged him to go play the field, especially since he'd been doing it the entire time we'd been together. That should have hurt me, right? But it didn't. All I feel now when I think of Jeremy Toussaint is relief.

Relief that I'm free.

Relief that the relationship finally ran its course.

I can finally breathe.

Even if no one in my family is on board.

Even on the night of the restaurant opening, he's pressuring me to get back together. I look around the new restaurant, proud of how I helped it take shape to become what it is, yet still not feeling tied to the place. Probably because I've been trying to do everything I can to *cut* ties with Jeremy, not get more sucked in.

"Mon amour, where are you running off to?" my mother asks, as she walks toward me with Louie in her pink Chanel purse.

Don't let my mom's faux French accent or handle of the French language fool you. She only spent a year and a half there when she was eighteen, but my dad, on the other hand, was born and raised there. They fell in love and moved here when my mom was twenty, raising my sister and me in the States with occasional visits to France. My dad's family lives there, and my mom and sister have spent the equivalent of maybe a year there over the course of my life.

It's all about how she's perceived. She grew up poor and on the outside looking in. Even now, married to someone extremely wealthy, it's very important to her that she appears to be a woman of mysterious upbringing and distinguished beyond measure. It just doesn't always add up, like the accent.

She insists I call her Maman. We all do what we can do to make Maman happy.

And poor Louie. The dog has been traumatized since he ate the French chocolates that my aunt sent and had to have his stomach pumped.

Again.

My mother's obsession with this dog is fascinating. I'm fairly certain I accidentally ate raw tobacco as a child, and I do not recall having my stomach pumped. Nor do I recall ever vomiting on her, because I knew better. And there's no way in hell she would've ever let me get anywhere near her Chanel purses, much less crawl inside one.

I see my dad and wave at him. He comes over and I hug him.

"I miss you," I tell him. He's canceled on our weekly lunch dates for the past three weeks in a row.

He doesn't say anything and I can't help but wonder if I've done something to upset him.

"Are you okay?" I ask him, my hand on his arm.

"What, my dear?"

"I asked if you're okay."

"Of course," he says, but he glances over my shoulder and I know he's too distracted to tell me otherwise.

"I'm just going to greet a few guests," I say, rubbing the top of Louie's head. His eyes are closed and his snaggletooth is on full display. He's wearing a ruffled puff-sleeved white button-up and a tuxedo onesie. Yes, this dog's clothing is custom-made and he's always dressed to the nines. My mother thinks he's the most beautiful creature on the earth even if people gasp at the sight of him. And *not* in awe and wonder either.

"That's wonderful, darling. Did you hear anything back about the condo search?"

I've been looking for a condo of my own for several weeks. My parents have a grand home in Manhattan and they've urged me to stay, but I need a place of my own. I've been living in New York for almost a year, and it's time.

"Actually, Caden Taylor thinks that one of their buyers fell through, so I'm going to look at it tomorrow after work."

"Ewwww, isn't that in Brooklyn?" she scrunches her face up, but not a whole lot moves. My mother and botox are very well-acquainted.

"Yes. I happen to like that area. It's young and alive. There's tons of culture and art exhibits," I say, hoping she'll understand.

I need space. I need to find my own way.

She shakes her head. "Fine. But that's far from Jeremy as well."

My jaw drops.

"Not this again. Maman, I came back here after school and I gave it a shot, I truly did. Jeremy and I will always be friends. He's part of the family. But we are long done. It's been months. And besides, we're in Brooklyn right now!" I laugh. Sometimes she amazes me with her snobbery.

She makes a face. "I tried to talk your father out of this location." She sighs. "But Jeremy is your soul mate…"

"He is not." I can't help but laugh. Jeremy is a lot of things, but a soul mate … no. He's a complete narcissist, so the only person he'd be a soul mate for is himself. "He wasn't even faithful when we were together. How does that not bother you?"

"Boys will be boys, darling. It's very French of him. He'll outgrow it. He's a *Toussaint*," she says the word like the name is royalty. "Our families go way back, you two were meant to be together."

"We're over. You all need to get on board with that."

"Get on board with what?" Jeremy's voice startles me as he comes up behind me and wraps his hands around my waist. I don't miss the way the hostess watches us when I look up to find her staring. I'm quite certain they were sleeping together when we were still dating. "Are we getting on board with a possible engagement?"

Yes. He has the nerve to speak of an engagement when we aren't even together. And the man is not grieving our breakup. He has a weird obsession with my family and keeping me as his side piece works to his favor. My father is a well-known restaurateur and he brought Jeremy in as a partner to Dussaint Cafe. Yes, they merged our two last names, Dubois and Toussaint, to create a unique one. Just like Jeremy wants to do with our two families. Apparently old money joined with old money makes for lots of new money.

His words, not mine.

But much like our merging, the name means nothing. It's a pretty word with no substance behind it. I think the name is ridiculous and have told Jeremy and my parents so. And like everything else, they have ignored my feelings and gone ahead with it like we're all in this together. Another reason I most likely don't feel any connection to the place. The most hurtful part of this entire situation is my father's reaction. I feel like he's completely pulled away from me. He's always had my back and I never thought he would react this way to me ending things with my boyfriend.

"Engagement? You have lost your mind. Both of you. I-I don't know how to even say this. I've tried gently and I've tried yelling it. We are over. And in fact … Jeremy..." I take a deep breath and go for it. "I am seeing someone. He won't appreciate the fact that you aren't letting this go."

Jeremy looks stunned for a moment and then his head falls back in laughter. "Please, Cosette. We both know that's not true. Where would you have met someone? All you do is work these days."

"We've been broken up for three months. And we weren't happy the few months that we were together. You've certainly moved on with more than I can count. Why wouldn't I?" I've shaken him off me and turned to face him. My hands are on my hips. I don't want to be cruel, but I'm done being walked on by both him and my mother. And I'm hoping my father will realize how he's hurt me most of all. I expected Jeremy and my mother to react this way. They are completely predictable. But my father— never in a million years would I have thought he'd be so distant.

"Who are you dating then?" Jeremy smirks, and Louie lunges from my mother's purse and catches his forearm with his snaggletooth. Jeremy jolts away and my mother gasps as if this is shocking. Louie has hated my ex-boyfriend since the first time they met. This is not new.

I look up to see the front door swing open, and Caden Taylor steps inside with more swagger than should be allowed for one man. Tall, with light brown hair and dark eyes that are impossible to look away from. His gaze locks with mine and he smiles. He has a smile that reaches his eyes, and my breath catches at the sight of him.

"Hello? Earth to Cosette. Why are you staring at him? Is he the guy? Isn't he a construction worker from the Bronx?" Jeremy says with such disdain, I can't help but roll my eyes.

The man is so snobby I can barely stand to be in his presence any longer. If it weren't for the love I have for his family, I'd have walked away and never looked back.

"Yes. We're together. And he's an incredible developer, so I'd appreciate it if you'd show him the respect that he deserves." I raise a brow at both Jeremy and my mother. She's busy shoving Louie back down in the plush silk lining that he's grown accustomed to.

"Caden Taylor? You're dating him?" my mother finally says, as she glances over at him and back to me. "He's so … American."

"He sure is." I curtsy with a fake smile plastered on my face. "Now, if you'll excuse me. I'd like to greet him properly."

My hands are shaking when I storm away, and Caden's gaze doesn't leave mine as I close the space between us, ignoring all the people waving and smiling at me as I do so. I know my mother and Jeremy are watching and I need to make a point, once and for all. This madness needs to stop. I'm just hoping Caden is willing to play along.

"Hey," I say as a wide grin spreads across his face. His brother Gus is beside him, but I don't have time to greet him just yet. "I need a favor. Will you play along with something?"

"You don't even have to ask," his voice is smooth and confident.

I glance over my shoulder to see my mother and Jeremy watching me. Jeremy smirks, as if he doesn't believe anything about this.

It's time to up my game.

I push up on my tiptoes and wrap my hands around Caden's neck and pull his mouth down to mine. I only intend to peck his perfect lips, just enough to get my point across. But when his mouth covers mine and his hands reach up to hold either side of my face, everything changes. I step in closer, enjoying the hard heat of his body, and his tongue slips in, deepening our kiss.

I couldn't pull away if I wanted to.

And I most definitely don't want to.

I haven't been kissed like this … ever.

My first kiss was with Jeremy Toussaint on my fifteenth birthday. It was a bit traumatizing, if I'm being honest. But I assumed all first kisses were bad back then. I had a few boyfriends after I left for school to attend ESMOD International in France. And when I returned to the States, Jeremy had been shoved down my throat. Literally and figuratively, if that says anything about Jeremy and his aggressive tongue kiss.

But Caden's kiss is sweet. Soft. Yet commanding at the same time. His thumb caresses my jaw. Goose bumps cover my skin, and my heart races. His tongue is exploring and tasting like he's been dying to do this for as long as I have.

There's nothing about this that I don't like. So maybe I've been crushing on the guy since the first time we met. But I had a boyfriend, or at least I was supposed to give things with

Jeremy a try. I've always thought Caden was hotter than hot and now his kiss backs that up even more.

"Holy hellfire. I need to find me a woman or go take a cold shower," Gus says beside us and I'm brought back to reality.

I'm in a public place.

At the opening of my parents' restaurant.

And my ex-boyfriend is a partner.

I pull back, my eyes blinking up at Caden.

"That ought to do the trick," I whisper, as I pat the front of my periwinkle dress in place.

Caden chuckles. "I hope not. I wouldn't mind doing that again."

I can feel the heat on my neck and cheeks, and he slowly pulls his hand away from my face. I miss the contact the minute we aren't touching.

My mother walks up behind me and breaks my trance. "Well, this is such a surprise. Hello, Caden. And is it—Goose?" she says when she looks at Gus, who's staring at her like she has three heads.

"Goose?"

"Your name. I've only met you once. It's Goose Taylor, right?"

His jaw drops, because Gus can't even fathom that someone would forget his name. I turn to my mother. "Maman, this is Gus Taylor. You've met him several times."

This is a little trick my mother likes to play when she wants to intimidate someone. I know this because I've been on the receiving end of her spite many times. Not that she could forget my name, but she has a gift for making her opponents feel small, including her daughter when I'm not on board with her plan. Not my sister, Juliette. She can do no wrong in my mother's eyes. I look around for Juliette. She probably had a facial that she couldn't miss.

"Oh, yes. I must be mixing you up with your other brothers, Splinter and Jackal."

Now Caden's head falls back in laughter and Gus looks like he's been slapped.

"Spence and Jesse," Caden says as he straightens himself, extending his hand. "Hello, Vivienne, thank you for the invite."

"Well, had I known you were dating my daughter, I would have personally invited you." She eyes him, flashing her best smile, but I know she's conspiring.

"I'm sorry. We were waiting for the perfect time to speak to you about it," Caden says, and he reaches for my hand. I can't believe he's willing to cover for me like this.

I lean into him and smile.

"I see. How long have you two been carrying on? I hope not during the time that Cosi was dating our Jeremy?" she says, turning sharply to face Caden. Her purse has now shifted beside Gus who just noticed Louie inside the purse. I want to warn him, but I'm too caught up in the conversation at the moment.

Our Jeremy.

"Well, seeing as *your Jeremy* was carrying on with other women while he and I were together, it's tough to know exactly what the timeline really is," I hiss, surprising both my mother and myself with my hostility.

"Tell the truth, baby." Caden squeezes my hand, and I swear I melt into a puddle right there. He's laying it on thick and I am so here for it. "We waited a respectable amount of time, because even though *your Jeremy* didn't show my girl the respect she deserves, *my Cosette* would never stoop that low. We've been together for six weeks."

I bite down on my bottom lip and look up to see Gus reach his hand into the purse as I come out of my Caden-induced daze. No sound leaves my mouth as I shriek for him to stop, just a loud squeak rumbles from my chest. Louie lunges out of the purse like a warrior under attack. My mother gasps, and Louie locks onto Gus Taylor's pinky finger like it's a piece of bologna. He squeals and cries out in pain, and Caden moves toward the dog.

"Hey, there, buddy. Let go." He rubs the top of Louie's head and the dog is putty in his hands. Louie releases Gus, who rubs his pinky fervently after he yanks it away.

"What the fuck was that? That little bastard gummed me something fierce," he says, leaning down to investigate Louie's mouth. "Well, I guess that makes sense now seeing as the little dude doesn't have a lot of teeth."

"That is so out of character for Louie François," my mother says, trying to shove him back into her purse, but he's licking Caden like his hand is wrapped in beef jerky.

Out of character? Gus isn't even the first person Louie's gummed *tonight*. The dog has bit everyone we know. Even in my own family, he's bit my mother, my father, and my sister. Our doorman needed two stitches after Louie tried to take his hand off for handing my mother a flower delivery. I'm the only one he's never attacked, and apparently, Caden Taylor just made the cut.

"So this makes sense why you've found a condo for my Cosi. You want to keep her close. How convenient."

"Not much I wouldn't do for her," Caden says, sounding completely genuine, and I shoot him a look of thanks. I don't know how long he'll be willing to keep up this escapade, but I'm thankful for the reprieve tonight.

"Well, I'll let you get back to it. Cosi, I expect some time with you in the morning before you head to the hotel to work." This is my mother's way of letting me know we will be discussing this further. This is not the time or the place. The Dubois are all about appearances. "Caden, it's been a pleasure. Why don't you and Goose go get a cocktail? They're free. I'm sure you'll like that."

I close my eyes at her words. The woman never misses an opportunity to stick it to someone. Caden just chuckles. Gus doesn't even attempt to correct her this time. She marches off, and I release a breath that I didn't even realize I'd been holding.

"I don't even know what to say. Gus, I'm so sorry about Louie and the whole Goose thing. And Caden, I don't want you to worry. I'll get you out of this quickly. You won't have to keep this charade up after tonight."

"Do I appear worried?" he asks, and his voice is so sexy that my tongue swipes out to wet my bottom lip because my mouth has gone dry. I glance down at Gus' hand and don't see any teeth marks. I think Louie really did just gum him this time. If he catches you with the snaggletooth, it can do some serious damage.

"Listen, you two figure it out. Goose needs a cocktail. I'll be back." He moves past us and heads for the bar.

"Your ex keeps staring at us. How about we send the message home?" Caden says, trailing the pad of his thumb along my cheek.

"I like the sound of that," I whisper, and he wraps his arms around me and holds me against his chest.

"Good. Because I'm just getting started."

CHAPTER THREE

Caden

"What's up, Goose?" I say when Gus walks into the lobby of The Lux Hotel where we spend most of our time.

"Shut the fuck up, you fake-dating dickcracker."

Laughter breaks out behind him as Spence and Jesse stroll in. "What did we miss?" Jesse asks.

"I believe the lovely Vivienne Dubois thinks your name is Jackass," he says to Jesse, and Spence's head falls back in laughter. "Don't laugh, dude, she called you shit for brains."

Now I'm laughing, which I don't have time for because we have a lot going on today. The top floor is almost finished and we're working our way down. We've got guys in the lobby working on the ceiling details, and Cosette has shipments arriving daily. She had a meeting at her office with her mother this morning, so she hasn't shown up just yet. After that kiss last night, you could say I'm slightly eager to see her again.

"She did not. She called them Splinter and Jackal," I say over my laughter.

"Is that any better? What the hell does that mean?" Spence grumps before holding his finger up when his phone rings. "Got to take this."

"Jackal's kind of a cool name. I'll take it." Jesse shrugs.

"You *would* be agreeable to Jackal." I wrap my arm around Hot Hair, my youngest brother's fitting nickname. His hair reaches the heavens and then some. "You're agreeable to everything."

"Is that so bad?" he asks, grinning.

"Not one bit."

My phone vibrates and I grin when I see that it's Cosette.

I'm dying a bit about last night. I should've never asked you to lie for me.

It doesn't even take me two seconds to start typing back. **Lying for you was the most fun I've had in a while.**

I see the dots and then nothing, dots and then nothing. Finally, another comes through.

Well. :) If you really mean that, how would you feel about ONE dinner at my house? My mom is having a hard time buying into us dating and I would dearly love to get her off of my back about my ex.

I grin at my phone and Spence laughs, nudging me as he walks by. "This girl's got Caden all twisted up. I like her already."

I text back. **I'd be happy to come to dinner. When? What time?**

Tonight at 7.

Damn. She's not messing around.

Count me in. And my sweet darling?

Yes, lover?

Fuck, I like the sound of her calling me that. **You have a wonderful day. XO**

You're really good at this.

I aim to please.

I cannot stop smiling. On a whim, I call up one of the florists we've used for our lobbies in the buildings we own. She answers on the first ring.

"Whimsy Floral, this is Alice."

"Hey, it's Caden. How are ya?"

"Caden, my favorite Taylor! I'm great. What can I do for you?"

"Well, if I didn't know you said that to all of us Taylors, I'd be feeling on top of the world right about now. Doggone it, Alice."

She giggles and I realize making a seventy-year-old woman giggle is right up there with cotton candy at a baseball game. Pretty damn sweet.

"If you have time today, I'd love the biggest floral arrangement you can pull off in a short amount of time. Something sophisticated, yet whimsical ... like you'd see a beautiful blonde fairy tucked in the wild blooms on a summer day…"

"Oh wow. Mr. Caden *Taylor*." She laughs. "You have me all twitterpated. I love the sound of this. I'm busy this morning, but your description makes me want to drop everything and work on this instead."

I don't know what came over me. Those words just sort of dropped out of my mouth. I look around to make sure my brothers aren't still close. Fortunately for my ass, they're across the lobby and in conversation.

I chuckle awkwardly, trying to get some semblance of manhood back. Did I really just say *fairy tucked in the wild blooms* out loud? Fuck me to France, I did.

Alice still sounds swoony when she says, "Don't you fret, I will have this whipped up for you within the hour. I cannot wait. I am already envisioning the magnificence."

"It's why we love you so much, Alice. Thank you."

"Anything for you, Caden. Now … who is this fairy dream for?"

"Miss Cosette Dubois."

"Oh, what an elegant name. Can you spell that for me?"

I do and give her the address of Dubois Designs. When she wants to know what should be on the card, I hesitate. What do you say to a fake girlfriend of one day?

I clear my throat and go with simple. "To my sweet Cosette. Love, your Caden."

"Short and so sweet. I heartily approve," Alice says.

I can't help but smile when talking with Alice. "You're a delight, Alice. I can't thank you enough for fitting this in. It does not have to be ready within the hour—in fact, if you're not able to get to it until the end of the day, let me know and I'll have you deliver it to her house instead."

"My mind is already on the bouquet. I am already creating," she says. And she hangs up on me without saying goodbye.

My sister Pen has called us *the brothers* since she was little and still does, so it's what we all say now when referring to each other. I'm meeting the brothers and their girls at the Mean Mug, our favorite pub, before my dinner with the Dubois family. A little liquid courage before I go get insulted behind Vivienne's fake smiles and pleasantries. I wonder what Mr. Dubois will be like. I've never even seen the man.

"Shut the motherfucking French door," Gus shouts before barking out an earth-shattering laugh.

Everyone at Mean Mug turns to face us, and I shake my head. The two of us are the only unattached brothers in the family and it's easy to see why.

"First off, the whole point of saying *shut the front door* is to avoid saying fuck. You continue to use it incorrectly." Jesse tips his head back and slams his beer.

"Po-tay-to, po-tot-o—damn, I feel like some tater tots." Gus flags over our server and orders yet another appetizer.

Welcome to my life.

"Help me understand this. Gus has been trying to get us up to speed on this little arrangement you've got with our designer, but you know he's clear as mud. So, she told her mom she was dating someone because her mother was *that* upset that she broke up with the dickspackle?" Spence asks, and I glance at my watch and push to my feet.

Sitting in this bar in my best suit makes me feel very out of place. I'll probably lose the jacket before I get to Cosette's.

"I don't know all the details. I'll find out more tonight when I speak to her. All I know is that she needs me to pretend to be her boyfriend for another night, and I'm happy to do it."

"You know that means that you can't date anyone else, if you're fake-dating Cosette," Mya says with a wide grin on her face.

"I don't think he minds," Jesse adds, as he leans into his girlfriend.

Emma moves to her feet and straightens my tie. "Even if you're pretending you're dating her, you know Mya and I need to meet her. It won't seem real if we haven't had a girls' night. You know, the girlfriends need to initiate the newest GD Taylor girlfriend."

"Fiancée," Spence corrects her.

Her head tips back in laughter and she leans into him. "Soon to be Mrs."

"Damn straight, woman."

"Okay. I need to go. I don't even know what the fuck I'm walking into," I say, shaking my head.

"Hopefully into a real relationship. Or some damn good sex at the very least," Gus says, clapping his hands together when an enormous platter of tater tots is set in the middle of the table.

"Eat your tots and stop talking," Spence demands.

"Text us with updates," Mya and Emma both shout as I walk away and wave my hand over my head.

I need to focus.

It's game time.

I nearly turn around and go home when I pull in front of the Dubois mansion. We keep a car around that's mostly Spence's, but we all use it from time to time, me probably least of all since I Uber everywhere. I should've Uber'd here tonight so I would feel the extra pressure to get out of the car. I'm fifteen minutes early, so I have too much time to stare at the house.

My phone buzzes at two minutes till seven.

I just want to say that these flowers—I am speechless! I've never seen anything like them. THANK YOU. I can see you from my bedroom window and am officially letting you off the hook. You do not have to do this. The flowers are more than enough. However, we are having lamb chops with a cognac dijon cream sauce and passion fruit and lemon meringue tartlets if that persuades you at all. I promise I won't make it as awkward as last night by

kissing you in front of everyone. And if you just drive away right now, I'll completely understand.

I hop out of the car as fast as my body will carry me and try to find which window she can see me from as I walk toward the front door. I find it right before I reach the door and she lifts a hand up to wave, her smile so bright.

I blow her a kiss and she smiles even bigger before disappearing.

I hope you'll make it awkward as hell by kissing me tonight, I think before ringing the doorbell. I hear yapping right away. Little Louie must be feeling better tonight.

An older, more uptight, non-smiling, not nearly as beautiful version of Cosette opens the door. I'd be ashamed of my thoughts, knowing what it's like to be compared to my siblings. I'm between Spence and Gus, for crying out loud. And then comes Jesse darling and finally, a girl! I learned early on to not even bother competing for attention. That whole *comparison is the death of joy* that Mark Twain talked about. I'm okay with catching people by surprise when they realize I actually have a personality too. But the way this woman's mouth curls as she looks me up and down and doesn't bother hiding how I don't measure up—I don't feel too awful for seeing how Cosette outshines her.

Cosette steps behind her sister and the way she looks at me takes away every reservation I had about coming. I meant it when I told her mom I'd do anything for her. Didn't fully realize how much I meant that until just now.

"So you met my sister," Cosette says, motioning for me to come inside.

"Hello." I nod politely.

She holds her hand out primly and I shake it, which seems to be the wrong move. Her nose crinkles up and I forge ahead.

"I'm Caden Taylor."

"Juliette Jacobs," she says. If haughty is a tone, she has it perfected.

"Nice to meet you."

She presses her lips together and doesn't say anything else. Louie is still barking his head off, but I don't see any sign of him. Cosette loops her arm through mine and smiles up at me. Everything feels instantly better.

"Come with me quick. I want to show you the flowers. I couldn't stand to leave them behind at work."

She grabs my hand and we go up the stairs and down the hall. The house is extravagant and we walk past room after room, coming to a stop in front of a blue bedroom. Everything is blue.

"Blue is your favorite color?" I ask and she laughs.

"Pink is actually my favorite color, but Juliette claimed that one when we were little." She shrugs. "So I got the blue room."

I want to paint the entire room pink right then and there, but I remember she's wanting to move out. I'd want to move out too if I had to live in this museum every day.

She holds out her arm and that's when I see the masterpiece. Alice outdid herself. It's more of an enormous terrarium than a bouquet, with greenery and tiny flowers filling it so that it's like an exquisite forest. And there, tucked in the moss and miniature ferns, sits a fairy with blonde hair looking wistfully in the distance. Damn, Alice. I need to give *her* a present.

"I've never seen anything so dreamy," Cosette gushes. "It is so beautiful, Caden. And it came right when my mom was trying to talk to me about this relationship, so perfect timing." She laughs. "We had nonstop clients all day long, so Maman is dying to grill me and hasn't had the opportunity to yet. So dinner should be interesting." She leans up and kisses me on the cheek. "I should've known you'd find a way to make this craziness something special."

My cheeks heat up and I reach out and take her hand. "You make it so easy." I kiss her hand and the skin beneath her freckles turns rosy. "That was quite the kiss last night."

Her flush deepens and she looks shy. "I am so sorry about that. You didn't know the mess you were walking into when you agreed to come."

"I am not sorry. Not at all." I smirk. "Here, at your service for as long as you need me."

"Oh, I'm sure tonight will do the trick," she says under her breath.

A bell rings and her whole posture changes. I can almost see the strain and stress hit her like a tidal wave.

"Okay. Time for the performance of your life," she whispers.

I don't tell her that this won't be a performance for me at all, to pretend to be interested in her. I find Cosette Dubois completely captivating. I'm already wondering how I can lengthen this role so I'll have more time with her.

CHAPTER FOUR

Cosette

Caden and I walk into the dining room hand in hand, and I get such satisfaction out of seeing everyone staring at us in shock and dismay. Not because I want to hurt my family or even that I want them to pay such close attention to me, but because this has been a long time coming. They have backed me into a corner about Jeremy and I have put up with it for far too long.

Beecham stands behind Juliette's chair as if he's guarding her from the new hottie in the house. His ears and his forehead shine, the light bouncing off of his frowning face.

My father doesn't look much more hospitable, already seated at the head of the table and looking bored. He's probably tired. He's getting on up there in years and going by his expression, I'm guessing he didn't get his early afternoon nap today. He's been avoiding me every time I make an effort to be alone with him, and I'd be lying if I didn't say it's the reason I want to move out of here so badly. His rejection stings. I don't know what I've done, and I'm hoping once he accepts my breakup with Jeremy, this will all blow over.

"Père, this is Caden Taylor. Caden, this is my father, Alban Dubois."

Caden reaches out to shake his hand and my dad nods before announcing that he has a headache and excusing himself.

"Nice to meet you, sir," Caden says, as my father forces a smile and leaves the room. My heart tugs as I stare at his back. I turn my attention back to the table.

"My brother-in-law, Beecham." I hold out my hand toward Beecham, and again, Caden is the one who makes the first move. I feel a wave of pride about him.

I look around and don't see my mother or her sidekick. "Where's Maman?"

Just then, my mother comes in and Louie is on her heels, dragging a ragged stuffed animal. No. No, no, *no*.

"Maman, please don't let Louie bring Raffi in here tonight."

She glances at me and flicks her cream pointy nails over her pink silk blouse. She looks lovely this evening. She even changed after work, something she doesn't normally do when it's just us. She must be trying to make an effort for Caden. The thought fills me with warm fuzzies for about .02 seconds. She still hasn't even looked at Caden. She smiles down at Louie and sits down, and Caden holds out my chair for me before sitting down himself.

"He won't bother anyone," she says, still looking at the dog.

We've not even put our napkins on our laps before Louie runs around and lies down between Caden and me. With Raffi. The completely desecrated giraffe. It's still quiet as a church between my family when the sounds start. Caden glances at me first with alarm and then realizes it's coming from the dog. The humping is severe. Louie is making love to Raffi and staring at Caden like he wishes it could be him. It doesn't help that Louie is also dressed in a red satin robe, channeling his inner Hugh Hefner. My mother has all of his clothes made, and I don't miss the way Caden studies the monogramming on the dog's back.

"Maman," I hiss. "Please."

She laughs and waves her hand like it's nothing. "He'll be done soon. He's French, darling, and he's had a stressful day. We won't even hear him once we start eating."

Louie came from a breeder in the States. The only thing French about this dog is his wardrobe.

"I am so sorry, Caden," I whisper. I can hardly even look at him, I'm so mortified, but when I do, I realize that it's taking every ounce of his strength to not lose it laughing. He's laughing but trying so hard to hold it in. It makes me laugh too. He reaches out and takes my hand in his, and everything inside of me instantly calms.

"Nice of you to join us tonight, Calden," my mother says.

I sag into my chair. Not this nonsense again.

"I'm starting to think you might be losing your memory, Maman, with your names. What a shame to be getting so forgetful at sixty."

Her eyes go wide as saucers and her hand flies to her neck. "I am nowhere near sixty, and you know it."

"Oh?" I ask, all innocence.

"I'm barely fifty," she cries.

Fifty-seven, but whatever.

"Maybe you should start a fish oil supplement. I heard that it helps with memory."

I wish my father was here. He always gives me that *go get*

em' tiger look when I stand up to her. I miss our chats. I miss having one person in my corner in this family.

"So Caden, how did the two of you meet?" Beecham asks.

"My brothers and I saw Cosette's work on the Ivy and knew she was the one we wanted for our hotel project."

I feel a burst of giddiness inside because the Ivy is the only project I've ever done solo. My mom bristles and my bubble pops, but then Caden lifts my hand up to his mouth and kisses it, and you could hear a pin drop. The entire table is staring at us, mouths hanging open.

"And of course, once I got up the nerve to ask her out, I never dreamed she'd say yes. She's so beautiful and kind … so talented, but so much more than that. She has an inner beauty that absolutely glows from the inside out."

My mouth is hanging open too. He is so, *so* good at this. And when he looks at me with adoration in his eyes, I have to remember that he's playing a part that I *asked* him to play.

This is not real. I have to repeat that in my head at least five times.

Apparently, Louie is not happy with how much attention I've been getting from his new favorite person because he ups his fervor with Raffi.

Putain de merde.

Of course, everyone is too distracted to say anything, so we're all quiet while Louie reaches his grand finale. When he's done—yes, thankfully, it *does* end—he drops Raffi at Caden's feet like he's presented him with a gift. He gazes up at Caden with his snaggle smile and Caden shakes his head at him.

"Glad you're feeling better, little guy."

I have to cover my mouth, I start laughing so hard, and

trying to hold it in just makes my shoulders shake harder. Caden's hand tightens against mine.

"As I was saying," Caden continues, his voice choked with laughter, "Cosette is a dream come true for me."

I glance at Juliette and she looks like she wants to throw up. Beecham looks perplexed, but that could be from the fact that the man can't make it through a meal without running to the bathroom. Between his irritable bowel syndrome and leaky gut, combined with my sister's penchant for French food—the man always appears to be in a state of discomfort. Regardless, both of them seem confused by the idea that I could stir up this kind of passion in someone.

I know. The idea is ridiculous. No one has ever spoken about me in such poetic terms before, and the fairy garden! Damn. What I wouldn't give for someone to really feel this way about me.

Nancy brings our food out, placing each plate in front of us one at a time and then removing the silver domes with a flourish.

"Nice presentation," Caden says under his breath.

We're barely two bites in when my mother decides to speak. I knew her quietness didn't bode well. She's been simmering that I said she was sixty, for one thing.

"What are your intentions with our daughter, Caden?"

"Maman! Give the man a break. It's his first dinner with us."

"I can't wait to hear." Juliette raises a brow and purses her lips.

"I'd be happy to answer that," he says.

Part of me wants to stop him because this is going to be brutal when my family finds out the truth. I'll never hear the end of it. But the rest of me wants to hear what he's going to say next.

"I am going to spend every day showing her how important she is to me until she falls so madly in love with me she won't want to live without me."

Again, every mouth drops. Mine included.

And then everyone concentrates on their food. I think my mother is afraid to ask any more questions about Caden's feelings because he's only making himself look like a saint in my eyes. The peace is short-lived.

Before the passion fruit and lemon meringue tartlets come out, Maman starts singing the praises of Jeremy. And Beecham and Juliette being the simpering sycophants that they are, quickly follow suit.

"So, I'm sure you know that Jeremy is practically a part of the family?" my mother says.

"That's great for Jeremy. I'm guessing he has a family of his own too, yes?"

"Yes, of course," Juliette says and her eyes double in size. "Do you not know who the Toussaints are?"

"Can't say I do." Caden continues eating, completely unfazed.

"The Toussaints and the Dubois are well-known families in France. Old money families with deep roots, if you know what I mean. Have you heard the term *old money* before?" Beecham says, with zero expression on his face, and I suddenly hope the cognac dijon cream sauce and tartlets will do a number on his stomach. The thought of my pretentious brother-in-law huddled over the toilet with a bad case of explosive shits, praying to the porcelain gods, gives me some pleasure.

Caden finishes chewing and nods. "Of course. But in my world, money is money. Old, new, yesterday's, next week's— doesn't much matter to me. I work hard every day and earn every penny I make. I'm proud of the work that I do. That's enough for me."

Juliette gasps and my mother chuckles, and Beecham, well, he's Beecham. I wish my father was here, because there is a lot of Caden that reminds me of my father.

"What is it that you do?" Beecham asks.

Caden lights up at this question. "My brothers and I moved to New York and started a business together. We've renovated a few apartment buildings so far, flipping them into condos that people can purchase. It's a way to get people into their first homes they might not be able to afford in the city with the prices these days. And now we've moved on to The Lux Hotel, which is a huge project for us."

My mother's mouth is so pursed I want to offer her a glass of water. My sister studies her French manicure like it's the most important thing happening at the moment. Beecham suddenly excuses himself and hightails it down the hall with Louie biting at his ankles the whole way. "The hotel is amazing," I say. "And the condos are gorgeous."

"Aren't you going to move into one of those shoeboxes?" Juliette grimaces and I'd love to slap the snobbery right off her face. I've often wondered how we were raised in the same household. Besides our pale blonde hair, we look nothing alike and have nothing in common. Never have and probably never will.

"Yes. It sounds like the one available is going to work."

"I was going to see if you'd like to head over after dinner. I can give you a tour." Caden wriggles his brows. He's completely unaffected by my family and I relax just a bit.

"Yes. Let's do it."

"I can't believe you're really doing this." My mother shakes her head with disbelief.

"I'm ready for all of it," I say, glancing over at Caden. He winks at me and my stomach does all these little flips.

Beecham hobbles back to the table, grumbling at Louie, who surprises everyone when he comes around the table and scratches for Caden to pick him up.

The dog definitely has good taste.

"Well, if you'll all excuse us. We're going to head to the building to take a look at the condo."

My mother pushes to her feet. "I need a moment, darling."

I glance at Caden and he's on his feet, attempting to clear his place. Nancy hurries over to stop him and I chuckle. Before I know what's happening, he has Louie cradled in his arms.

"I'll be right back," I say, and he nods as he laughs at Louie who is moaning in his arms with pleasure.

We step inside the butler's pantry and my mother closes the door. "You've made your point, Cosi. Let's move on. Jeremy is ready to change his ways. Sabine gave him a good scolding and we're all ready for you to get engaged." Sabine is Jeremy's mother. I do love her. But sometimes I think even she knows that her son is a bit of a weasel.

"Maman, I'm not trying to make a point. This is not a game to me. I don't love Jeremy. Not the way I should. I'm with Caden now, and I'm happy. You need to accept it."

"I won't. You and Jeremy were always supposed to get married. This isn't a new idea, Cosette. You're messing everything up."

I rear back. Is she kidding me right now? "Messing every-thing up? Why? Because he's a partner in your restaurant? I'm your daughter. My happiness should matter to you."

"Oh, please. Jeremy can give you a nice life. He has a trust fund that could buy this home ten times over. The restaurant is just to keep him busy. What are you going to have with this handyman? What kind of life can he provide? You're going to live in a condo? You think you can be happy living that way?"

My mom's view of life is about status, who you know, having someone at her beck and call. Her house is fully staffed and she thinks I should have those same desires too. Where she veers off course with her theories about lifestyle is with her desire to work. Maybe the way she was raised has her always thinking about what could happen if it's gone. I'm not sure. But I think even she must get bored with being rich and actually enjoys her design company. She certainly never needs to work another day in her life.

I rub my temples and yank the door open. Living away from my family while I was in college was a nice break. This year, being back at home has opened my eyes to so many unpleasant things about the people I love most in the world.

"I'm leaving with my boyfriend, Mother." I storm out of the pantry and hurry upstairs and throw a few things in a bag. I make my way out to the dining room, and when Caden's eyes lock with mine, I see all the empathy in the world.

"Are you ready to go?" he asks, and he reaches for my bag and throws it over his shoulder and then takes my hand.

"I am. Oh, don't wait up. I'm going to spend the night at Caden's," I say, before grabbing my purse and heading out the door.

I hear my mother gasp and Juliette whispering all sorts of nonsense.

I don't look back.

Because Caden Taylor is helping me find my way.

My fresh start.

And I am here for it.

CHAPTER FIVE

Caden

"Are you all right?" I ask after I slide into the driver's seat beside her.

"Yes." She's got her hands folded together in her lap and she's shifting them back and forth in frustration.

"Want to talk about it?"

"About the fact that I come from a family of pretentious snobs? What is there to say? Oh, is it okay if I sleep on your couch? I probably should have asked you first."

I laugh. She's so … different from anyone I've ever been with. "Family isn't always perfect, but they're usually coming from a place of care. They want you with Jeremy because he's got a lot of money, and that means something to them," I say. "And you never have to ask if you can stay with me. You're always welcome."

"They're so shallow. They want me with a man that cheated on me. Repeatedly. And why? Because he has more money than God? Who cares? My family has plenty of money of their own. I make good money. I'll make my own way."

"Of course you will. Tell me about Jeremy. Why do they want you with him so badly?"

"Well, his parents are best friends with my parents. My mom likes the sound of his last name and the attention that it would garner in her social circle, I guess."

"You dated him for a while?"

"We dated in high school for a little bit. In all honesty, we never had much in common. Jeremy isn't interested in design or in creating anything. I knew he was a playboy back then, but it was just sort of expected that we'd date. I was a bit of a late bloomer, and I wasn't really interested in dating anyone at all, so it worked at that time."

I glance over at her when I stop at the light. A pink hue is covering her neck and adds a little color under her adorable freckles on her cheeks.

"And then what happened?" I ask when the light changes and I pull onto the freeway.

"He left for college first, and then I left. I wanted to attend school in France. Be around my relatives there more. Find my own way. So we remained friends. I dated while at university, but nothing serious. But when I moved back to join my mother at Dubois Designs, there was all this pressure to get back together with Jeremy. You saw us in Vegas. We were hardly the happy couple. I think he likes showing me off, bragging about my family and all of that. But there's just nothing there. And I don't know why he cares to pursue this nonsense."

He cares because she's a fucking prize. Cosette Dubois is the gold medal of women. She's gorgeous. She's smart. She's funny. She's the whole fucking package. Of course he cares. He wants the best of both worlds. I'll never forget the first time I saw her. I met with her and her mom at Dubois Design and could barely string together a sentence when she walked into the room. It's been nearly a year ago now and I still get tongue-tied around her sometimes.

"He knows he has a good thing. Can't fault the man for that. But he should have treated you right, and maybe you wouldn't have left." I pull into the garage beneath the building.

"I would have left either way. I didn't leave because he cheated on me, Caden. I mean, that's not the only reason. I left because I knew there was something missing. I'm also only twenty-four years old. I don't want a lifetime of unhappiness. I want to live and travel and find a partner who wants the same things as I do." Her voice is so soft, I fight the urge to pull her onto my lap once the car is in park and I remind myself that none of this is real. It's all for show even though no one is here at the moment.

I turn to face her and reach for her hand. "You should have all of those things. You deserve the best, Cosette."

She bites down on her bottom lip. "Thank you. So, am I messing up your game by forcing you to have a fake girlfriend?"

"Nope. I'm exactly where I want to be."

She nods and her tongue swipes out to wet her lips. "Really? So how long are you willing to play along?"

"As long as you want me to, *lover*," I tease.

"You'd do that for me? Why?" she asks as I unbuckle my seat belt.

"Because you're good peeps, Cosette Dubois. And it's hardly a hardship. Hell, being your fake boyfriend is the most fun I've had in a long time." I jump out of the car and open her door before she steps out.

"You're good peeps too, Caden Taylor. Even Louie knows it," she says over her laughter as we slip into the elevator.

"That dog is a trip." I laugh.

"Uh, yeah, you could say that. But you tell me when you've had enough, okay? If you can't turn the ladies down any longer, you just say the word and we'll stage a great breakup."

"The ladies can wait. Not going to happen." I chuckle and she smiles. "You'll be jumping ship first."

We step off on the eighth floor and I walk her toward the vacant condo. When I push the door open, she walks in and I flip on the lights. Her entire face lights up as she takes in the space.

"I can only imagine how bright this is during the daytime. I love the floor-to-ceiling windows. Wow. Did you design these?"

I move toward the windows and stare out at the city. "I did. I felt like the view would be our selling point. Give people a bang for their buck, you know? We made up for it with the budget and the location, knowing that installing these windows in place of the wall would go a long way. I believe it's the reason they sold out so quickly."

"And this one is available? How is that possible?" she asks as she floats through the space like a living, breathing fairy.

"The person buying it decided to move abroad. We were just going through the waitlist to decide who to call when you spoke to me about it."

"And you gave it to me, just like that?" she whispers, moving to stand in front of me. Her chest rising and falling against mine.

I push the white-blonde hair away from her face. My God, she is gorgeous. "Just like that."

She wraps her arms around me and hugs me tight. "Thank you, my wonderful boyfriend. I'll take it. When can I move in?"

I laugh and kiss the top of her head. "The inspections are all done. So we'll get the financial stuff going, but you can move in whenever you want."

"I can't wait. So where do you live?" she asks as she pulls away and moves from room to room to check out the space.

"Funny you should ask. Surprising that you don't know, seeing as we're so in love and all." I laugh. "I'm right next door."

"No way. And you're sure you don't mind me sleeping on your couch tonight? I just couldn't resist with the way my mother was pushing Jeremy on me again."

I lead her to the door and we flip off the lights before moving toward my apartment. "I have a guest room and you're welcome to stay in it as long as you want."

I want to tell her she's welcome in my bed whenever she wants too, but I'll keep that to myself. Hell, I've felt the pull that lives between us. The force that has been there since the first day I met her. But maybe she doesn't feel it. Maybe she just needs a fake boyfriend, and I happen to be right here. The right place at the right time, and all that.

As I put the key in the door, there's a loud ruckus and we both turn around to see Gus, Spence, Jesse, Mya, and Emma heading our way.

"Well, well, well … what do we have here?" Gus says, and his cheeks are flushed.

I roll my eyes as Cosette and I pause at the door. "What the hell are you doing here?"

"We tracked your phone, you dicksquirrel. Knew you were home and wanted to hear about your fake date that appears to still be going strong," he says in a sing-song voice before making his voice ridiculously deep. "Hello, lovely Cosette."

Who's the dicksquirrel now?

I push the door open and everyone follows us inside.

Spence and Jesse greet Cosette, and Mya and Emma are bouncing up and down, excited to see Cosette again. They met her in Vegas when we were all there for a mini vacation and got all starry-eyed about her then too. I roll my eyes because I know they're going to try to make more out of this than it is. Cosette needs me to play the part of boyfriend to get away from her ex. Was there a smokin' hot kiss involved? Yes. But do I think she wants more? I really don't fucking know. And this is new for me. I'm not shy when it comes to women, but I rarely have to make the moves. Women usually have no problem telling me what they want.

Cosette Dubois is different. In every sense of the word.

The girls remind Cosette of their names before dragging her off to the couch to chat.

I pull out seven wine glasses and open a few bottles of wine.

"What's happening here, Sir Fakealot? Or is it Shady McFakey?" Gus purrs in my ear, which causes me to reach in my refrigerator to grab my secret stash of olives while he attacks a bag of pretzels. The dude has the attention span of a small flea. I drop an olive in his glass of red wine before handing it to him. Spence, Jesse, and I each grab two glasses and walk out to the living room and hand them to the girls.

We all settle on the oversized sectional, and I glance out at the twinkling lights in the distance. When I look up, Cosette is staring at me and she smiles. My fucking chest squeezes so tight I think it might explode. This is also new.

Before I can respond, Gus spits wine across the coffee table, along with an enormous chunk of an olive. My head falls back in laughter, and I'm thankful for the wood floors we've installed in all the condos.

"What the motherfucking hell? Juniper Holloway ... no fucking more!" he shouts, moving to his feet, and we lose it.

My brother is as theatrical as they come. And he has a sensitivity to olives ever since he binged on some of Mya's mother's secret recipes. Juniper fucking Holloway is a wives' tale that my brother has taken far too seriously.

He swore off all olives months ago. Every bar he's visited has heard the story, because he wants to be sure no one ever accidentally drops olive juice, or God forbid, an olive itself in his cocktail. And he's all about the bar garnishes, just not olives.

So ... in true Taylor form, I always keep a stash of olives in the fridge hidden in an old cream cheese container. Just in case. There is no one more fun to prank than Gus Taylor.

Cosette is on her feet, hurrying over to him like he's been wounded. "Oh my gosh. Are you okay?"

The rest of us are still trying to gain our composure, and she glances back at us with concern.

"He's fine. He's just ridiculous about olives," Emma says, swiping at the tears streaming down her face from laughing so hard.

"Brother. Did you do that?" Gus' face is so serious, it takes all I have in me to shake my head no. "Please say you're fucking with me. I can't take any more of this curse."

Spence covers his face with both hands and tries to stop himself from laughing.

"What curse?" Cosette asks, as Gus reaches for her hand and places the back of it against his forehead as if he has now come down with a fever.

"Juniper Holloway," he whimpers, and Jesse grabs some napkins and starts cleaning up the mess.

"Why would Juniper Holloway put an olive in your wine glass?"

Cosette asks before telling him he doesn't feel warm and returning her hand back to her lap.

Her lavender gaze locks with mine and she smiles and shakes her head with confusion.

"Probably because Gus was nosing around in my business again," I say, raising a brow at him.

"Noooooo. You wouldn't dare, Caden. Not when you know my sensitivity to olives. It brings it all back up for me. My asshole was on fire, man."

"I'm just saying. Maybe Juniper Holloway thinks you're barking up the wrong tree. And why the fuck are you tracking my location?"

"Because I worry about you. And what do you do? You invite the devil in to fuck with me." He pushes to his feet and shakes his head.

The dude really believes in this one, and I almost feel guilty. Almost. But when you grow up with three brothers and one sister, you learn how to have their backs and when to fuck with them. And I have Gus' number. He makes it far too easy. I basically just confessed, but he still isn't sure. He marches to the refrigerator and searches the shelves, never considering that they could be hidden in a decoy container. It isn't rocket science.

"I don't see any fucking olives in here, man."

Emma and Mya fall back in a fit of giggles again.

"He makes it too goddamn easy," Spence whispers.

"He really does," I say.

"Don't worry, brother. I've got your back," Jesse says.

Gus pours himself another glass of wine in a fresh glass and uses a fork to swirl in the liquid to make sure there are no surprises.

He drops back down to sit with us and we pull ourselves together. Even Cosette is struggling not to laugh now.

She fits right in.

"So, are you going to take the condo?" Spence asks.

"I am. Yes. Thank you guys so much for offering it to me. I'm really excited about it."

"Well, that will work out nicely." Gus smirks. "Living next door to Mr. Fake-A-Date."

Cosette's cheeks pink up, and I'm ready to drop another olive in his glass.

"Don't be a dicksausage," I hiss.

"So protective. Are you two kiddos certain this is pretend? Because I'm getting all sorts of feels over here."

"Gus, zip it. He's helping her out. Like that Hallmark movie about the promise. What was it?" Spence looks around like we'll know the answer and then snaps his fingers. "*The Mistletoe Promise*, that's it. It doesn't hurt anyone, so no harm, no foul, right?" He stands and offers a hand to Emma.

"You're such a poet when it comes to words, Old Solemn," she purrs.

"Fake, shmake. We don't care. Mean Mug tomorrow with me and Emma?" Mya asks Cosette, as if this whole arrangement is normal.

"I don't know what that is, but count me in," Cosette says.

"Perfect. We want all the deets on this little ... arrangement." Mya is on her feet and Jesse wraps an arm around her.

They all make their way out, but Gus stretches out on the couch. "I like you, Cosette. You're the nicest girl he's ever brought home ... even if it's not real, I'd like to keep you."

I groan. "She's not a puppy, dicknub."

Cosette snorts then slaps her hand over her mouth. "Dick-nub? What?"

I grin at her. "Welcome to the brothers." I point at Gus. "Go home. I hope you have many olives in your nightmares tonight."

Gus pulls me in for a hug. He's a teddy bear when you get right down to it. He stops to hug Cosette.

"You know, if you get tired of fake dating this guy … you can real date me anytime." He kisses the top of her head and I roll my eyes.

"Don't let the door hit you in the ass."

"Women happen to like this ass," he says, as I close the door behind him. He's still laughing as he walks down the hall.

I drop to sit beside Cosette on the couch.

"I like your family," she says. "They're so … real. And fun. And normal."

"You think what you just witnessed is normal?" I laugh as I take a sip of my wine.

"Well, you just had dinner with a dog wearing a satin robe who humped a giraffe the entire time. My parents are trying to push an arranged marriage on me with a guy who couldn't remain faithful for a week. My sister and her husband have nothing to say that doesn't involve dollar signs. Yeah … it was normal. And really refreshing."

I clink my glass with hers. "You're the best fake girlfriend I've ever had."

"Right back at you, lover boy."

CHAPTER SIX

Cosette

I wake up feeling better than I have in I can't even remember when. I think just being out from under my parents' roof and all the pressure that has come along with that … it's been exhausting. More than I realized. My mom is exhausting. I will never measure up to Juliette. And the one who's always had my back—my dad—has gone silent.

I check my phone and there are three missed calls from Jeremy. Two texts.

Answer your phone!

Don't be so childish, Cosette. We need to talk.

I set the phone down on the side table and stare up at the ceiling, feeling like all the good vibes I woke up with are dashed with this little exchange. Well, that's just it—it's not an exchange of words at all. It's him shoving his way into my life when I've made it clear I don't want him there. At least not as my boyfriend, or worse, as my husband. He just won't let it go. I honestly don't know why he even acts like he wants me anymore—if he's enjoying the challenge, or if he can't see past losing the money that our little union would've brought him if I'd cooperate. It's ridiculous considering the man has plenty of money all on his own.

I delete his voicemails without listening to them. I'm certain I've already heard his spiel before, countless times. Since I got back from France and have tried to start my new life at home in New York, I've been bombarded with all things Jeremy. If my family can bring him up in two conversations with a guy I'm supposedly dating, there are clearly no boundaries in place.

Enough of this. I need to get ready for the day. I can't remember when I last woke up without my alarm. I crawl out of bed and take in the view out the window. It's a lovely day. I grin when I think of this new arrangement with Caden. I've thought he was a great guy from day one, but I had no idea he was so hilarious and so … calming. I stretch and head into the guest bathroom to shower. That's what feels different this morning. The calm.

I take a quick shower, thankful that I brought a change of clothes and some makeup so I can head straight to work. I'll be at the hotel today with Caden, and I am glad that The Lux isn't too far from here.

I quickly make the bed and the smell of bacon fills the room. My stomach rumbles and I hurry out of the bedroom.

My mouth goes dry at the sight of him. Caden is standing at the stovetop in a pair of plaid pajama bottoms and no shirt. He has his back to me, so I take a minute to look at him. I knew he was gorgeous, but this … it's almost criminal. He's chiseled to perfection. Tanned skin. Muscular arms. There's some sort of ink on his left shoulder, but I can't make it out. His back goes narrow at the waist, and I fan my face before he turns around to catch me standing there.

"Hello, lover." He smirks, and I squeeze my hands together to keep from fanning myself again.

"What are you up to, boyfriend?" My voice is a bit gruff and I clear my throat.

"Just making my girl a little breakfast. I hope you like bacon and pancakes?"

I chuckle and mosey on up to the breakfast bar just as his door flies open.

"Do I smell bacon?" Gus says, and turns to me. "Ahhh … the fake girlfriend spent the night. I like it."

I can feel my cheeks heating, and I bite down on my bottom lip just as Caden chucks a piece of bacon at his brother and it hits him in the face, but he manages to catch it.

"She stayed in the guest room, dickweed. Get your mind out of the gutter."

Gus bites off half a piece of bacon and winks at me. "I'm just giving you shit, Cosette. But Caden, you do seem to be in an unusually good mood this morning."

"What can I say? My fake relationship makes me very happy." He laughs and sets a plate down on the breakfast bar and motions for me to take a seat.

"I can see that. I'm starving." Gus takes the barstool beside me.

Caden rolls his eyes but sets a plate in front of his brother. I can't help but scan his body. His front is as good as his backside, if not better. I guzzle half a glass of orange juice because I'm clearly parched from the view. His abs are chiseled, and they lead down to a serious V. I've never been one to fawn over a man's body, but this is more like art. Like someone sculpted this man into the most perfect male form.

"So, what's the plan for today?" Gus asks.

"Cosette and I are at the hotel all day today. You're

coming over to work on the top two floors this afternoon, right?" Caden asks.

I don't miss the ease between them. If I walked into Juliette's apartment unannounced ... her botox would most definitely get a workout. She doesn't even let me visit when I request an appointment. She says that her home is her sanctuary and she doesn't like other people's energy in her space. So the Taylors are a breath of fresh air.

"Yep. Spence and I are going to check out that new building that just became available, and Jesse is working with Doris on the books today, but we'll be over to join the crew this afternoon."

"Be prepared to be watched. My mother's coming to the hotel today to check out the progress. She is not happy about the design changes, so she's probably going to give you a little grief," I say, before forking an oversized bite of pancakes and groaning because it's so good.

"No groaning, lover. The big guy gets a little reactive to beautiful women groaning in his kitchen first thing in the morning," Caden says it so casually that it takes me a minute to process what he means, and Gus' head falls back in laughter. "What? I'm only human."

"He can back up the big guy bit, I'm just sayin'..." Gus points at me with his fork. "Runs in the family, but big brother here—" He nods sagely, and Caden bops him with an oven mitt.

My jaw drops open, but no words come to mind. I'm not used to this type of banter. This type of comfort. This type of genuineness. And *raunchy*. I giggle behind my hand and know I must be ten shades of pink.

"Cosi, I've got to tell you. I find your mother a bit ... terrifying." Gus drops his plate in the sink.

Caden bumps his brother with his shoulder. "Don't be a

douchestick. That's her mother. Show some goddamn respect."

"Oh. It's completely okay. She terrifies me too, most of the time. I love her, but she can be very intimidating."

I look up to see Caden staring at me before he quickly looks away. "All right. Give me five minutes to grab a shower."

I nod.

Gus and I make small talk until Caden comes out, and it's the most I've laughed in a very long time. Caden and I catch a quick Uber and head to the hotel.

"Thanks for everything. Letting me stay with you last night. Making me breakfast. Playing along with this ridiculous scheme. I really appreciate it."

He turns to look at me when we're stopped at a light. "Trust me. I'm enjoying getting to know you better. You don't need to thank me. And don't be nervous about your mom. I've got your back."

Something about his words settles me. Because when Caden Taylor says he has your back, my gut check tells me that he means it.

My phone continues to vibrate in my purse and I groan before pulling it out and silencing my ringer.

"Someone's trying to get a hold of you, huh?"

"It's Jeremy. I swear he never called this much when we were together. The man is having a temper tantrum because he thinks I'm dating you."

"Well, maybe it's time we step up our game, baby." He winks as our driver pulls up to the hotel.

My stomach flutters a little bit and I internally scold myself for reacting this way. Caden's my friend. Nothing more.

"You just might be right."

We make our way inside and my mother is standing there, eyeing me from head to toe. She scrunches her nose just enough to let me know she disapproves of my choice of dress today.

Buckle up, Maman.

You're about to disapprove of a lot of choices I'm going to make.

And I'm totally okay with it.

"Thanks for meeting us, Cosette. We've heard so much about you that whether you're fake dating Caden or not, we were dying to hang out with you," Mya says, as I pull up a barstool at the high-top table where they're seated.

Caden dropped me at my parents' house after work so I could change, and I had my parents' driver bring me over to Mean Mug because I knew I'd want to have a couple glasses of wine.

"I'm thrilled to be here. Thanks for inviting me." I mean it. I've been looking forward to this all day. I felt an instant comfort with Mya and Emma last night. They're both gorgeous, genuine, and from what I can tell, always laughing. And I don't have many girlfriends here in New York. I went to boarding school in Maine during high school, and I attended college in France. So, I am in need of some real girlfriends. I have a feeling these two would be keepers.

"Well, we're thrilled to add a cool chick to our little duet. I mean, your fashion alone has my attention." Emma pauses when the server walks up and we all order a glass of Chardonnay.

I chuckle when he walks away. "Thank you. My mother thinks my fashion choices are lacking."

"Girl, trust me when I tell you, you are killing the fashion game."

"I couldn't agree more," Mya says.

I can't help but smile. I like them.

"So, what's the deal with this ex-boyfriend of yours? He just won't leave you alone?" Emma asks, and my phone vibrates in my purse for the millionth time today.

I pull it out expecting it to be Jeremy once again, but instead, it's Caden.

Be safe tonight, sexy. Call me if you want to stay here, or if you need a ride.

"Sorry. I thought it was Jeremy. But it's Caden being sweet," I say, before I type out a quick response and turn off my ringer.

Careful, boyfriend. A girl could get used to this.

I giggle and they both lean over to look at what I'm typing.

I'm counting on it. Call me when you're done and I'll give you a ride home.

"This is the best fake relationship I've ever seen," Mya says with a laugh.

So bossy.

Only when it comes to my girl getting home safe. <winky face emoji>

I put my phone down and face them, and they are both watching me as if they want all the details.

"Spill it, girl," Emma says as she takes a sip of her wine.

I fill them in on my history with Jeremy. My mother's obsession with our families joining. The way my father has been so distant since Jeremy and I broke up. And we spend the next hour and a half laughing and talking.

And drinking all the wine. Two and a half glasses, I think. Maybe three?

And a shot of tequila because Emma insists we all do shots as we toast to Jeremy biting the dust.

And then there's that martini with extra olives as they fill me in on the whole story behind Gus' fear of olives.

And Mya's mother's horrible cooking.

And then there is another shot of tequila as we toast to Emma's grandmother's nipples, which were originally the butcher's wife's nipples.

My head is spinning and I can't remember a time that I've had more fun.

My mother and my sister think laughter is very American. They don't believe that a sense of humor is a redeeming quality.

"I'm so glad you kicked that guy to the curb. You don't need that in your life. You're too good for that. But I'm sorry your family isn't being supportive," Mya says, and I think her words are slurring a bit.

"I say *good riddance* to Jeremy, the boring, cheating bastard. He wants what he can't have and doesn't appreciate it when he does have it."

I'm laughing so hard that tears are streaming down my face. They are more upset about Jeremy than I am.

"It's been eye-opening because I don't feel anything but relief to be done with him. And it's been a few months. But now that he thinks I'm with Caden, he's being relentless."

"So, you and Caden are just acting, huh?" Mya asks, and her cheeks are rosy from all the cocktails.

"Yeah, he's been so great about all of this."

"You don't find him attractive?" Emma purrs.

My head tips back in laughter. "Of course I do. I mean, I'm only human. Oh my word, I saw him with his shirt off this morning, and let's just say… the man is too much. But he's just helping me out."

"I say we drink to him helping you out with anything and everything," Emma whisper-shouts and then raises her hand in the air for the server to bring more drinks.

"Easy there, she-devil," a deep voice says from behind me. I turn around to see Spence standing there smirking at Emma, and Jesse and Caden walk through the door.

A woman stops Caden and his gaze locks with mine as he talks to her. My vision is a little blurry from one too many cocktails, but he looks agitated, the way he rubs the back of his neck and shifts on his feet to move away from her. I quickly turn away. I don't need to ruin his game. It's a good reminder that we're just playing a part right now. Caden isn't mine. He's just pretending to be.

We're friends.

Good friends.

"I think you've had enough, baby," Spence says to Emma and he nuzzles her neck.

Swoon.

"Awww, don't ruin all the fun, Old Solemn. We're just cursing the ground that Cosette's ex-hypocritical boyfriend walks on."

"Ooohhh ... I feel a little woozy," Mya says as Jesse helps her to her feet.

"Damn lightweight. This one has a sensitive stomach." Emma thrusts her thumb in Mya's direction.

"I can hear you. I may be tipsy, but I'm not stupid." Mya stumbles a bit on her feet and we all three burst out laughing.

Before I can get to my feet, Caden is there. He wraps his arm around my waist and helps steady me.

"Hey, lover boy. I hope I'm not ruining your chance with that lady over there," I say, and my words feel far away, like they're dragging underwater. But the thought that I could be in Caden's way sends some sort of weird feeling through my body.

Anger?

Jealousy?

No. I must just be too intoxicated to think straight. But I'm glad that Caden's by my side at the moment.

Mya and Emma can't stop laughing and neither can I.

"You're not ruining anything. Let's get you home. See you guys in the morning."

"Wait a minute, *lover boy*. We didn't get to hug her good-bye," Emma shouts and she and Mya both hurry toward me.

A barstool gets knocked over in the process, which only makes us all laugh harder.

"Cosette Dubois…" Emma says, pushing the hair out of my face.

"Yes?" I ask, and I can't hide my smile.

"We found our missing piece that we didn't even know was missing," she says.

"We realized what was missing after we met you. You complete us, little rosy Cosi," Mya says, looking at me all weepy and then she bursts into tears.

"Oh boy. Time to go," Jesse says, wrapping his arm around her. She's at the door and still yelling how much she loves us, and we follow Spence and Emma out the door.

Caden's car is waiting at the curb and I wave goodbye before he helps me in.

My lips are numb and I can't feel my feet.

But I look up at Caden and I know I'm exactly where I want to be.

CHAPTER SEVEN

Caden

Holy shit. Drunk Cosette manages to be sexy as hell with the way she keeps looking up at me with those doe eyes. The more I get to know this girl, the more protective I feel over her.

And she needs it.

Her family doesn't have her back and that bothers me.

"Your place or mine?" I ask her and she grins.

"I should go back home. I can't crash in your guest room forever and also, I need clothes."

"You can crash at my place as long as you need."

"Did I ruin things for you back there?" she slurs, and she's so fucking cute it makes my chest squeeze.

She's turned in her seat facing me, and her cheek is resting against the leather seat. Lavender eyes are looking up at me like I hold the fucking moon.

"You didn't ruin anything."

"Is that your girlfriend? I mean your real girlfriend?" she asks, and when I glance back over, her eyes are closed.

"No. I hardly know her."

"She'd be lucky to date you, lover. You're the best boyfriend I've ever had," she whispers, and then bursts out in laughter at her own words. "You know what I mean."

"I do." I nod, and we're quiet until I pull down her street.

"Thanks for coming to get me. I could have called my parents' driver. Herb's a nice guy even if he smells like sauerkraut and pine needles."

Now it's my turn to laugh.

"Well, I wouldn't want you dealing with that kind of smell when you're feeling so good," I tease, and I turn off the car. The house is dark.

"You're so thoughtful. And handsome. I see why that girl was all over you, the way you're looking in this fancy … what is this?" She taps her hand against my chest but rubs it all around, which makes my dick go hard immediately.

Can't go there with Cosette.

We have a good thing going right now.

"It's a T-shirt," I say, and I can't help but laugh.

"Yep. It is. It just fits you so nicely. And, I get it. I really do." She still has her hand on my chest and she looks up at me and gasps before patting my cheek. "I think I might throw up."

Now I'm laughing as I hurry out of the car and get her out as well. She leans forward and vomits several times, and I hold her hair back for her. She keeps apologizing between hurls.

"You're okay," I say, as I rub her back.

"Oh my gosh. I can't believe I just puked in front of you. This has to be some kind of rock bottom. But I had the best time, so I guess it's a sign of a great night, right?" She looks up and sways into me.

I lift her off her feet and she rests her head against my chest. "It's definitely a sign of a great night. Do you have a key?"

"We have a code. My mother thinks keys are for peasants," she says, and she bursts out in laughter again. Cosette's laughter is one of the best fucking sounds I've ever heard.

She tells me the code and I push the door open as she guides me upstairs. The house is completely quiet and she covers her mouth to keep from laughing. I set her on her bed and she looks up at me.

"Thanks for being such a good friend, Caden."

I smile at her and reach out to touch her cheek. "Goodnight, my sweet friend. I'll see you tomorrow. Take all the time you need, coming in."

She falls back on her bed and watches me as I walk out. It's really hard to leave when she's staring up at me like that.

I shut the door behind me and nearly trip over Louie who is now looking up at me much like Cosette was. He's wearing a pajama-looking thing with pink flamingos and I shake my head. I don't know about people who never let their dogs go naked. If you can't even be free as a dog, what's even the point in life?

I reach down and pet him and he falls out on his back, paws up in full surrender.

I can't help but laugh, the little guy is so stinking cute. He's got three teeth poking out of his mouth, otherwise he's all gums.

When I try to move away, he gets up and follows me all the way down the stairs. From somewhere in the distance, I hear Vivienne calling him, but he stays on my trail. I reach the door, and he pants up at me like we're going somewhere exciting. He even throws a little twirl in there.

"Louie. You have to stay," I whisper. "Go to your mother."

He jumps on my leg and waggles his tail some more. I sigh and scratch his head again, looking around for something to distract him. I don't want to get caught looking like I'm snooping around, so when he doesn't even go after his stuffed giraffe, I pick him up and head back up the stairs toward Cosette's room. I knock lightly and when she doesn't answer, I open the door just enough to put Louie in her room, shutting the door before he follows me back out.

I decide to text her when I get home to explain my crazy reasoning, but she texts me first as I reach the car.

Thought you were coming back for a kiss, but it was just Louie licking my face off. Thanks for that. ;)

My laugh sounds loud on the quiet street. **At your service,** I type back.

As I drive back to my side of town, I think about how much fun I'm having with Cosette. There aren't many girls I meet in New York that I'm interested in seeing again. My mom thinks I still haven't recovered from the heartbreak of losing my college girlfriend, Leah, but I rarely think about her at all. My heart doesn't feel broken. I don't pine after her like a wuss or wish I'd done anything different—except I do wish I hadn't dated her as long as I did. She dumped me when I wasn't ready to get married while we were still in school, and she was married to someone else within the year.

Yeah, that did a number on me. Made me a little skittish about getting in deep with anyone else, I guess.

I need to be careful with Cosette too. Because I am thinking about her way too much. She needs a *friend*. Pure and simple.

I can do that. Hell, I need more friends in my life too. It can be easy to think I have all I need with my family because, the truth is, I do. They fill me up and then some. But Spence and Jesse have already settled into relationships and I know once kids start, I won't have unlimited access to them at all times. I don't see Gus settling down anytime soon, Pen either … but who knows? Things didn't exactly go slowly with either Spence or Jesse's relationships. Hopefully our family will all grow together, whether we're in romantic relationships or not. All I know is, a few friends wouldn't hurt.

Still too introspective for my own good, I walk into our building and drop the keys off at Spence's place. And when I close the door to my apartment and look around, that nagging feeling persists. For someone who's always relished the quiet at night and a little space at the end of the day, why do I suddenly feel like something is missing?

Is it too soon to apologize for being a drunkard?

I laugh when the text from Cosette comes through.

You don't need to apologize for anything. What are you still doing up? I thought you'd be long passed out with Louie and Raffi.

I watch as the three little dots move across my screen.

I puked a few more times. Louie is not happy with me. He's turned his nose up at me multiple times. He's as judgy as my mother. <rolling eyes emoji>

She's so fucking cute it's hard not to laugh. I scrub a hand down my face.

Proceed with caution. This girl is off-limits.

He has no room to judge. The dude humps a giraffe out in the open. The bastard has no shame.

I know she's laughing and we're not even together. But Cosette has a wicked sense of humor. It's one of my favorite things about her.

That's very true. Thanks for reminding me. Thanks for taking care of me tonight. I owe you one.

My mind goes to a million different places of favors I'd like to get from Cosette, before I pull my thoughts out of the gutter.

You're older than her, dickhead.

She needs a friend, not a hookup.

She's not that girl.

You owe me nothing. Get some sleep. Drink some water and hydrate. Prepare for the hangover from hell tomorrow. I'll see you at the hotel.

I drop down to sit on my bed and wait for her response.

Thanks, Caden. See you tomorrow.

I stay up watching late-night TV until I can't see straight and fall asleep on the couch. My dreams are tormented with Cosette and her sweet smile, that expression that looks like she has so many fun secrets I'd like to hear all about, and when I wake up the next morning, I feel like I've been put through the wringer. I take my shower and lecture myself in the mirror when I get out.

"Lighten up, dude." I point at myself, leaning closer to the mirror. "Life is supposed to be fun. You'll be an old man overnight if you start contemplating the meaning of life."

Feeling better already, I try to put it all out of my mind, determined to have a good day.

I wait for the elevator and hear a ruckus as the doors open. Gus charges out, and Emma and Spence are on his heels.

Gus is dry heaving and gagging so dramatically it's impossible not to laugh.

"Dammit, Kingsley. You got vomit on my new shoes. You

know I'm sensitive to smells." He bends over and makes all sorts of gurgling sounds.

"Keys," Spence shouts to me, and I toss him my apartment keys as he runs ahead of Emma toward my apartment.

"Don't be a baby. You've puked on me before," Emma hisses and she looks like the walking dead. Her hair is a tangled mess, and she stumbles toward Spence who has my door opened for her.

My God. How much did these girls drink last night?

"That's because you aren't sensitive to these types of things," Gus shouts back, leaning against the wall like he's just been shot.

"Dude, are you hungover too?" I ask after Emma beelines it into my apartment.

"No. I had a relaxing night at home entertaining a lovely lady friend." He holds his hand to his forehead. "But Kingsley gets on the elevator and hurls right onto my new Nikes. None of it landed on her or Spence or even the elevator. She aimed for me. I can't deal with this madness." Gus looks up at me and shakes his head and I can't help but laugh.

"Let's go clean up your shoes, you little dickprincess."

"You know I can't handle vomit. Ever since Pen puked on me a few years ago. It's not my thing." He has a hand over his mouth and he's stumbling behind me like he's been in an accident.

Yeah, Pen projectile vomiting all over Gus at his own college graduation goes down as one of my favorite sibling memories. He'd pressured her to go shot for shot with him on the tequila, and after she put the last one down, she high-fived him and proceeded to shoot liquid from her mouth straight into his face, exorcist style. Spence, Jesse, and I couldn't contain our laughter that night. And then we consoled Pen, and Gus threw a massive temper tantrum as he dry heaved and whined all the way home.

Classic Taylor shenanigans.

"I don't think puke is really anyone's thing," I said, pushing the door open and reaching for a towel. "And no offense, but that looks like spit-up. There's hardly anything there. You're being a huge ass baby."

"It's not the amount of vomit that matters, it's the idea of it. Of regurgitated shit coming out the wrong end. I'm a visual learner, and I am not okay with this. You hear that, Kingsley," he shouts, as he takes his shoe off and wipes off the quarter-sized white goo from his shoe.

"Well, I feel like a new woman. Sorry you had to take the brunt of it. Love you, Gussy boy." Emma is standing in front of us now looking like she's raring to go.

"Why do you look better than I do?" Gus whines.

"Because I clearly needed to get that tequila out of my stomach. I hurled a few times, and now I'm good to go. Let's go get greasy breakfast sandwiches on our way to work," Emma says, grabbing a bottle of water from my fridge and kissing me on the cheek.

"Why does he get the kiss when I'm the one you desecrated?" Gus asks as he slips his tennis shoe back on his foot. "And yes to the breakfast sandwich. I need a pick-me-up after all this drama. This is not how I like to start my day."

"Listen, dickweasel, shit happens. Stop whining and man up," Spence says, as he takes Emma's hand and leads us out the door.

"You coming with us for breakfast?" Emma asks me when we step on the elevator.

Gus pinches his nose between his thumb and his pointer finger because he claims he can smell the vomit.

"This isn't even the same elevator we were on before, you

dufus," Emma says and then she turns back to me to wait for my answer.

"Yep. I have a hunch you aren't the only one who needs a greasy meal." I think of Cosette.

"You're right about that, brother. All of this excitement has worked up my appetite," Gus says as we step outside, and I roll my eyes because I wasn't thinking of him.

"I thought you were nauseous from the puke." Emma raises a brow at him.

"Stop saying that word. It's bringing it all back to me," Gus whines and rubs his stomach.

We all burst out in laughter as we walk down the street in typical Taylor fashion. And I suddenly feel an urgency to get to the hotel. I'm anxious to see how Cosette's doing.

Because that's what fake boyfriends do, right?

CHAPTER EIGHT

Cosette

I wake up to rapid knocking on my door and then my mom steps inside.

"Louie!" she cries. "What is he doing in here? I looked all over for him and thought he must have gone to get Raffi and fell asleep."

"He found his way in here last night," I say, grinning at him. Ow, it hurts to grin. I put my hand on my head and wince. That hurts too.

"You've been avoiding me for days now," my mom says. "Just when were you planning to discuss this new relationship with me?"

"We've discussed it. He's been over here for dinner. What more do you want me to say?"

"I want you to say it's a cruel joke and that you're just doing your best to show Jeremy what he's missing." She points at me. "Which is an excellent idea, by the way. That is what this is all about, isn't it?"

I reach for the water on my nightstand and guzzle it. She's still waiting for an answer from me when I stop.

"No, Maman. I don't know what to tell you. But I have to get ready for work. I slept right through my alarm."

"Well, Jeremy and his parents are meeting us at the restaurant tonight. I expect you to come and act like a civil adult."

"I won't be going to dinner tonight." I get out of bed, and the room slightly spins. Yikes. This is why you don't drink as much as I did last night. I've never been drunk, not even in college. A memory of me throwing up last night and Caden holding my hair back comes to mind and I groan. No. How humiliating.

My mom thinks I'm groaning about dinner.

"You most certainly will. I've already told them you'll be there and they're expecting you."

"You shouldn't have done that without checking with me first."

Louie follows me into the bathroom and I can hear my mom walking toward the bathroom too. She whisks him up in her arms, nuzzling his neck as he tries to squirm away.

"Just please be there, Cosette," my mom sounds tired and I look at her in concern. Dark circles are around her eyes.

"Are you okay, Maman?"

"No!" she cries. "You are breaking my heart! Sabine and I are devastated. Your father is too, although he will never show it. And we needed this marriage … especially now." She presses her lips together like she's said too much.

My eyes narrow in on her and she backs out of the room. "What are you not telling me, Maman? What do you mean, we need this marriage, especially now?"

She makes a choked sound and glances around the room wildly. "Oh, just after the year we've all had. And your father is getting old, Cosi. We need to make sure we are all secure for the future. No one knows what tomorrow brings. The heaviness in the world, the state of our—" She waves her hand around like I should understand what she's talking about, but I am completely lost.

I start the shower and stand at the bathroom door, while she stands at my bedroom door, looking like she's going to burst into tears.

"If I come tonight, I'm bringing Caden. I don't know if he can be there yet or not, but that's my condition."

Anger flashes in her eyes, but she nods grimly. "Very well. You're being ridiculous, darling. But maybe you need to see how these two men line up against each other when they're in the same room. Maybe that's what it will take for you to come to your senses."

I close the bathroom door before I lose it. I don't know how many more ways I can say it, but okay, I guess I'll have one more dinner with the Toussaint family. Maybe *they* will get the message after they see me with Caden.

My mother's control has been stifling me my whole life, but I've been willing to put up with it to keep the peace. I couldn't feel more like the outsider in this family than I do, and so I've tried to make all of them happy by going along with what they want me to be. It's just never enough. And with the distance I feel from my father, I feel very alone in this house. It's always been me and him against the world—and now it's just … me. I tried again to set up a time to talk to my dad and again he had some excuse about a golf priority.

Pretty sure my mom only sees me as someone she can marry off to increase her standing with the rich and powerful. I have been groomed to be Jeremy Toussaint's wife and there's no room for me to step outside of that. Juliette was glad to fit in that mold. And I tried. I dated Jeremy as long as

I could stand it, but I just know I can't do it. I will never be happy being someone I'm not, and being with someone I don't love.

All I long for is a home where I can relax, be myself, and be appreciated for exactly who I am. I think that only happens in the movies. But I'm so excited about my new condo and the freedom it will offer. I can't wait to move in. I got the ball rolling with the financial stuff, and it looks like I will be in my own space very soon.

Gah, that outweighs all the depressing thoughts. *I'm shaking off the foul mood now*, I think as I step into the shower. Let's hope Caden can help me put on one hell of a show tonight and that I can move out of this stifling house stat. I don't even need the life I dream about, just get me out of this godforsaken one!

My mother is waiting in the driveway with Herb when I step outside. I open the door and Louie's tail wags when he sees me.

"Nice seersucker suit," I tell him.

"I've given some thought to the direction you took the hotel—I'm not pleased that you went about this without me. Not pleased at all. But if it's more freedom in the business you're wanting, I concede. I'd much prefer you let out your little rebellion in that area than in this business with Jeremy."

"That's just it, Maman. I don't want to look at the man I'm supposed to marry as a business at all. I want to marry for love. I can't be like you and Papa."

She gasps, but she knows it's true. She's twenty-two years younger than my father and married him for his money. I'd like to think they have a fondness for one another, but I haven't seen much evidence of that, at least not from my mother's side as of late. And Juliette followed that path with Beecham.

I lean up and smile at Herb. "Please drop me off at the hotel instead of our office." He nods. I take note of his new car air freshener. It's lessened the garlic smell by at least fifty percent. It's the little things. "Thank you."

Maman huffs next to me and all I can think about is how nice it will feel to breathe. The sooner I can put some distance between myself and my family, the sooner I will feel like I can catch my breath.

My head is pounding as I walk into The Lux, but already, I feel better. Caden is in the lobby and he waves something at me.

"There you are, and looking lovely, I might add." He grins at me and it feels like everything will be okay. "I have an extra greasy breakfast sandwich. Thought of you when I ordered it."

My face flames and I put my hand on one cheek to try to cool it down. "I am so embarrassed about last night. I don't even remember everything, but the parts I do remember are —" I shake my head and grit my teeth, making a face.

"—Are not bad at all," he finishes for me. "You were fine. Don't worry about it. I hope you're feeling okay though."

"Yeah, not the best, but that's what I get for trying to drink my body weight. Never again, lesson learned." I laugh. "And yes, I will take that sandwich. Thank you."

Someone calls him and he hands me the sandwich before hurrying to help the guy. I unwrap the greasy goodness and dig in, moaning as I take the first bite.

"What *is* this?" I ask out loud.

Caden walks back over just then. "Sausage Egg McMuffin."

"Where do you find these things?" I gasp, taking another bite. It is heaven.

And I think he's going to pop an eyeball out with his

shock and laughter. "You've never gotten an Egg McMuffin from McDonald's?"

My eyes widen. "We were never allowed. This is from McDonald's? I always saw the commercials and wanted a Quarter Pounder so bad, but my mother insisted that was the devil's food."

He laughs harder. "Well, some would say you're right. But who doesn't need a little devil in their life every now and then?" His tone and the way his gaze dances across my face and down my body leaves heat licking across my skin.

I finish chewing but can't look away from him. I know my cheeks are pink, but I can't care about that right now. It's really hard to tell sometimes if he's flirting for real or playing this boyfriend role. He was nice before, but things have definitely kicked up a few notches.

I fan myself. It's too hot, he's too hot. I take another bite of the sandwich because it's so damn delicious and I can't seem to think in clear sentences when I'm around Caden Taylor.

He doesn't seem in any hurry and when I finish my sandwich, I grab his arm, catching him by surprise. He grins and I melt. Again.

"I forgot—and don't feel like you have to, it's all last minute, but I just wanted to ask—" I run out of air and he chuckles.

"Deep breath," he says.

I listen and take a long, cleansing breath. When I'm done, he's still waiting patiently for me to say whatever I want to say.

"Are you always this laidback?" I ask.

He has a dimple. My God, he has a dimple and it is out in full force now. "That's what you wanted to ask me?"

"No. Yes. Well, and something else too." I wave my hand. "Sorry, I'm all over the place today."

"You're fine. And I guess the answer is yes … I've never seen the need of stressing over things that I have no control over."

"And what about finding control in the first place? Have you always been this self-assured guy who does whatever he wants?"

He puts his hand on my shoulder and squeezes. "I wouldn't say I always do whatever I want, but yes, I've tried to shape my life into doing the things I want to do, being the kind of person I'm proud of. It helps that my family has always cheered me on along the way."

I sigh wistfully at that. Maybe it's not just in movies after all.

"What else did you want to ask me?" he asks when I'm quiet for a long time, mulling everything over.

"Would you be willing to go to dinner with me tonight?"

He's already nodding his head and smiling when I shake mine, holding my head up.

"With my parents, Jeremy, and his parents?" I add.

He whistles and then takes my hand, twining his fingers through mine. He leans in a step and my heart gallops ahead of me.

"Is it time to pull out the big dogs?" he asks, leaning his forehead onto mine.

"I don't know that expression, but I'm thinking the answer is yes."

"I would be glad to go to dinner with you tonight."

Just then someone calls my name and it's a delivery person holding a massive bouquet of white flowers. Are those lilies? Caden lets go of my hand and takes the flowers from the man since he's closer.

"This is Ms. Cosette," Caden says. "Looks like you have another admirer."

I sneeze twice. Oh no. "Weird that they'd come here and not my office. Are these lilies?" I frown and sneeze again.

"I don't know. I'm just the delivery guy. Where would you like these?"

"Wherever is convenient, I guess." I look around and there aren't many surfaces that aren't cluttered with all the projects going on. The lobby reception desk is the only place I see. There are roses and hydrangeas and only a few lilies, maybe I've outgrown the allergy by now.

He sets them there and watches while I open the card and back away a bit just in case. My anger boils when I read it. And my eyes blur, burning, as I sneeze five times in quick succession.

"Are you okay?" Caden asks.

I grab a tissue from the box sitting a few feet from the flowers and wipe my eyes and then grab another tissue and sneeze into it.

I try again to read the card, between more sneezes. My throat feels kind of weird too.

If two can play this game, count me in. You belong with me, Cosi. I won't give up until my ring is on your finger.

~Jeremy Alphonse Toussaint

I wave the card toward Caden and he stares at me in alarm. "Cosette, I think you're allergic to these flowers." He grabs my arm and pulls me away from them.

"Those are definitely lilies. I've always been allergic, but I've never reacted quite this badly." I sneeze again and again. My skin itches and I glance down and see a bunch of red splotches all over my arm. I move farther away from the flowers and he takes them and quickly leaves the room.

When he hurries back, he reaches in his back pocket for his wallet and hands me a Benadryl. "I should've given you this first," he says.

"You carry Benadryl in your wallet?" I ask.

"Pen has a nut allergy, so we each carry it with us at all times just in case."

My eyes get glassy as I take it from him, and I lean my head on his chest for a second. "Thank you," I whisper.

I think about what it must have been like to grow up in the Taylor household. To have someone always looking out for your best interests.

I may have grown up with marble floors and a trust fund that will last me a lifetime, but they have something that money can't buy.

They have a family.

And love.

CHAPTER NINE

Caden

"You sure you're up for this?" I ask Cosette after she settles into the passenger seat beside me. She's been off all day since taking the Benadryl. I found her slumped over against a wall in my office at the hotel when it was time to leave for dinner.

"Yes, of course. Benadryl just makes me sleepy. I can't believe how long this is lasting. I've never had such a strong reaction to lilies. Thank you for getting rid of those." Her words are soft. I don't think the hangover mixed with the allergic reaction is making her feel very well at all.

"My pleasure. I think Anthony was more than happy to take them home to his wife and score some brownie points," I say, referring to the painter that was working at the hotel all day. "Plus, I don't need Jeremy sending my woman flowers, right?"

She chuckles and turns to face me. She looks tired. "Right. Thanks for doing this tonight. Truly, you're going above and beyond."

I chuckle. Hanging out with Cosette Dubois is not a hardship for me. I enjoy her company, so I'm happy to help.

"Of course."

"Well, prepare yourself. My family is no walk at the park, but Jeremy's family can also be a handful. I love them because I've known them most of my life—but his mother, Sabine, is not pleased with me for ending our relationship. You'll like his father, Gerard. He's my favorite. But, I've never been on the wrong side of the Toussaints."

"Well, too bad that they don't get to decide who you date, or who you marry." I shake my head because I still can't wrap my head around the fact that they're trying to arrange a marriage in this day and age. "So let's turn things up a bit tonight. Really send the message home."

She chuckles. "Okay. We should probably know more about one another if we're madly in love, right?"

"Good idea. What do you want to know?"

"Favorite color? Favorite food? Favorite season?" she asks as I pull into the parking lot at the restaurant.

"Blue. Tacos. Fall because of football. How about you?" I put the car in park and turn to face her. Her cheek is resting against the seat, and she looks like she could fall asleep if we stopped talking.

"Periwinkle. Pizza. Summer because I love the beach."

"Nice. What's your favorite holiday?" I ask.

"Christmas. You?"

"Same. The presents, the food, the snow. I fucking love it," I say. "Favorite movie?"

"*Little Women*. I've watched the old version and the new version more times than I can count. You?"

"*Rocky. The Godfather. Jaws.*"

Her eyes double in size and she laughs. "*Jaws* traumatized me. I refused to swim in an ocean for years after watching it."

I unbuckle my seat belt because we're going to be late.

"Oh yeah? Well, *Little Women* traumatized me." I jump out of the car and come around to open her door.

"How does *Little Women* traumatize anyone?"

"Because Pen made me watch it when we were young and then she insisted all of us act it out. I was cast as Jo." I shiver at the memory as I reach for her hand. "I still break out in a sweat every time I remember her trying to force us all into her dresses that were far too small anyway."

Her head falls back in laughter. "I think if you saw the new version, and no one forced you to act it out, you'd really like it."

I guide her in the door, my hand resting on the small of her back. She smells fucking good.

She looks fucking gorgeous, even hungover and with a severe flower allergy.

My fake girlfriend is fucking perfect.

"Why's that?" I ask as we make our way inside.

"Because it's all about family—and so are you." She winks, and it takes all I have not to dip my head down and taste that sweet mouth of hers.

Get it together, asshole.

This girl is not looking for a hookup or a boyfriend. She's looking for an exit strategy for her current situation. She wants to be free. Single.

"Your party is already here. Follow me," the hostess says, and she stares at me a little too long.

"I think she likes you," Cosette whispers close to my ear so only I can hear. Her lips graze against my ear and my dick springs to action.

Shit.

I mentally curse him. I have a feeling I'm about to walk into the lion's den, and I certainly don't want to do so with an award-winning erection. The thought makes the big guy calm down and I chuckle.

"Too bad for her, I'm crazy about my girlfriend," I whisper close to her ear this time, and I don't miss the way she shivers just a little at the contact.

She looks over her shoulder and smiles. Lavender eyes so trusting and sweet. "You ready for this, lover?"

"I was born ready, baby."

The restaurant is a lot stuffier than where I normally dine, but it smells damn good. The tables are covered in white cloths with candles and flowers sitting atop, and the dim lighting sets the mood. The hostess stops at a large round table and Cosette squeezes my hand.

I take in the group. The dicklicker, Jeremy, moves to his feet and I don't miss the way his icy gaze moves past me.

"Cosi," he says, moving toward her and kissing each side of her face. "Did you receive my flowers?"

He speaks loud enough for everyone at the table to hear him and he reeks of booze.

"I did." Cosette's posture is stiff and her hand does not leave mine.

"You don't look pleased? In fact you look a little *off*, are you feeling all right?"

"I actually had a horrible allergic reaction to the lilies," she says, and I fight the urge to laugh at the douche kabob's reaction. He looks like he's been slapped.

"What? Since when are you allergic to lilies?" He's aggravated and he doesn't hide it.

"*Since birth.*" She delivers it so perfectly that I try to cover my laughter with a cough.

"Oh, nonsense. You'll be fine, Cosi. The point is that he

sent you the gorgeous arrangement," her mother says and I'm startled that there is no concern whatsoever for her daughter having a severe reaction.

"Hello, Maman." Cosette displays little emotion in her tone. "You remember my boyfriend, Caden." She turns and looks at each person at the table and they all move to their feet at once.

"Yes. Nice to see you, Calden," Vivenne says, and I bark out a laugh as Cosette corrects her.

Again.

"You as well." I make my way around the table shaking hands. I get a chilly greeting from Sabine Toussaint, but I'd prepared for that. Alban Dubois isn't chilly nor warm, he appears completely distracted and disengaged. Perhaps put out that he's even here. I don't get the feeling it's my presence that annoys him, but that *everyone* seems to be bothering him.

The surprise of the evening is Gerard Toussaint who appears to be clueless that I'm stepping on his son's turf. Or he just doesn't care. Either way, he claps me on the shoulder and pulls me in for a hug.

"Nice to meet you, young man. Any friend of our Cosi's is a friend of mine."

When I step aside, he pulls Cosette in for a long hug. I can see that he adores her. More so than his son who just appears to want to lock her down.

Cosette takes in the table, and there is one vacant seat next to Jeremy and one empty seat beside Gerard on the other side of the table. She comes to a stop and stares at her mother. "You're kidding, right? I'm not sitting away from Caden."

"Come on over here, I don't mind moving," Gerard says, shooting his wife and Vivienne a look of disapproval.

"Thank you," Cosette leads me to the two seats.

"You look tired, darling," Vivienne says, studying her daughter.

"I have a mean hangover and I've taken Benadryl to stop my throat from closing due to my twenty-four-year allergy to lilies." She places her napkin in her lap and I laugh. The girl is witty as shit, and I'd be lying if I didn't say that I'm charmed by Cosette more and more each day. She is full of surprises. I've always appreciated her strength on the job, her no-nonsense attitude, but she's even stronger than I'd originally thought. Maybe she's just finding that side of herself, and I'll do whatever I can to help support her.

"It was pretty bad," I say, and Sabine's eyes double in size when she looks at me. Was I not supposed to speak at this dinner? These people are fucking crazy and I'm just getting started. "She had welts all over her body."

A gasp echoes around the table as if I've just committed a mortal sin. Vivienne rolls her eyes. "We don't need the gory details."

"Well, I needed to make sure my girl was okay, and that meant checking every inch of her beautiful body. You know, to make sure the welts were going down."

Cosette's hand finds mine beneath the table and she squeezes. I glance over to see her covering her mouth to hide her smile.

Just getting started, baby.

"Oh my. Well, that's more details than is appropriate for dinner talk where I come from," Sabine says, and Jeremy nods before waving over the waiter and ordering a double whiskey straight up and another bottle of wine. We all place our dinner orders before the server hurries off.

"I'm just thankful she made it to dinner. I almost took her to the hospital. Probably best you stop sending flowers to my girlfriend anyway. It's disrespectful *where I come from* to send flowers to a woman who has made it clear that she's in a relationship."

"Amen to that," Gerard says, holding up his glass and shaking it for the server to bring him another.

"Of course, you don't have your own son's back," Jeremy hisses.

Cosette is leaning against me as if she can barely keep her eyes open, while Vivenne and Sabine are giving me death stares. Jeremy downs his whiskey and asks them to bring another. Alban looks like he's taken Benadryl himself as he keeps nearly nodding off, but I don't miss the way he glances at his daughter with admiration, yet still appears completely disengaged.

"I like that you aren't afraid to call out another man if he's not respecting your lady. My son has always had a hard time with boundaries," Gerard says. "He's a bit entitled."

"No one needs your opinion, Father." Jeremy turns to face me. "And maybe you're disrespecting me by dating Cosette at all. Have you considered that? We had plans to be engaged this summer." He tips his head back and finishes yet another cocktail. No one appears startled by his behavior, so I get the feeling this is the norm for the old dickwhang.

"We have never discussed an engagement before you sprung it on me at the opening … when we were broken up," Cosette says, sitting up now, cheeks pink and eyes full of fire.

"Jeremy." I wait for him to look at me, but I don't miss the way Vivienne's eyes are bulging out of her head that I'm calling him out. When he finally turns to me with complete annoyance, I speak. "It takes two people to get engaged. One to ask and one to accept. Cosette did neither. And she wouldn't have agreed to go out with me if she were even remotely considering an engagement with you. So I suggest you check yourself, buddy."

"*Check myself?* Why don't you check yourself?" he says, and I try not to laugh.

The guy is so pretentious it's not even funny. At least be original. He's just throwing my words back at me. He wouldn't stand a GD chance in the Taylor household.

"Excuse me, but this is a fine dining restaurant. I won't have this low-class banter at my table," Sabine says as she stares at me.

"Not a problem for me, as long as he understands the situation."

"You don't even know her," Jeremy shouts, and everyone looks stunned by his loud outburst. But I'm guessing this guy is one too many cocktails in to compose himself.

"Jeremy, stop this. You are the one who doesn't *know* me and we've grown up together. Aunt Sabine, Uncle Gerard, I'm sorry if you're disappointed, but I have moved on. If none of you can respect that, then we have no business being here." Cosette pushes to her feet, and before I can stand, Jeremy jumps up and stumbles back, probably because he's three sheets to crazy town by now.

Two waiters have just approached the table with our plates decoratively arranged along their forearms like something you'd see in the movies. Jeremy flails his arms, knocking one waiter into the other and the plates go flying. Vivienne looks so surprised, which is shocking in itself because the woman's face is more frozen than the goddamn Arctic Sea. Sabine gasps and hurries over to her son, who is attempting to help one of the waiters to his feet, and she slips in what I think is the mashed cauliflower because God forbid these people eat a real fucking potato. Cosette hurries over to help her, because Sabine has fully yard-saled it across the floor. Her legs are up in the air and she's trying to move to her feet like a pig rolling in shit. I try to help the waiter, but I can't stop laughing because you can't make this shit up. Jeremy has the audacity to order another cocktail when he helps the waiter to his feet, and he completely ignores his mother. Vivienne and Cosette are trying to help Sabine right herself, patting down her dress in place as she fixes her hair, completely ignoring the fact that mashed cauliflower is smeared across her entire backside. A few stalks of asparagus have landed on the table and Gerard Toussaint reaches across the table for one and takes a bite and chuckles, making no attempt to help anyone with the mess they've made. Several waiters are there now, trying to help with the chaos, and Cosette turns to look at me before breaking out in a fit of laughter.

"Oh my gosh. This is the worst dinner ever," she says over her laughter. "Sorry, lover."

I shrug before grabbing a piece of asparagus from the table and taking a bite. "I've had worse. You've met my brothers."

Tears are streaming down her face from laughter and her mother and Sabine are looking at her like she's lost her mind. Her father and Gerard follow suit and start laughing along with her, and Jeremy shoves his chair into the table and stalks off. Not to help clean up the mess he's made, but the bastard makes his way to the bar and drops down on a stool and orders a drink.

These people are motherfucking batshit crazy. And I'll be damned if I'm not having the best time watching Cosette laugh her ass off about it.

She doesn't fit in here. She never has. She's special, and it's obvious to everyone at this table, which is why they all want to control her.

"Mother, we're going to head out. I'm sorry about the mess. I think it's best that we leave." Cosette kisses her cheek and she kisses Sabine's cheek as well, as the two older women huff off to the bathroom to clean up, shooting me daggers as they leave the scene of the crime.

"Sorry about"—she holds her hands up and gazes around still laughing—"all of this."

"Not your fault, sweetheart." Gerard leans close to Cosette and whispers something in her ear and she nods.

"Goodbye," she says, as she leans down to kiss her father. He grasps her hand and pulls it to his lips. It's a much more tender moment than I've seen from him before, and Cosette wraps her arms around him and hugs him tight.

"Thanks for having me," I say, smiling at the two men.

"Caden, it's been a pleasure. You've got a good one there, young man. Hold on tight," Gerard says.

"I intend to." I reach for her hand and we make our way out of the restaurant, everyone turning to stare as we do.

"That went well, huh? I think they like me," I say as I hold the door open for her.

"I think that went better than expected. They definitely like you." We both burst out in laughter as we walk to the car.

Another remarkable night with Cosette.

I could get used to this.

CHAPTER TEN

Cosette

"Thanks for coming," Caden says as he takes a long pull from his beer.

"Of course. I wouldn't miss your birthday. The big 3-0! Never dated an older man before." I clink my wine glass with his.

He clutches his chest. "Ouch. I'm thirty years young, lover."

"You sure are," I tease. "I'm excited to meet your sister."

"Yep. Pen's a character. She's looking forward to meeting you as well. Gus is on his way back from the airport with her now. She had an exam this morning, so she couldn't fly out last night."

"You told your sister about me?" I cock my head to the side and study him. He's so freaking good-looking it takes my breath away most days. And the more I know Caden Taylor, the more I like him. His insides match his outsides.

He's kind and loyal and fiercely protective of the people he loves.

Not that he loves me.

No, no, no, no.

We're friends. But he definitely has my back. The way he handled everyone at dinner two nights ago was unbelievable. He didn't react or get his feathers rumpled by the craziness that is my family and Jeremy's family. He put them in their place, and unfortunately, they just unraveled more as the night went on. For everyone else, it ended in disaster. For me, it was highly entertaining.

"Of course I did. You're my girl." He winks.

"That I am, bel homme."

He chuckles. "I don't know what you're saying, but I love it when you speak French to me."

I smile. "Handsome man," I whisper. "That's what I said."

His eyes light up and he looks the tiniest bit shy for a moment.

"Well, now I really love it," he says. He rubs his hand down his face like he's trying to wipe some of the smile off. "So before things get crazy, I wanted to ask how it went today at the hotel with your mom? She seemed pretty tense."

"Her face makes her look tense because you can't tell if she's smiling," I say over my laughter. "But she's still upset about the dinner. Not at you. She blames me for that whole scene that played out."

"How was any of that your fault? Jeremy was three sheets to the wrong side of trouble. He was sloppy and the cause of all of it."

I nod. "I know. My mother has never been super logical. And you can't really reason with her."

"I don't like her blaming you. What does your dad have to say about it?" His pinky finger grazes mine as we're sitting at the bar. As if touching one another has just become second nature through the show we've been putting on. Or maybe he's trying to comfort me because he feels badly about the way my mother is treating me. Spence, Emma, Jesse, and Mya are playing darts, and Caden and I made our way to the bar for a drink. The simple contact has my stomach doing all kinds of flips. I sink my teeth into my bottom lip to calm myself.

"He hasn't said much. That's been his MO lately. He just takes it all in, I guess. He's been pretty distant."

"Yeah? Are you two close?"

"We always were. Sometimes I felt like it was me and Dad against the world. My mom and Juliette are power-houses, you know? They run the roost. Always have. Dad and I tend to blend in the background. But ever since I've broken up with Jeremy, he's been pretty distant. I don't know. I miss our chats, but every time I try to go there, he's just so closed off."

He nods and runs his finger up and down mine. "Keep trying with him, Cosi." It's the first time he's ever called me that. It's always grated on me the way Jeremy and my mother say it. I thought it was because I didn't like the nickname. So not true.

I freaking *love* the way it sounds rolling off Caden's sexy mouth. Those plump lips.

Dear God. Where did that come from?

Well, there's no shame in speaking the truth. I think it's okay to think your friend is gorgeous. He just happens to be a hot, sexy guy who's pretending to be my boyfriend.

A girl can admire a beautiful man, right?

It's like admiring a gorgeous piece of art.

As long as you don't touch it because it's not yours.

And Caden Taylor is definitely not mine.

I need to figure myself out on my own.

I am woman ... hear me roar.

That's my new mantra. I've waited a long time to get here. A long time to find myself. To find my voice. The last thing I need to do is get mixed-up feelings with a guy I really care about. A guy who has become a really good friend in a short period of time.

I don't have a lot of those, and I don't want to mess this up.

"I will. Thanks for that. You're right. I need to fix things with him. I'm so used to tucking tail and running away when it comes to my family, and my mom has encouraged me to give him his space. But it's time I do what I think is right."

"I agree. Did Jeremy reach out and apologize?" Something crosses his dark features, but I can't read it.

Anger?

Jealousy?

"Of course he did. He apologized about the lilies and then insisted he's sent them to me before and that I'm wrong about my allergy." I chuckle.

Caden doesn't laugh.

"That dickswab is clueless. You were covered in hives and your throat was closing up. How is that not real?"

I cock my head to the side and try my best not to laugh. "Do you want to know what he thinks it is?"

"Oh, I can't wait for this one."

"He believes that my body is reacting to us breaking up and to my new relationship." My head falls back in laughter, and I pull my hand away because the alcohol mixed with his nearness is doing funny things to me.

"How were you ever with that guy?"

"I honestly don't know," I say, just as a gorgeous woman with long brown hair and beautiful blue eyes approaches.

"Hey there, birthday boy," she purrs. If you looked up voluptuous in the dictionary, there would be an 8 x 10 glossy of this lady. She's wearing a red body-hugging dress that fits her like a second skin. There are more cutouts than there is fabric. Her overzealous breasts are barely contained by the strip of fabric trying to hold them in place. It doesn't look like they need the help. Gravity appears to be on their side. I mean these are some serious breasts. I glance down at my chest and I suddenly feel self-conscious that I'm wearing a white sheer blouse with jeans and heels. I've been the president of the itty bitty titty committee for many years, and my boobs are having some serious breast envy at the moment. Sure they've filled out since high school, but there's still barely a handful there.

"Veronica, hey," he says, as he pushes to his feet and gives her a hug. He introduces us and we both say hello. Her gaze runs from my head down to my feet before she turns her attention back to Caden.

I suddenly feel the need to get out of here. Veronica runs her hand up the back of his neck and I have the overwhelming urge to claw her eyes out.

I'm not that girl.

Nor will I ever allow myself to be that girl.

It's his birthday. He's been playing a role to help me out. What kind of friend am I to hold him back from enjoying his birthday?

I'm sure Caden is used to sleeping around. I'm not blind. Women notice him when he enters a room. He's never talked to me about his relationships. I only know that he isn't in anything serious, which is why he agreed to help me out. But that doesn't mean he isn't sleeping with other women when we aren't together.

Although we're together a lot. He'd have to have some pretty quick booty calls to pull it off.

Why am I even thinking about this?

It's not my business.

I skirt around them and head for the back of the bar where the others are gathered, but I don't quite make it that far. A hand wraps around my bicep.

"Hey, hey, hey. Where are you running off to?" Caden asks, and I turn around and laugh.

"I thought I'd give you a minute with your friend. It's your birthday. I want you to have fun."

He smiles and I squeeze my thighs together because all sorts of things come alive in me when Caden Taylor smiles at me.

He's just a friend.

He's just a friend.

He's just a friend.

He just happens to be terribly sexy.

"I have fun with *you*, lover."

I straighten myself. I don't want to joke about this right now. "Caden, I appreciate all that you're doing for me. But it's your birthday. My family isn't here. We can stop playing for the night so you can do … whatever it is you do on your birthday."

"I've had plenty of birthdays that I don't care to even remember. Right now, I want to hang out with my fake girlfriend and my family. Veronica is a friend."

"A friend with benefits, I'm guessing." I don't know why I say it, but I want to know.

"What makes you say that?" He smirks.

"Something about the way she was claiming you, I guess. Call it instinct, but that woman does not want to be your friend."

He laughs and it's contagious. Even all green-eyed-monster feeling, I laugh too.

"Damn, you're cute, Cosi. Come on, lover. Let's go beat these fools at darts."

He leads me to the back where everyone has just finished their game and moved to a tall table near the dartboard.

"Hey, hey, hey," Gus shouts. "The party is here."

I turn around to see a beautiful girl, who I assume is Penelope, Caden's sister. She has long dark hair and piercing blue eyes, but she favors the brothers. They all look so different from one another, and yet also have strong similarities. She's petite and looks to be about my age or close to it.

"Bring it in, birthday boy." She wraps her arms around Caden's neck, and he lifts her off the ground and spins her around.

"Thanks for being here, Penny girl." The closeness between these siblings makes me ache for something I've never had. I've always wished for a big family, and the Taylors make it all look so fun.

"Are you kidding? I wouldn't miss it for the world."

"How'd that econ test go?" He sets her down on her feet.

"Killed it." She sings out and everyone laughs.

"Before you make your rounds, I want to introduce you to Cosette," he says, and she turns to look at me.

Before I even say a word, she's got her arms wrapped around me. She's most definitely a Taylor. Beautiful. Warm. Kind. I'm guessing she has that wicked sense of humor like the rest of them just by the way she carries herself. Like she's ready to dish out whatever they serve up to her.

"It's so nice to meet you. I've heard so much about you from—well, *everyone*, but mostly Caden," Pen says and Emma comes over to hug her next.

"Hey, I've been telling you all about Cosi the past few

days. No way has Caden given you more deets than I have," she says as she moves to stand beside me. "She's our missing piece to the puzzle."

"You got a lot more missing pieces to that crazy puzzle of yours, baby," Spence says and everyone laughs.

"Ignore them. I'm happy to meet you finally," Pen says to me.

"I've heard so much about you as well. So glad you were able to come all this way for Caden's birthday."

"Are you kidding? You've met *the brothers*. They'd have a meltdown if I didn't come for their birthdays. These boys love to be celebrated," she says, as Caden rolls his eyes. "Oh please." She nudges Caden in the chest. "Your birthday celebration lasts an entire month. You're the worst."

"You *are* the worst," Gus says, and Jesse and Spence both agree.

"I won't argue with you. I enjoy a good birthday month." Caden puts his arm around Gus' shoulder. "I do think I'm tied with Gus though, for being the worst."

"True." Pen laughs, as the server comes over with a round of drinks for everyone.

We spend the next few hours laughing, drinking, dancing, playing darts, and laughing some more. The girls fill me in on the GD behind the G.D. Taylors.

"Oh man, you should see my mother when these boys curse like sailors. She loses her…" Pen pauses.

"Shiiiii … take mushrooms," Mya says and we all burst out in laughter.

"Wait until you meet my parents. You're going to love them. They make up for all our craziness. My mom can't wait to meet you." Pen smiles at me and my eyes widen. I'm surprised that Caden told his sister about me, and never in a million years would I think he'd speak to his mother about me. We aren't a couple.

We aren't anything really.

"Don't be surprised, girl. These boys tell their mother everything. It's a G.D. Taylor thing." Emma laughs.

"A friend of Caden's makes you a friend of all of ours," Pen says, bumping me with her shoulder.

And I'm GD fine with all of it.

CHAPTER ELEVEN

Caden

"I can't believe how far along you are. Wow, your vision really came to life. Proud of you," Pen says after we finish touring the property. The hotel opening is in ten weeks, and though we have come a long way, we still have a long way to go.

"Thanks. I was excited to show you the progress. The interior is all Cosette. It's her vision, and she executed it flawlessly." We settle next door at the cafe and order coffee.

"She told me that the interior was all inspired by you." My sister smirks, as she sips her coffee.

"Cosette is humble as shit. I'm hoping some of that rubs off on Gus soon." I laugh.

"So what's really going on there? Just friends? You sure about that? You two sure gush about one another. And I didn't miss the way the sexpot in the red dress kept looking over at you at your birthday party the other night. She looked disappointed that she wasn't leaving with you." My baby sister is nosy as hell, but she's also very perceptive. You can't get much by Penelope Layne Taylor. The girl was born to sniff out a lie. And no one enjoys calling you out on your shit more than she does.

Was Veronica disappointed that I didn't go home with her the other night? Sure. We've hooked up a few times, but I'm not feeling it at the moment.

Whether I'm in a real or a fake relationship, I don't fuck around. And right now, Cosette needs me. I'm good with it.

"She'll get over it. I'm not giving Jeremy any wiggle room to call me out and try to get her back." I've filled Pen in on the situation.

"I see. So you think Jeremy would know if you took another woman home?"

"Maybe. I'm not willing to risk it. The dude is not playing with a full stack. She needs to be free of him."

She smiles and I know a lecture is coming. "So you're not willing to cheat on your fake girlfriend. That's some serious loyalty, brother."

"What can I say? I'm a loyal guy."

"That you are. And there's nothing going on between you two?" she presses.

"Nope. I mean, we spend a lot of time together. She's young. She's trying to find herself. She's finally free of that dicktaco and she needs to be on her own right now. I respect that."

"She's twenty-four. She's hardly too young. She's older than me. So you've asked her if she wants to be alone?"

I groan. I'm not in the mood for a Pen grilling. "She wants to get away from her ex-boyfriend. Her family wants to shove him down her throat because apparently he has more money than God, and they care about that shit. I'm a means to an end. Nothing more."

"Would you care if she dated someone else? I mean, other than the dicktaco?" she asks, as she sips her coffee like the true shit stirrer she is when it comes to my personal life.

I growl. "Don't say that. She needs to be on her own."

She cracks up at that. "Sure she does. And she's moving next door to you next weekend, right?"

"She sure is. Finally getting out of crazy town."

"How's that going to work, you know, when you two stop playing house? She'll be your neighbor. She'll probably bring lots of men home at some point. You going to be okay with that?"

I push to my feet and my chair makes a loud skidding noise when it moves across the tile floor. I'm done with this conversation. "I'll cross that bridge when I come to it. Let's go. I need to get you to the airport."

We have plenty of time, but her questions are agitating me.

I don't care who Cosette dates in the future. Of course I don't.

But she needs to be on her own right now.

The thought of this ending has me all sorts of uncomfortable and that pisses me off.

"I have four hours until my flight leaves, you stubborn ass." We walk out of the cafe and back to the hotel. "I'm meeting Cosi when we get back. We're going to the cafe for coffee too."

I roll my eyes. "Do not stir shit up, Pen. I'm not fucking around. She's trying to figure things out. We have a good friendship and I don't want to mess it up."

"Because you messed things up with Leah? You know she wasn't the right one for you, right? She was dating her current husband a week after the breakup. That's not a soul mate, that's a speed dater. You made the right call. Your gut told you she wasn't the one. Even with all that pressure she put on you. Just because you weren't ready back then, it doesn't mean you never will be."

Did it sting that my ex replaced me in record time and found her way down the aisle that she'd pushed so hard for us to walk down just months before? Sure. Was I the most trusting guy on the earth? Probably not. I didn't buy into that happily ever after shit then and I still don't. I've never found anyone to make me believe in it. My parents have it and I'm happy for them, but not everyone wants it.

Not everyone needs it.

I like my life. And there are plenty of women that are open to doing the casual thing.

It works for me.

Speaking of which, I have a nasty case of blue balls, which isn't helping me practice patience with my sister's rapid questions about Cosette. I haven't been laid since this whole thing started, and I'm fine with it. But my dick is a different story. He hasn't been a part of this negotiation.

So, I've been rubbing it out to thoughts of my fake girl-friend every morning in the shower. Sue me. I'm not acting on it. Hell, I'm even loyal to the girl in my fantasies. She is hot as hell. She smells like heaven. Her laughter is like the best song I've ever heard. And those lavender eyes put a spell on me every time I look at her. But we're friends and I won't cross that line.

Cosette needs to figure out how she wants her future to play out, and I'm just helping her get there.

"Done with this ridiculous conversation, Pen. Don't bring this up with her, or I swear I'll shave your eyebrows off in your sleep."

Her head falls back again and she pats my cheek. "Love you, brother dearest."

I roll my eyes. No matter how much she gets under my skin, I can never stay mad at my baby sister. I've never been able to.

"Hey, there. I just finished up in the suite and have time for a break. Did you want to go grab a coffee?" Cosette's eyes land on Pen's hand and the coffee cup she's holding. "Or a muffin?"

My sister laughs. "I'm a senior in college. If I haven't had three cups of coffee before 9 AM, I'm behind for the day. I was just coming to find you to head next door."

"Great. Do you need anything, lover boy?" Cosette teases, and I don't miss the way Penelope watches our interaction.

I need to be careful.

I don't do gray areas, and Cosette Dubois could easily become a gray area.

"I'm good. Thanks. Have fun."

"Oh, we GD plan to," Cosette says and she winks.

They both wave as they head out the door. I'm immediately hit with dozens of questions from the electrician and I shift to work mode.

It's what I do best.

Cosette moved in next door yesterday, and she invited me over for dinner tonight to thank me for helping her. Hell, I didn't do much. Most of the furniture was new and had been delivered. She hired movers for the rest of it, and they did most of the work. I helped her hang a few things and move some furniture around after they left. Her style is more comfortable than her office. Whites and pinks and a lot of fresh flowers. It's cozy, just like her.

I knock on her door, and she yells for me to come in.

"Honey, I'm home," I call out when I step inside.

"I've been waiting for you, lover," she coos, and my dick goes hard once again. This is happening more often now, and I need to figure it out. I don't know how long I can go without sex, as this is definitely the longest for me. I'm starting to not think straight.

Gus called me a dicknoodle more times than I could count last night at Mean Mug. We'd gone for a few beers. I'd spent the day with Cosette and I needed something.

Air.

Space.

Distance.

Her.

I'm drowning in this girl, and I've never felt that way before. So it's time to check myself. Draw a line and stay on the right side of it.

Turns out the air, the beer, the space ... none of it worked. I missed her today and couldn't wait to come over. How lame is that?

My fake girlfriend is the only girlfriend I've ever missed.

That is fifty shades of fucked up.

I hand her the flowers and her face lights up with surprise.

"No lilies, I promise."

"Well, that's because you know me, dear. And how in the world did you find periwinkle roses?" she gasps.

"Hey, it's your favorite color, right? Could you not have picked a more basic color like pink or red? Alice, the florist, was not happy with me."

She laughs and her cheeks turn pink. I want to kiss that perfect little nose with the few freckles scattered across it.

No, dicktit.

Wrong direction.

"I've never seen periwinkle roses. You're full of surprises. Let me get you a glass of wine and put these in water." She turns around and I take a minute to appreciate her fine ass. The way her jeans hug her curves. She struggles to reach for a vase, and I move behind her. Even in her heels, I tower over her. I pull down the one in front.

"This one?" I ask, looking down at her. My chest to her back.

Close enough to taste her. She nods, but she doesn't speak. Almost like she's holding her breath. I stay there longer than necessary because I'm a greedy bastard when it comes to Cosette.

I hand it to her, and my fingers graze hers.

Crap on a cupcake.

Just the simplest touch and my dick thinks it's go-time. I back away and turn around to take in the space.

"Wow. You're all settled. This looks amazing."

She sets the vase down on the island and pours us each a glass of wine. She places mine on the counter, and I wonder if she's avoiding handing it to me because she feels the same thing I do every time we touch.

"Thank you. I've been busy today. Thanks for hanging that curtain rod. I love having that window open, but I like having the option to close the white linen panels if I need the privacy."

For what?

Is she taunting me?

Visions of Cosette dancing around her apartment naked fill my head. I sip my wine and settle on the barstool, adjusting myself as inconspicuously as possible as she continues working in the kitchen.

"Did your parents end up coming over today to see your place?" I ask, desperate to change the subject about what

Cosette would be doing in her living room that required privacy.

Is she going to start bringing dudes over here?

Oh, hell no. That shit would not fly with me.

You're friends, dickhead. Get it together. I sigh. I know I'm in trouble when I can't even get creative with my dick names. Geez.

"My mom ended up going to lunch with Juliette and they didn't want to leave their side of town. But my dad came over and we had a great visit." She chuckles as she sets a tray of cheese and crackers and fruit in front of me. Mya and Emma like these things and they have a funny name for them.

A chartitty board?

No, that's not it.

My eyes zero in on Cosette's top. Her perfect tits press against the fabric and my mouth waters.

Sick puppies.

Estella's cooking.

Yaya's Nipplegate story.

These are all the things that can pull me out of a desire-filled haze at the drop of a dime.

"Oh yeah? What did he think of the place?"

"He liked it. We were reminiscing about my childhood. It's the first time in a long time I felt like I was communicating with him. It was really nice," she says. "I mean, he wasn't feeling great. He has allergies and his ears were plugged, so I felt bad about that."

"Well, I'm glad he came by."

"Yep. And he asked about you."

"Damn, this is good cheese." I finish chewing. "What did you tell him? Is this the breakup dinner? Are you dumping me, lover?" I keep my tone light, but my chest squeezes as the words leave my mouth.

This is going to end at some point. It can't go on forever. And Cosette and I will finish up the job at the hotel and go our separate ways.

Sure, we'll be neighbors, and we are most definitely friends, but we won't be spending all of our days together when we're done. And the reality of that bothers me.

More than I thought possible.

"No, I mean, unless you want to call it done. I will understand, you know. But they seem to finally accept the fact that I've moved on. Jeremy isn't quite there yet, but my parents are. So you say the word and I'll pull the cord."

"Nope. You're not getting rid of me that easy, baby." My words are all tease, and she smiles.

"Dad seemed genuinely happy for me, so I feel bad about lying to him. If I didn't think he'd tell my mother, I would have told him the truth. But the only way they're going to let me find my way is to think that you and I are together. At least for now. I wish they could respect that I want to be on my own. Free of Jeremy. Free of their expectations. Does that make sense?"

It sure as shit does. She wants to be on her own. She can't say it any more clearly than that.

"Absolutely."

"My dad never brought Jeremy up once, so I don't think he's as upset about the breakup as my mom wants me to believe."

"Well, that's good to hear. It sounds like you're on your way to being free of everyone."

Including me.

I need to respect her wishes too.

Cosette Dubois is off-limits.

We are friends.

And it's time for my dick to get on board with that.

CHAPTER TWELVE

Cosette

I had a really nice time with Caden the other night when he came over for dinner, but something has felt a little off ever since then. I can't put my finger on what it is. He's just not coming around as much when I'm at the hotel, not as flirty. It's only been a few days, but today when I called him *lover*, he didn't even smile.

I'm back at my office now, catching up on a few things I've missed from being at the hotel so much lately.

"Cosi!" My mother sashays into my office, smiling. Louie squirms out of the Chanel bag she's carrying him in, leaping to the floor and Maman squeaks. "My baby!"

I pet Louie and appreciate his Louis Vuitton romper. His whole body shakes with his excitement to see me.

Maman sniffs. "You must've just had salmon or tuna or something, luring him in with the stench."

"No, I actually skipped lunch today." I push back in my chair and gather a few papers from my desk. "But let's hope I wouldn't have a stench about me even if I'd eaten," I say under my breath.

She waves her hand. "Oh, pay me no mind. I have the most wonderful news. We're going to have a pool party this weekend. You won't believe who's coming. Alexander Fontaine! Can you believe it?"

"Really?" She's right for once—I can't believe it. Alexander is only the hottest designer in the States and Europe right now. He's in his forties and I've been watching his work closely since I was a teenager and decided I wanted to follow in his footsteps.

"How did this happen?"

"Oh, Gerard and Sabine set it all up. He's in town and can you imagine—he loves to swim." She shudders like the thought is preposterous. "Since we have a pool and the Toussaints don't, of course I offered our beautiful pool. It will be an intimate pool party, only a couple dozen of us or so. You must come. He asked specifically for you."

"What?" My hand flies up to my throat. "He asked for *me*?"

She laughs. "Oh, I'm sure he just wants you to model in one of his spreads or something."

I deflate a little bit at that. I did some modeling in college, but I hated it. I'd hoped he'd heard I was making a name for myself with Dubois Designs, but knowing Gerard, he probably exaggerated the whole thing to my mother to make me sound good. I'm grateful there's one Toussaint who seems to have my back. But it will probably mean seeing Jeremy too, with his family involved.

My mom winks. "You know this could really be the thing to knock some sense into Jeremy. A man of Alexander's *caliber*."

The heat slaps my face like a physical punch. I see red

instantly. I don't bother reminding her that I'm seeing Caden, because how many times can I say it?

But seeing Alexander Fontaine—I can't turn that down.

"Wear something beautiful," she says, reaching into the Chanel and pulling out a credit card. "My treat." She pauses before handing it to me. "Just please don't go over … a thousand."

"Well, that's a first. You don't normally give me a budget, but rest assured, I would never spend a thousand dollars on a bathing suit."

"You'd wear a bathing suit?" she gasps.

"Did you not say a pool party?"

She covers her mouth in horror. "Do people really swim at those things though? Oh, merde."

She's so flustered she leaves the office and then flies back in. "Louie? Louie, come here, love."

Louie is hiding under my desk by my feet and he stays as still as he can, not moving an inch.

She looks at me wildly. "Where did he go? Please tell me he didn't go find more chocolate."

"He's under here," I tell her, leaning down and scooping him up. It would be too mean to let her worry about him, although I was tempted with the way he was cuddled up to my feet. He bares his teeth at Maman when she walks toward him.

"Sorry, little buddy," I whisper into his fluffy neck.

He looks at me longingly as she stuffs him back into the bag and sashays out of the room.

"Saturday at three," she calls out.

"I'll be there."

I don't hesitate. I have the text written to Caden in three seconds flat.

You up for a pool party on Saturday at 3? My parents' place?

It takes a little longer for him to answer and when he does, it's jarring. I don't think he's ever pulled the one letter man-text with me. Not once.

K.

K? I feel hurt and the tiniest bit like I want to go off on him but realize it could be my snobbery getting in the way right now. I know it's not the worst thing he could do, it's just so Jeremy. So typical male. So *not* Caden.

Now I'm certain I've done something wrong or that he's done with this little arrangement.

If you're not able to, no worries! Just thought a little pool time might be nice with how hot it's been.

Sounds good, he says back. No cute nickname, no emoji.

Dejected, I shut everything down and pull a Vivienne Dubois. I go shopping and I spend too much money.

Caden is sweet when I see him the next day at work. I almost think I imagined the whole thing. He's still not quite as attentive as he usually is, but I think I'm expecting too much out of a fake relationship. The poor guy can't be on 24/7, especially when he's put his dating life on hold. When Pen was in town, she let it slip that he definitely *isn't* seeing anyone else, and that he's taking his job as my fake boyfriend very seriously. *"He doesn't want to give Jeremy anything to run with,"* she'd said.

That made my heart nearly burst with butterflies, but it also made me feel so guilty. I guess the sooner all of this can be resolved, the easier it will be for everyone.

So I guess I'm going to enjoy this time with him while it lasts. Can't say I love the thought of being his best buddy when he starts bringing all the Veronicas home. The thought makes my stomach twist.

Oh no. What if the insulation isn't the best? What if I could hear him with someone?

I'm so shaken up by where my thoughts are taking me, I avoid Caden as much as possible in the days leading up to Saturday. It's hard to do, but I manage to do it without a single confrontation. The work gets done, and Caden and I haven't had a second alone. Not one lingering look either. I've been very professional.

And I haven't brought up the pool party again either. It's killing my little organized brain to not double-check to see if he's going or not, but I resist. The last thing he needs is a clingy fake girlfriend.

Saturday morning, he texts while I'm still in bed.

Should I bring the pizza slice floats for the party today? You think Vivienne would approve?

He sends a picture of the Taylor siblings, Emma, Mya, and Caden's mom, on individual pizza slice floats, and they're all in a circle to make the full pizza. I crack up. If you look up fun in the dictionary, there would be a picture of the Taylor family.

I cannot think of anything more perfect than this for a Vivienne party. I haven't even told you about our special guest.

Louie in a bikini?

I lose it again. And feel so relieved that he seems back to himself again that I can't even contain it. I jump out of bed, excited for the party. Because Caden will be with me.

Louie will definitely be in a bikini.

He doesn't say anything else and I clean my apartment, do laundry, and take my time getting ready.

When it's almost time to go, I unplug my phone from the charger and see that I've missed another text from Caden.

It's a photoshopped picture of Louie sitting next to Hugh

Hefner in front of the Playboy mansion. They're both wearing long red robes and Louie's sash is open. He's standing up—I don't know how he found a dog standing to make this work, but it's freaking hilarious and a tiny Speedo is showing between the open flap.

I laugh until I cry.

I'm still laughing when he knocks on my door.

He's smiling so big, but it drops when he sees me. I glance down at my ensemble and back up at him.

"Too much? I didn't want to take the time to change when we got there, so I thought I'd just wear this on the way."

He swallows hard. "Fuck, Cosette."

My eyes widen and I'm pretty sure my nipples reach out to the heavens in hopes that they can touch him somehow.

"You look fucking amazing," he says in a husky voice.

Damn. I fan myself with the huge hat I'm carrying to cover myself in the sun with later. Fortunately, his eyes are still scanning my tiny white bikini that's showing through the long sheer black and white polka dot cover-up that reaches the floor. It's all very old Hollywood with my black kitten heels and fire engine red lipstick. I have the long glam waves going too, and Caden takes note of it all.

Do I normally put in this much effort to attend a party of my mother's? Absolutely not.

But thoughts of my fake boyfriend on my arm had me putting a little more effort in than usual.

"You look incredible," I whisper. And he does. He looks ready for a beach wedding in his white linen shirt and pale grey linen pants.

"Not even fit to be seen next to you." He holds his arm out and I loop mine through it.

"Not true even a little bit. You look good enough to eat."

The words leave my mouth and my eyes fly to his, mouth open. "I mean. That. Well, it's true, but…"

He is stunned at first, but he quickly recovers, laughing all the way down the hall. We reach the elevator and step inside. The air feels expectant, like something good is about to happen.

Instead of turning to stand beside me in the elevator, he stands facing me and puts his hand on my waist.

Mercy me. Every part of me is straining to get closer to him and it's like he feels it too, our bodies colliding into each other's. His head lowers and I think—*this is it, it's happening for real this time!*—when the elevator opens and Gus gets on.

"Well, Hot Cheetos and Takis, what do we have here?" He slaps his hands together and rubs. The guy is too good-looking and hilarious for his own good, because if it were anyone else interrupting whatever the hell that moment was between Caden and me, I'd want to inflict some kind of punishment. Instead, a little nervous laugh escapes me and I look down at my feet as if they'll save me.

When I look up, Caden looks like he might throttle Gus and Gus is grinning so wide, I'm afraid it will stick.

"Hot damn, you guys look scorching hot." His eyes widen when he takes in my whole outfit. "Uh, Cosette, I can see right through that dress."

Caden bops the back of his head and Gus yelps.

"Well, I can!"

"It's a swimsuit, and get your eyes back in your head, dickwaffle." Caden's usual teasing tone is gone and Gus' grin is back.

"Okay, brother, my apologies to the lady," Gus says, reaching out for my hand. "For the record, it is *never* a bad thing if I can see right through a dress. Just so we're clear."

He's about to kiss the back of my hand, when Caden puts

his hand between Gus' lips and my hand. Gus cackles and I get the giggles too. Caden bites the inside of his cheek, trying so hard not to laugh now. Gus lets go of my hand, and the elevator stops.

"Love you, brother," he says. "You are nailing the method acting."

He takes off before Caden can grab him again, his laughter echoing through the lobby.

Despite the Gus segue, the heat between Caden and me is still in full swing all the way to my parents' house. We're quieter than usual, but it feels necessary. I, for one, need time to regroup and remember that I like my newfound independence. Because my body is telling me I want to climb Caden like a tree and never come back down to earth.

CHAPTER THIRTEEN

Caden

I wasn't sure what to expect at the Dubois pool party, but Alexander Fontaine was not it. Cosette tells me he's here right as we're walking through the gate and into the lush gardens surrounding a pool I've only ever seen on reality TV shows about the rich and famous. I am an admirer of his work, having studied his concepts of designing sustainably yet elegantly. He was the mastermind behind the Devereaux House in Paris, and I was obsessed with his creativity for a long stint in college.

All of that to say this: I almost can't even care. That's how bad my lust-filled thoughts are wrapped around Cosette Dubois. She is driving me fucking insane with her cherry lips and the way she always smells like the sweetest flowers. Her smile and the way—

"Cosette, over here," Vivienne calls out, her hand on Alexander's arm. He looks taller and better looking than I expected in person. And his eyes are honed in on Cosette. She does make quite the entrance without even trying.

She clasps my hand and I've never been more grateful to have her by my side. I stand tall and proud, and yes, I'm still sporting the blue balls, but little Louie runs by and it's like my photoshopped picture was prophetic. He's wearing a little black Speedo with a hole in the back for his tail to hang out. It's enough of a comical sight to put the brakes on all my dirty thoughts.

Alexander smiles warmly at Cosette, and Vivienne clutches her daughter's arm like she's just able to breathe again now that she's back in her presence.

"Alexander, I'd like for you to meet my daughter, Cosette. She is a rising star on my design team and has long held you in such high esteem. Cosette, this is Mr. Fontaine," Vivienne says with a flourish. I've never seen her smile so big. And it only gets bigger when Jeremy steps into place beside her.

Alexander reaches out and takes Cosette's hand, lifting it to his lips, and I have the same urge I had with Gus, to hold my hand out between them to keep the contact from happening. Only this time, I don't act like a child and the effort to be an adult about someone touching Cosette makes me itchy.

Cosette smiles up at him, her cheeks flushed and her face all aglow like an angel. My heart pitter-patters and it is not the only one, if Alexander's smile is any proof.

"It is my pleasure to meet you, Cosette." And damn me, if his French accent doesn't kind of make me swoon myself. "I admire the beautiful work I've seen of yours. When Mr. Toussaint told me it was your vision that captured his restaurant so beautifully, I knew I must meet you."

Jeremy clears his throat and tries to cut in to say something, but Cosette jumps in. "It is an honor to meet you, Mr. Fontaine. I love your work," she says.

"Please, call me Alexander."

She smiles. "Alexander, I'd like to introduce you to Caden Taylor. He's renovating The Lux, another project I'm working on, and it is going to be spectacular."

"Thanks to Cosette here," I add. I reach out to shake Alexander's hand and I feel him sizing me up, possibly wondering what I am to Cosette. Should it bother me that she didn't introduce me as her boyfriend? Nah. I'm here, aren't I? "I've long admired your work," I tell him.

"Thank you," he says politely before turning back to Cosette. "I'd love to hear your thoughts behind some of the decisions you made—like the beautiful curtained-off booths in the back." He holds his arm out and Cosette looks at me wide-eyed as she takes it and walks away.

Damn. That was smooth. And fuck him for taking my fake girlfriend right out from under me.

"Doesn't feel so good, does it?" Jeremy says, as we watch the two of them walk away.

"Don't compare our situations. They're not even close." I walk away before I say more than I should. The dickcaca is working my last nerve, and I have no patience for him.

There are a couple dozen people milling around, and it looks like a movie set. Mr. Dubois and Mr. Touissant are both stretched out on lawn chairs beside the pool, each donning some sort of colorful Hawaiian shirt. They both have cock-tails and Jeremy's father is talking a mile a minute, while Cosette's father appears to be looking off in the opposite direction. Everyone else is drinking a cocktail in a fancy glass and looking too cool to get in the pool. I'm tempted to strip down and do a cannonball in the water … but there's commotion near Vivienne that puts that on hold. I move a little closer to see if I can help. She's trying to pick up Louie and he has something in his mouth and is headed right toward the pool.

Next thing I know, she's shrieking, "My baby! Louie, no!"

And the little guy isn't watching where he's going with what looks like a big pork rib hanging out of his mouth. He goes sailing into the water and sputters.

"He can't swim," she cries. Even though Louie seems to be gathering strength, his dog-paddle instincts kicking in.

I kick off my shoes, ready to jump in, but what happens next is the most shocking. Vivienne Dubois goes flying into the water, hat, clothes, and shoes be damned, and is the one that comes up sputtering and not gathering strength. She goes under and I don't hesitate.

I pull my shirt over my head and step out of my pants, glad I'd thought to wear my trunks underneath. I dive in and lift Vivienne out of the water, as she spits water in my face. While I'm at it, I gather Louie in close too, and drag them out of the water. Vivienne is huffing and puffing, her mascara running down her cheeks as she cries.

She's still saying, "Louie, my baby," so I'm not sure she even realizes her life was the one who seemed in the balance for a second or two. Louie licks me, the rib still floating in the water, and trots off before Vivienne can grab him. She cries harder.

"He's okay. Good as new," I assure her.

Her hat is wilted and dripping as I try to help her to her feet. It's then that I notice the guests are staring at us in various levels of shock and dismay. And then I hear laughter starting to rumble. I turn around and see Mr. Dubois, head thrown back, laughing so hard he's holding his chest. It takes a moment, but then Mr. Toussaint joins in. It's the first time that Cosette's father appears to even be engaged in what's happening around him. Interesting. He doesn't miss a beat to laugh when his wife looks like a drowned rat.

Vivienne squeaks and pushes my arm away, where I'm still making sure she's steady on her feet. She has one heel on and one heel still in the water as she hobbles, up and down, up and down, toward the house.

Everyone else looks too terrified to move until she's fully in the house and then there's a collective sigh of relief and the scattered chuckles begin.

Cosette makes her way toward me, Alexander still by her side, and her eyes have doubled in size.

"I wish I had a video of that," she manages to get out when she finally allows herself to laugh. "That memory will live on in my head forever." She presses her hand to her mouth and her eyes are overflowing as she loses it again.

"Your poor mother," Alexander says, chuckling. His laugh even sounds dignified, the bastard. "I hope she will join us again soon."

"She'll be back. She won't want to miss the action."

We all look over when we hear the sounds of Louie having his way with the stuffed giraffe. It's something that's hard to ignore and yet hard to look away from. I try to give him privacy as he's finishing, but the little dude is really giving it his all. Cosette moves toward him to try to distract him, but he has quite the finish and then trots over to me, Raffi hanging from his mouth.

Same as before, he drops the stuffed animal at my feet and looks up at me.

"Uh, you're welcome?" I say. "If this is your thanks for saving your life, I think the full thanks should go to your mother."

Cosette loses it again and Alexander stares between the two of us, looking perplexed. I may not be head of the design universe, but making Cosette laugh makes me feel like I'm the luckiest guy alive.

. . .

Things settle down after we've eaten. The drinks are flowing freely, but I'm keeping my intake to zip. Cosette and I are finally in the pool, and the last thing I need with her exposed skin in such close proximity is alcohol running through my veins. I feel drunk without it. Especially when she looks at me with that flirty expression in her eyes that I've been seeing more of lately. I can't tell if I'm just wanting to see it so badly that I'm imagining it or if it's really there. I've never been in this position before, so I feel unequipped to know. I need to ask Mya and Emma what their take is on Cosette and any feelings that might be stirring up. Honestly, I don't let myself go there most of the time.

"What are you thinking about?" she asks, swimming toward me.

She gets so close that I put my hands on her waist under the water and she floats in even closer. Her legs wrap around my waist and I can't remember what she asked me. This feels too good.

"Caden?" she asks, her voice all tease. "You okay?"

"What? Yeah." I tighten my grip on her, and she gasps when my hands grasp her thighs. "We playing it up today?" I ask.

"I'm game for anything," she whispers.

Things like that. She's been saying things like that more often, where it could be perceived all kinds of ways. And the way I'm perceiving it is with me sliding her swimsuit to the side right now and impaling her with my cock. Pretty sure she didn't mean that exactly, but—

Her eyes get wide when she feels how hard I am.

"Sorry 'bout that. It's been a while." I try to play it off to that, but I'm almost certain it's all her. My dick doesn't seem to realize that this is a little game we're playing.

She surprises me by looking over her shoulder and then back at me, grinning. And then she kisses me. Not a *sweet, keep it simple in front of your parents* kind of kiss, but *a full-on, I am going to knock you right off your feet* kind of kiss. Her tongue and mine duel for control and I forget that we're at a party at her parents' house. I have to hold onto her glorious cheeks underneath the water to not go down, which makes her push into me harder. Not what I thought I'd be doing today, but I am here for it one thousand percent.

Until there's a huge splash next to us and Cosette takes her plush perfect lips off of mine. It's a sad moment. But probably for the best. I was about to rock into her or sneak my fingers underneath her bikini bottoms and that wouldn't have been the best decision in front of the fam. Or at all. Right, *right*. Good internal.

Jeremy splashes water on us—of course it was him jumping in. "Get a room," he says under his breath.

"Good idea. Thanks, Jeremy," Cosette says, staring up at me. Her lips are parted, and it takes every ounce of willpower in me not to finish what we've started.

It's a show. It's a show. I repeat those words to my dick. *Fake, fake, fake.*

Fortunately, most people are by the bar or in conversation and haven't noticed the full make-out session in the pool. Everyone but Jeremy, and when I glance around, I see that Alexander and Vivienne seem to be paying close attention too. Hmm. Well, I guess we were playing to the intended crowd.

I just have to keep reminding myself that this is not what it appears to be. Not even what I'm feeling. I can't get lost in the moment. But it's not as easy as I'd planned when I signed on for this gig.

And that thought alone is a bit alarming.

Time to pull back a bit and keep my head in the game.

CHAPTER FOURTEEN

Cosette

I'm toweling off and glancing back to see Caden doing long strokes back and forth across the pool. Damn. I did not want to untangle my legs from his waist. That was the single hottest moment I've ever experienced. My mom moves in next to me and clucks her disapproval.

"A beautiful man is only good for a distraction," she says, as she watches him swim too.

"He's more than a beautiful man, but damn, he sure is that." I sigh and she turns to me, taking my hand in hers.

"That scene in the pool was appalling, but if you would only let your good sense return, you'd see that it seems to have worked. Not only is Jeremy walking right into your hands, more than ready to commit, but Alexander Fontaine can't keep his eyes off of you. The world is your oyster, Cosi. It's time you stop this rebellious streak and grow up."

I'd been honored by Alexander's attention earlier, but I couldn't help but feel he was more about a fun time while he's in New York than wowed by my job skills. He asked me out to dinner and I told him I'd have to check with my boyfriend to see if his schedule was also open. He'd grinned politely but didn't pursue the topic.

I love having a fake boyfriend. Is that okay to admit? It's the perfect excuse. And it's endless fun. No complications. Well, maybe a couple. The only time it ever gets weird is the guilt I have for holding Caden back. I know he's horny as hell after that experience in the pool—I'd love to think that's all me and that I turn him on so much he can't see straight, but I've always been the realistic one in the family.

The other complication being me. I don't know how long I can keep this up without blurring the lines. It's like my brain knows this is short-term and we're just having fun tricking my parents and Jeremy, but my heart and body are at war with that theory.

Caden gets out of the pool and my mouth goes dry. He gives his hair a good shake, and I watch his every move. The way the sun glistens off his tanned shoulders, his hair that's lighter than Spence's and Jesse's but darker than Gus'—is my favorite shade and slightly wavy, and I love winding my hands through it. His chocolate brown eyes that are so kind and caring and that seem to see straight through to my soul.

"Cosette," my mom says, and I jump. She shakes her head and mutters under her breath.

I walk toward Caden because he's really the only one I care to be with at this party, and Alexander steps in front of me before I reach him.

"You and your boyfriend seem quite close," he says. "I wonder if the two of you might want to join me for the evening. Something tells me we'd have unforgettable experiences together." He looks at me and then at Caden, who has picked up his clothes and is walking toward us.

I swallow hard. Can't say I've ever had this kind of invitation before. But Caden does that to people. He makes us see things through rose lust-colored glasses.

"Oh, my boyfriend doesn't like to share," I say to Alexander just as Caden walks up.

Caden's eyebrows reach the heavens. "Doesn't like to share what?" He smirks.

"Me." I wink and his pupils dilate, his mouth parts, and he is by my side in an instant, his arm around my waist.

He lowers his mouth to mine and I think I'm floating. Too soon, he pulls back and I crash back down to earth.

"No, I don't," he says.

"Too bad," Alexander says under his breath. "If you change your mind, here's my card." He holds it out to me and I take it, only because I don't want to be rude, not because I will ever contact him in a million years. "I'll make it worth your while, both of you." He gives us a sexy smile and strolls away.

I don't look at Caden for a few seconds because I know once I do, I'll be a goner. His hand tightens around my waist and I feel his shoulders shake.

"Stop," I hiss. "I won't be able to get it together if I start laughing now."

"I'll make it worth your while," he says in my ear, in an exaggerated Alexander accent. "Did the man really just proposition both of us?"

I place my hand on his chest, not because I care if anyone's watching. Not because I want to put on a show.

Nope.

I touch Caden because I want to. I need to. This isn't a game to me at the moment.

I don't know what it is.

"He did. That's definitely a first." I laugh.

He puts his hand over mine and his mouth moves to my ear to whisper. "Are we putting on a show again? I hope I didn't come on too strong in the pool. Just trying to be the perfect fake boyfriend."

His words are a literal punch to the gut, but I tap my fingers against his chest before pulling my hand away. I smile up at him. "I think we've put on enough of a show for the day. Should we head out?"

His gaze narrows and he studies me. "Yeah, sure."

"Okay, let's make our rounds and we can head home." He takes my hand and a lump forms in my throat.

This is me getting carried away. Reading the signals all wrong. I asked him to do me a favor and now I'm making more of it than it is. The guy is doing everything I've asked, and for what? Just to help me out. And now I'm going to start crushing on him and make him feel awkward for shutting me down.

I feel sick to my stomach when we say goodbye to my mother. She's been carrying Louie in a BABYBJÖRN ever since the pool accident. His hair has dried slightly spiky and he's wearing a white V-neck.

"Goodbye, buddy. Is he wearing scrubs?" Caden asks as he pets the top of Louie's head.

"No. He doesn't work in a hospital. He's wearing the finest Egyptian cotton known to man. After the trauma, I thought comfort was most important. Thank you, Caden. You saved his life."

I close my eyes for a minute because my mother has clearly lost her mind over the incident. At least she's not shaming me for my girls-gone-wild-spring-break-edition escapade in the pool any longer. Caden is the hero of the moment.

Hell, he's been the hero for me since the day I met him. I

look up and watch as he hugs my mother. He's so kind. He didn't think twice about diving into the pool. No one else made an effort to move. My father chuckled as if he'd completely forgotten the fact that my mother can't swim very well.

Mom's hair looks a bit shellacked into place, but considering the woman took the plunge into the pool in the midst of her shindig, she's pulled it together well.

"You saved his life, Vivienne. I was just there to help you out."

My mom has treated Caden like the dirt beneath her Manolo Blahniks ever since we started this whole fake dating thing, and yet he jumps into a pool to help her out for no other reason than he's just a good man.

Such a good man.

A man who hasn't had sex in weeks because he's being loyal to his fake girlfriend who's too afraid to stand up to her own family.

What does that say about me?

"Well, I appreciate it all the same." My mother turns her nose up once again, as if her mask has slipped back in place. "Cosi, Alexander has invited your father and I to his home in France for a visit. I can't bring Louie on this trip because we'll be yachting part of the time and with the water trauma he just had, I am not willing to subject him to it. You know you're the only person aside from me that he loves, so I need you to watch him for me. It's not for two weeks yet, so you have plenty of time to prepare your schedule. I'd like you to stay at the house with him."

No better time than the present to take control of my life.

"I'm happy to watch Louie, but I will be doing so at my home. That's where I'm comfortable."

"But it's a condo? I don't know if *he'll* be comfortable."

Caden cracks up next to me. "As long as he has Raffi, I think the little dude will be happy."

My mother sighs a few times before looking at me. "Fine. If those are your conditions, what choice do I have?"

"You're welcome, Maman. I'll be happy to help you out." I kiss her cheek, and she looks completely perplexed by the conversation.

Caden takes my hand, and we say goodbye to everyone on our way out. My father has retired to his room in the middle of the party and no one seems to find that odd. My mother shushes me when I ask if he's okay. I completely ignore Jeremy when he kisses my cheek and tells me he misses me.

"You okay?" Caden asks, when he opens my door for me to slide into the passenger seat.

"Yes, of course. Just a little tired."

"Yeah? Proud of you for putting your foot down with your mom. That was impressive."

"It's about time, right? I'm making you put on this show because I'm afraid to say what I want. The least I can do is demand I watch Louie at my own place."

"She's not an easy woman to stand up to. I get it. And I'm not complaining about our arrangement. I'll do it as long as you need me."

"You shouldn't have to though," I say, as I stare out the window and the reality of what I've done sets in. I've fallen for a man I asked to pretend to be my boyfriend. A man who isn't looking for a relationship. A man who agreed to do this because he has a good heart.

"Are you hungry? Want me to grab something on the way home?" he asks.

My heart is pounding because somehow, I lost control of the situation. I want him to grab dinner. I want him to come to my place and eat. I want him to spend the night with me ... not as my fake boyfriend ... but as someone who wants to be with me. But that's not the reality.

How did I get here?

"Thank you for the offer, but I think I'm just going to head home and get in bed early. It's been a long week."

He nods, and we're quiet the rest of the drive home. When we arrive at the building and take the elevator to our floor, he leans against the wall across from me.

"I'm really sorry if I took things too far in the pool, Cosi. I was just having fun," he says.

I think about the elevator ride on the way to the party. I swear he almost kissed me before Gus stepped on. Am I crazy? Did I misread that too?

"You didn't at all. Can I ask you something?"

"Anything," he says, as he studies me.

"Before we started this..." I use my hand to motion between us. "This whole big fake relationship thing. Did you date? I mean, I know you're uncomfortable because you're going without sex while we keep up appearances, so you obviously used to have it. But you didn't date the women you slept with?"

The doors open and he holds it for me as I step off.

"Cosette." The word flutters around like there's so much more meaning there than he's saying.

I pause and lean against the wall, waiting for him to answer.

"I haven't been with anyone since we started this whole thing. You know that, right?"

"I do. But before me, what did you do? Just sleep around?"

He's standing in front of me and he looks wounded. "I do all right."

Of course he does all right. The man is a Greek god on a bad day.

I've let myself get carried away.

I've let myself fall for an unattainable guy.

"I'm sorry this went on for so long. I messed up asking you to do this. I think we need to call this done. It's just getting too … messy."

His gaze narrows as he watches me and he takes a step back. "All right. Got it."

"Thanks for playing along. I think we fooled everyone."

Including me.

"Happy to help." He shoves his hands in his pockets.

His words sting. "I guess you can go back to sleeping around. You don't have to put up with me or my crazy family anymore."

"Sure. I'll see you at work on Monday, I guess." He starts walking down the hall and I follow him, pausing when we get to his door.

"Goodnight, Caden."

He nods but doesn't say anything as he puts the key in the handle.

Once I'm inside my condo, I lean my back against the door and cover my mouth. There's a lump in my throat that's making it difficult to breathe.

But I need to call this done, because if I get in any deeper, I won't survive when he walks away.

And he most definitely will.

CHAPTER FIFTEEN

Caden

What the fuck just happened?

I toss my keys on the counter and fight the urge to punch a wall. Maybe the lapse of judgment in the pool scared her off. I mean, I certainly didn't hide how much I wanted her.

Fuck me. That was stupid.

Maybe it was about Alexander? He most definitely propositioned her. Maybe she wants to date him.

There's a knock on my door and I hope it's Cosette telling me she was just messing with me.

Spence and Emma stand on the other side and I hold the door open to invite them in.

"Where have you been all day?" Spence asks.

"Pool Party at the Dubois."

I go to the fridge and grab a beer. I hold one up for Emma and she takes it. I hand one to my brother and pop the lid off of mine before taking a long pull.

"We were going to see if you and Cosi wanted to go grab dinner," Emma says. "Jesse and Mya went to a show."

"Cosette and I ended our little arrangement," I say, tipping my head back and drinking the rest of the beer.

"Oh. Well, you don't look too happy about it." Emma hops up on the counter and studies me.

"It's fine. We knew it would come to an end at some point, right? Now I can get back out there."

"Back out there, my ass," Spence says.

"Why? It's been a while. I'm ready to get back in the game."

They both laugh and that pisses me off. "What the fuck are you two laughing at?"

"You, little brother. You left the game the day Cosette Dubois asked you to pretend to be her boyfriend. The whole thing is bullshit. We all see it."

"You all see what? Enlighten me, old wise one," I hiss.

"You like each other. A blindfolded man in a darkroom could see that," Emma says.

I roll my eyes. "Well. You read the signals wrong, because Cosette just ended it. She told me to go back to sleeping around."

"That's a very odd thing to say when you're ending a fake relationship? Am I right, Old Solemn?"

"You're always right, baby."

"Good answer." She turns back to me. "Caden, wake up. She clearly doesn't want to end it or she wouldn't have said for you to go back to sleeping around. She would have just thanked you and acted like a buddy. Something happened at that party, and she got scared."

She's not the only one.

My feelings for Cosette Dubois scare the shit out of me.

"Listen, I'm not good at this. I don't think she's looking

for anything, and I haven't been in a relationship in a long time. We're good friends, and I would hate to mess that up."

Spence nods. "Spoken like a true coward."

I reach into the refrigerator and grab another beer. "Takes one to know one, I guess."

"Probably right, but at least I can admit it."

"Fuck you, Spence." I stalk into the living room and drop down on the couch.

"Okay, let's tone down the GD snark." Emma laughs as she comes to sit beside me, and my brother chimes in with her when he drops down in the chair across from us.

"You're frustrated and I get that. But it seems like you and Cosi had a really good thing going," Emma says.

"It was fake." I lean back against the couch and shake my head.

"Was it though? It sure didn't seem like it to anyone else."

"She wants to be free. I was acting like her boyfriend so she could get rid of the last dude that tried to tie her down."

"The last dude that tried to tie her down was a dick-nugget. You're a motherfucking Taylor. Start acting like it. If you like the girl, go get her. If you lose her, you have no one to blame but yourself."

"So eloquently stated, Old Solemn." Emma laughs before turning back to me. "He's right. Maybe she thought she wanted to be alone, but I think you both were pleasantly surprised to find out you like spending time together. Trust that. But you've got to tell her how you feel and put yourself out there. What's the worst that can happen?"

"I fuck it up, because that's what I do."

"Bullshit. You're basing this all on the words of a woman who wanted to get married right out of college. Who does that? I wasn't a fan of hers, by the way." Spence throws a pillow at me and I catch it. "It was her way or the highway …

she didn't give a shit about what you wanted. And she found some other sap who was on board with doing whatever the fuck she wanted. So stop blaming yourself for that, and go after what you actually do want."

Leah told me I was emotionally unavailable and a commitment-phobe. Maybe I was back then. But I never once felt like I was suffocating when I was with Cosette. I always wanted more. But fucking up this friendship is not an option. So I need to proceed with caution.

"Yeah, all right. I'll talk to her."

"Yes," Emma shouts as she pushes to her feet and fist bumps the sky.

"Thanks for coming by. I can take it from here."

"I know you, brother. Don't sit on this too long. I almost made that mistake myself," Spence says, as I move to my feet and he claps me on the back.

"I wouldn't have let you get away even if you tried," Emma says, kissing my brother on the cheek.

"All right, you guys go have your date night. Love you, but I need you to go so I can think."

"Too much thinking never leads to good things." Spence pulls the door open and waves.

"Did you seriously just steal Gus' mantra?"

"It occasionally works," he says over a laugh as he moves down the hall.

I close the door and think about what I want.

I want Cosette Dubois, and there's no way around it.

I don't want to fuck it up.

But this is worth fighting for. My fake girlfriend is the first person I've ever felt the need to fight for. It makes no sense, but everything in life doesn't need to make sense.

I yank the door open and take a few strides toward her door, just as she steps out into the hallway at the same time.

"Hey," I say. "Are you going out?"

"Nope." She tucks her hair behind her ear. "I was actually just coming over to talk to you."

"Oh yeah?" I ask, as I move into her space and she backs up against the wall.

"Yeah," she whispers. "Where were you going? Out to find yourself a one-night stand?"

I laugh. "Would that bother you? You've mentioned it a few times."

"Actually, yes. It would bother me."

My hand is on her cheek, and I caress her jaw with my thumb. "Why is that?"

"Because I don't want you to be with anyone else."

"Because you're afraid Jeremy or your mom will find out," I ask, and my voice is gruff. We're standing so close I rest my forehead against hers.

"No. Because the thought of you being with another woman makes me feel sick. I don't know what happened, Caden. This wasn't supposed to be real, but nothing's ever felt more real to me."

Her raw vulnerability makes my chest squeeze.

"It's real to me too, lover." I tease because saying the words scare the shit out of me. "I just don't want to fuck it up because I care about you so damn much."

"Do you think maybe it's just a physical attraction?" she asks, and I pull back and look at her.

Lavender eyes and pouty lips. Her skin is creamy and soft. Her white-blonde hair tumbles over her shoulders and the woman nearly drops me to my knees with the way she's looking at me. Like I hold the universe in my hands, and I have all the answers to life's problems.

She's changed since I saw her and smells like whatever goodness she washes with—I want to bury my head in her.

I come to my senses, realizing I've been staring at her for a while.

"I don't know what it is. It's been a long time since I've been in a relationship, Cos. I don't recognize all of these feelings. I just know I don't want to blow it."

"Is that what you're worried about?"

"Hell, yeah. I would never want to hurt you." My lips graze hers and she closes her eyes.

"There's no pressure. Everyone already thinks we're dating. So maybe instead of fake dating, we can step it up to friends who like to…" she pauses, and her voice is raspy and strained.

"Kiss? You want to up the game a bit?" I tease, and I nip at her bottom lip.

"I do. But I'm fairly certain I'm not as experienced as you. I've only been with two guys, and neither were all that exciting. So you need to be patient with me."

I press myself against her, needing her to feel how badly I want her. I want to pummel any man who's ever touched this woman. I've never been a jealous man, nor a possessive one.

But everything is different with Cosette.

"Don't you worry about any of that. You're absolutely perfect to me. I just want to make you feel good. Are you all right with that?"

Our breaths are coming hard and fast and I haven't even touched her yet.

"Yes," she says as her fingers tangle into my hair. "No pressure, okay? Let's just see what happens."

I smile. This girl is too perfect.

I lift her off the ground and her legs wrap around my waist as my mouth covers hers and I walk her toward my apartment.

When we're inside, I keep kissing her, her back against

the door. "You taste so fucking sweet," I whisper against her mouth, licking the seam between her lips for more. Her little pink tongue meets mine and she makes this perfect moan that shoots straight to my dick. I'm a goner. I fly down the hall toward my room. Once we're there, I set her on the edge of the bed and get an instant rush when she pulls her tank top over her head. Her bra is cream lace and I can see her pink rosebud nipples through the lace. She falls back on her elbows looking up at me and I pull her shorts off so I can see whatever lacy bits she has going on down here too. Her stomach is flat and defined, so delicate that I'm afraid of crushing her, but she tugs me toward her with pure greed and drags my shirt over my head.

"I would want to take it slow if I hadn't been imagining this all day long," she says. "There will be time for slow later, yes?"

"Holy hell, I love the way you think." I'm out of my pants and briefs faster than she can blink and the sinful look in her eyes is all the foreplay I need. "But first things first. Get naked," I whisper, grinning. "Take it all off and we'll see how fast you want to go when I have my tongue between your legs."

Her mouth parts and her whole body flushes. I've always wondered if it did that. And then my mouth is hanging open when she takes her bra off and throws it at me, all tease, then lowers the lace down her legs.

I lean over her when she falls back into my pillows, enjoying the insanely beautiful picture she makes on my bed.

I kiss her then, the way I've wanted to every time we're together. It's different this time without an audience, knowing we're both here in this moment and meaning it.

There is nothing fake about this kiss.

My dick tries to reach out and seize the moment, but I'm

determined not to speed this part up, no matter how fast she thinks she wants it.

We kiss and kiss and kiss, until I'm drunk on her. Her tits against my chest are making me crazy and she's squirming up to meet me, while I try not to let the lower halves of our bodies touch all the way just yet.

Patience, my sweet Cosette.

I do what I've always wanted to do—I bury my face in her neck and inhale. "You always smell so good." I don't stay there long though because every part of her smells like this. I bury my face in her breasts next, enjoying how they feel and taste and how responsive she is to my every touch. "You're so pretty all over," I whisper into her skin, gradually making my way down her body while still tweaking her nipples. "Such a pretty pink pussy."

She giggles and it's cut off with a moan when I take a long swipe of her with my tongue.

"Mmm," I moan into her and she latches onto my hair for dear life.

Time stands still until I hear her chanting my name.

She looks completely sated when I come up for air. Like a fucking angel. I'm about to ask her if she's okay, if she needs more or feels done, but she pulls me down on top of her like a woman with super strength.

"Hi," I whisper, against her mouth.

"I need you *now*," she says.

I don't need to be told twice. Once I'm covered, I sink into her wet warmth like a man starved. She's so wet that it doesn't take as long as I thought it might for her to adjust to my size, but still I take my time. I can't stop staring at her, the way her teeth clutch her bottom lip as I go deeper.

"You're filling me up so good," she whispers. "I've never … it's never … more, please."

Damn. She's killing me. I have to give her what she wants, and oh when I do, it unleashes the beasts in both of us. Her hands are all over me, a sheen of sweat covering her skin, and the sounds she makes are the best kind of torture. I impale her and she clutches my ass with her feet and hands, wanting more and more. It's the best goddamn experience of my life. I can feel every twitch she makes, thank God for ultra-sensitive condoms, and when she's close, I dive in even deeper, hitting her G-spot and making sure I rub against her clit at the same time. Every part of her begins to tremble and she squeezes my cock so hard I see the fucking stars.

"Caden, oh my God," she shouts.

And I am right behind her. "Fuck, fuck, fuuuuck."

I practically blackout when I explode.

There is absolutely no denying that our bodies were made for each other.

CHAPTER SIXTEEN

Cosette

Sacre dieu, merde, zut ... French curse words flood my brain as I replay the events from last night. I never knew it could be like this.

But my fake boyfriend is full of surprises.

He's actually upgraded to so much more.

There is nothing fake about what went on last night, and late into the morning.

The man delivered more than I ever knew possible.

And Gus was not lying at all about what Caden's been hiding in his pants. I flush and get hot all over just thinking about it.

I think about my time with Jeremy, the urgency that was always there when we were together. The dread that I felt every time he wanted to have sex. It was a task, not an experience. I thought that was the norm. But Jeremy was clearly just a selfish lover. And Jacques was very similar the few times that we were together in college, though he didn't strike me as selfish, just inexperienced. I'd decided back then that I just wasn't a super sexual person. Jeremy all but agreed, but made me feel like it was okay for him to chase his own pleasure and it was my fault that I didn't feel any of those things.

But oh my, Caden could teach a course on pleasing a woman. In fact, he should.

He moves just a little, letting me know he's waking up.

"Have you ever considered sharing your talents with other men? You know, spread the love around," I say when I rest my head on his chest and look at him.

His eyes are just opening, though I've been up swooning for the past thirty minutes.

His hand wraps around the back of my neck and he blinks a few times as he takes me in.

"What are you talking about, lover? I love that I can call you that now and it's actually true." His voice is gruff and sexy, and I have to bite down on my bottom lip because Caden makes me feel all the things.

I smile. "You're pretty amazing at the whole sex thing. I think you should share your knowledge with the other struggling blokes."

He barks out a laugh. "You're so fucking beautiful, Cosi."

My breath catches in my throat and my mouth goes dry.

What is this man doing to me?

His dark eyes are studying me, and his lips are still swollen from kissing me for hours last night. His skin is tanned velvet muscle, and his stomach is chiseled with defined abs that make it impossible to keep my hands to myself.

"You're beautiful," I whisper.

"Where have you been hiding all my life?" he asks.

I feel my eyes well with emotion. I've never felt such a

connection to another person before, but I've felt it all along with Caden, haven't I? And now that we've been together, I feel almost overcome with emotion.

Maybe he's the push that I've needed all along to get out of an unhappy relationship. To start standing up to my mother, and to take control of my own life.

"Right here," I croak, and he pushes to sit up a bit, concern laced in his dark gaze.

"Hey, hey, what's going on?" He tips my chin up, forcing me to look at him.

"I just feel…" I pause and swipe at the single tear trailing down my cheek.

"Feel what? Is this too much?" He's stroking my hair away from my face.

"No, it's definitely not too much. It's not enough." I shrug. "It's overwhelming to feel things you've never felt before, you know? Oh my gosh, I probably sound crazy. We have sex for the first time and now I'm all weepy and emotional. I swear I'm not that girl, not normally at least."

"Stop. I love that you're feeling weepy. I'm feeling it all too, Cosette. I think I've been feeling it for a while. But I know you want to be on your own, and I don't want to rush you."

I push up on my knees and face him. "I wanted to be away from Jeremy once and for all. I wanted to find myself and what I wanted. And all of that led me to you. This is everything that I want right here." I intertwine my fingers with his and really put myself out there.

I've never felt more vulnerable and I don't even mind it because it's Caden. I know I'm safe with him.

"That's what I want to hear, because I've been fighting these feelings for a long time. And I don't want to fight it anymore," he says, using his thumb to gently stroke my jaw. I close my eyes and relax.

"So what does this mean?" I whisper and open my eyes to meet his gaze.

"It means we go all in, right?" he says.

I nod. "But you aren't used to being in a monogamous relationship, right? I need to make it clear that I don't share, Caden. It's not a gray area for me. I've been with a guy who cheated on me, and I'm not settling for anything less than being all in this time around."

He nods. "I've never cheated on a woman. Yes, it's been a while since I've been in a relationship, but when I'm in, I am all in. And sharing you is not an option, Cosi. I thought I made that clear with Alexander." He growls at the thought and my head falls back in laughter.

"So possessive," I tease.

"Only where you're concerned." He pushes up and rolls me on my back as he hovers above me.

"So we're really doing this, huh?"

"Hell, yeah, we are. I think it's been real for me for a long time." He smiles down at me and my stomach does these little flips. I suck in a long breath.

"Me too. Maybe it was real the whole time," I say, because I think that's probably true for me.

"Maybe." His mouth covers mine, and I get lost in Caden Taylor once again.

"Hey, baby," Caden whispers in my ear as he comes up behind me and wraps his hands around my waist.

The past few days have been dreamy. We spend our time at work together and our time outside of work together.

I've never been happier.

"Hey," I say, as I turn around to face him.

The hotel is quiet as most of the workers have gone home for the day. The opening is fast approaching and Caden and I have been working long hours here to wrap things up.

"Did they get everything hung for you on the top floor?" he asks, and I run my fingers through his hair.

"They did. It's looking so good. Did you get everything completed in the restaurant and meet with the chef?"

"Yep. It's all coming together. It feels good, right?"

"It does. Proud of you," I say, pushing up to graze my lips against his because when he's near, I can't help myself.

"Proud of you, lover." He smiles. "You want to go christen that suite?" he asks, and now he covers my mouth with his. His tongue slips in as his hands glide down my body, stopping to squeeze my ass.

I giggle against his mouth and pull back. I'm panting and ridiculously turned on, but I fight the urge to do exactly what he's suggesting. We haven't kept our hands to ourselves since the minute we decided to give this a go. And I'm not complaining about one minute of it. I've never been so attracted to a man before, nor have I ever felt all the things that he makes me feel.

"We have dinner at my parents' house in fifteen minutes. You know how Maman is about tardiness. It's her second biggest pet peeve."

"What's her first?" he asks, tilting his head to the side as his grin spreads clear across his handsome face. His dimple is on full display, which happens every time the man smiles at me. It does all sorts of crazy things to me.

"Jorts."

"Jorts? What is that?" he asks as his gaze dances with

anticipation. Pops of gold and amber dancing in the dark orbs.

"Jean shorts. You know, jorts."

He barks out a laugh and it bounces around us as we stand in the hallway leading to the corporate offices.

"Jean shorts are your mother's number one pet peeve? Don't tell Pen. I think those are her favorite item of clothing. Preferably the shortest ones she can find."

I chuckle. "Mine too. I just don't wear them around my mother to save myself the long lecture that always follows. And she'll be in rare form tonight because she's going to be a wreck about leaving Louie."

"This is the first time she's ever left him, right?"

"Yes. I'm actually shocked she isn't taking him. But she said the long flights are too much for him these days and she thinks he'd be better off with me. I don't mind. I love the little guy. Hell, he's the warmest member of my family lately." I can't help but laugh as he links our fingers together and leads me toward the front door. We shut off the lights and set the alarm, before making our way outside.

We talk about all the things we will be doing with Louie over the next two weeks as we Uber to my parents' house. I'm preparing to be inundated by my mother about my responsibilities to her favorite child, Louie François.

When we arrive at my parents' house, we find my father sitting in the den staring at a piece of art.

"Hey there," I say and move closer, leaning down to kiss his cheek. "You doing okay?"

He nods and squeezes my hand. His gaze doesn't meet mine. He's been avoiding my gaze for too long and it's time to remedy that.

"Yes, darling," he says, eyes back on the art. "How are you?"

"I'm well. Caden's with me." Caden comes around and shakes his hand, but my father doesn't get up. That's also a new habit of his, but the man is getting up there in age, so I'm guessing he's tired.

"Stop fussing over the man. Come here, you two. I need to go over Louie's itinerary before we sit down to dinner." My mother moves to stand directly in front of my father, which startles me. "Alban, we'll be back shortly. Caden, I'm glad you're here because Louie has a lot of luggage that you'll need to carry to Cosi's *condominium*." She always says the full word, over-enunciating every syllable.

Condominium.

As if she's a toddler who's just learned a new fascinating word. She thinks condo sounds too informal. This word she likes.

"Luggage?"

I glance over at him and chuckle. "His outfits, of course."

We follow my mother down the hallway into the mudroom, where three Louis Vuitton bags sit. An overnight bag, a garment bag, and a duffle.

Yes. The dog has monogrammed luggage.

"What could he possibly need a garment bag for?" Caden asks as he studies the pile before him.

"His robes. His dinner jacket if you two decide to take him out. His Hawaiian shirt in case you take him to a pool."

"I don't even have a dinner jacket," Caden says under his breath while Maman is busy shuffling things around.

I smirk. "You're a bit less formal than Louie."

"The dude humps a giraffe. He's not better than me," Caden whispers in my ear as my mother moves across the room to gather Louie in her arms.

It takes all I have not to laugh. Louie is wearing what looks like a navy and green silky gown with a little hole in the back for his tail. The arms are wide and make his walk look extremely awkward.

"Maman. What is he wearing?"

"It's a caftan. You know, for travel."

"A what?" Caden asks.

"Travel attire, dear. His jammies are in the duffle. We brush his teeth twice a day. I've left extensive notes for you in the bag."

"I don't think you brushed my teeth twice a day," I say as I glance inside the duffle bag.

"We didn't know the importance of dental care back then." She waves her hand around and sets Louie on his feet.

I'm fairly certain brushing twice a day has been a known rule for much longer than I've been alive. And it doesn't appear to have done Louie much good in the teeth department.

"Is Raffi in the bag?" Caden grunts, because he knows that if there is one thing we need to bring with us, it's definitely Louie's four-legged lover.

"Yes." Maman pulls a silk hanky out of thin air and dabs at her eyes. I don't see liquid there, but maybe she's considering crying?

I've only ever seen her cry over Louie.

"Are you okay?" I ask. "Dad seems a little out of it too."

"No one is out of anything, Cosette," she says defensively. "Let's go take our seats for dinner. Your father is starving."

My father didn't appear to be starving or interested in anything aside from staring at a piece of art that we've had since before I was born when I saw him a few minutes earlier.

We head to the dining room, and I look over at Caden and shrug. My mother is not the most predictable woman normally, but she's acting even more erratic than usual. He wraps an arm around me and kisses my cheek.

Nancy has brought my father to the table and before I take my seat, my mother stops me.

"Wait. Cosi, I need you to help me in the kitchen. Caden, you can sit and visit with Alban."

Help in the kitchen? My mother has a staff that works for her. She's never so much as placed fruit in a bowl in the kitchen. She shows up to meals. She helps plan the menu. But assisting in the kitchen is definitely not something I've ever seen her do.

She pushes through the swinging door and I follow.

"Maman, what is going on with you?" I ask, as she leads me to the far corner near the breakfast banquet.

"Nonsense. You know how I get about leaving Louie," she says as she shakes her head. This is not a true statement as I've never actually seen her go anywhere without the dog. "What is going on with you and Caden?"

"What do you mean?" I ask.

"You seem so touchy. It's so unbecoming. People don't want to see that kind of display, Cosette."

"What? We've just been holding hands."

"Exactly," she says, with one brow raised. "Take your lead from Juliette. She's proper about those … things."

"Maman. Stop. I'm happy. I'm not going to not hold my boyfriend's hand because you think it isn't proper. Maybe you and Juliette should consider being a bit more affectionate with your own husbands." I cross my arms over my chest. I'm not going to be judged over something this silly.

"I do not know what has gotten into you, but I promise you that kind of show will not sit well with Louie." She rubs her hands back and forth as if she's just cleaned up this little mess.

I can't help but laugh. I cover my mouth with my hand to try to stop it before I compose myself. "I am happy to watch Louie while you're gone. You know that I adore him. But if me holding my boyfriend's hand is going to upset your dog, then perhaps he should stay with Juliette at the ice palace."

She gasps and then leans in to whisper as if she's telling me the most scandalous of secrets. "You know Louie is not a fan of your sister."

"I do."

"Fine. I guess I can't force you to respect my wishes while I'm gone. Apparently, it's too much to ask of my youngest daughter." She turns and starts to walk back toward the dining room.

"Pack your bags, kids. We're going on a guilt trip," I sing out behind her and she whips around. She has the faintest smile on her face. There just might be a sense of humor buried deep under her Gucci caftan.

"I do not know what has gotten into you, darling."

We join my father and Caden at the table, and it's the first time I've heard my father speak tonight. He actually has a smile on his face as if he's enjoying the one-on-one time with my boyfriend. My father hasn't enjoyed being in a group for a while. He is approaching eighty years old, so Maman says it's all very normal. But I'm happy to see him share this moment with Caden.

Caden is relaxed and content and I can tell he's enjoying the conversation.

My mother starts barking orders at Nancy to bring out the food and my father turns to look at her.

"I have a headache. There's too much shouting."

I meet my mother's gaze and silently ask her what's going on. Her eyes widen and she snaps her fingers over her head.

"Nancy, take Alban to bed. He's exhausted."

"I thought he was starving?" I say, shaking my head with confusion.

"Cosi, will you please stop arguing with me? We need to discuss Louie's bedtime routine."

"I can't wait to hear it," Caden says over a chuckle. "Good night, Mr. Dubois."

I watch as my father gets to his feet and I hurry over to kiss him on the cheek before he leaves the dining room.

I want to ask my mother what's going on, but she's so hellbent on giving us a detailed breakdown of their evening routine, I don't dare interrupt.

CHAPTER SEVENTEEN

Caden

We just had the most bizarre dinner at Cosette's parents', and I can tell she's bothered by it, but we're both so consumed with getting Louie settled we don't discuss it.

For the first time since I've met the Dubois' family, I actually had a nice conversation with her father. I think getting some time alone with him worked in my favor. He's a nice guy. Not snobby like Cosette's mother at all. He asked a few questions about my business and seemed genuinely interested. I didn't feel any anger or disappointment from him about the fact that I'm dating his daughter.

"Okay, he's in his jammies and ready for bed." Cosette walks out with Louie in tow. He's wearing cheetah print pants and a button-up top and I can't help but laugh.

"He has multiple pairs of jammies? And are those monogrammed?" I ask.

"Yep. He has several pairs. Don't ask. My mother is all

about this guy." She drops down to sit on the couch, and Louie moves to her lap.

I take the seat beside her and pet his little head. "You okay?"

"Yeah. I hate seeing my dad get older. He seems so distant and fragile. I'm not used to that. And the way my mother dismisses him every time I'm there is alarming. Like she can't stand the idea of anyone being around him. Did you two have a nice visit?"

"Yeah. He was actually great. I'm glad I was able to have a moment alone with him."

She smiles, but I don't miss the concern etched on her face. "Me too. Well, I'm exhausted. It's been a long day. Are you ready for bed? Do you mind sleeping here tonight?" We usually trade off apartments, but I figured we'd be staying here while Louie was visiting.

"I'll sleep wherever you are, lover." I lean over and kiss her. Louie yelps and I scoop him up and head toward Cosette's bedroom.

"Good answer." She follows me into the room.

Louie has a dog bed at the foot of the bed and Vivienne even sent a small wooden step stool so he could get onto the bed. This dog has more gear than most newborn babies. I was thankful that the Dubois' driver Herb was able to give us a ride home, as the amount of gear for the dog would have been embarrassing to try to shove into an Uber.

Cosette and I head to the bathroom to get ready for bed. We brush our teeth, and I watch as she scrubs her gorgeous face and applies moisturizer. I glance at Louie curled up in his bed and stop to scratch his belly before we climb into bed. He might not be as high maintenance when he isn't with Vivienne.

"Hey, maybe we shouldn't put him in all the clothes while

we have him here. Make him a little more normal, you know?" I ask.

Cosette chuckles. "I don't know if we should change up his routine. Being away from home might be traumatic for him."

"Whatever you want, baby." I pull her closer and my mouth crashes into hers. I push up on my knees and pull away just long enough to tug the tank top over her head.

"You're insatiable." She laughs but then pushes herself up and kisses me hard. I didn't bother putting on a T-shirt, and Cosette's hands are in my briefs tugging them down my thighs as we speak. It doesn't take long for us to both get naked, and her breath is coming hard and fast, which only urges me on. I flip her on her back and prop myself above her.

"I love you, Cosi."

"I love you, too," she whispers. "So much." A tear runs down her cheek and I catch it with my thumb.

I haven't said these words to a woman in a long time, and I'm convinced this is the first time I actually mean them. I love this woman with everything I have. I don't know how it happened, or when it happened, but I'm all in.

I lean down, claiming her sweet mouth.

Something latches onto my ass and I pull back and howl.

What the motherfuck is going on?

I scramble to my knees and see a leopard-clad Louie hissing at me as he stands on the bed.

"Dude. What the fuck?" I say as he lunges at me again. I have no choice but to pin him to the mattress. The little guy is out of control.

Cosette is on her feet beside the bed and she cries out. "Don't hold him down. He doesn't like to be restrained. Please, Caden. Let him go."

"Are you serious? He's acting fucking crazy." I hurry off the bed, keeping the little bastard in place as I move to stand beside her. He may be a little guy, but his eyes make him look like a crazy motherfucker at the moment.

"Yes. He must just be scared. Maybe my parents don't have sex in front of him? I don't know, but I promise he won't do anything if you let him go," she pleads.

I lift my hands slowly, as I'm standing there butt naked beside a naked Cosette, terrified that this eight-pound bastard is going to attack me.

"You're okay, buddy," I say, hoping to soothe him.

Before either of us can react, he launches his body through the air. I'm so stunned I reach for Cosette to cover her, pushing her forward onto the bed, and he sails past both of us like a magic bullet on a motherfucking mission. I hear the crash before I turn around and Louie Francois is face-down on the wood floor. Cosette flails out of my hold and hurries over to him. When she picks him up, he has a tooth dangling from his mouth, there's one shark-sized tooth lying on the wood floor, and there's blood spilling out onto her hands. The bastard only had three teeth, and after this one falls out, he'll be down to one.

"Oh my God, Caden. He knocked his tooth out. We need ice," she cries, and she uses a sheet to wrap around her body as she cradles the crazy Tasmanian devil that is currently throwing me major stink eye.

Yeah, I rang your bell, you one-toothed motherfucker.

I just told the girl I loved her, and now I'm getting this cheetah-clad ball of motherfucking fluff an ice pack after he tries to rip my face off? What the fuck just happened?

I grab some ice and wrap it in a paper towel. When I return to the bedroom, Cosette is wrapped in a white sheet cinched just above her perfect tits. I'm guessing I won't be seeing those again tonight. She's cradling the four-legged cockblocker and I move to sit beside her on the edge of the bed.

"How is he?"

Her eyes well with emotion and her bottom lip trembles, and it makes my chest squeeze. Even when I ended things with Leah after years of dating, I felt nothing. Aside from a bit of relief. But Cosette being upset that her dog tried to kill me and knocked his own teeth out—that makes my chest squeeze?

This girl clearly owns me.

"Caden," her voice breaks on a sob. "One tooth fell out and one is dangling." She holds her hand out to show me the single tooth and I'll be damned if the little dude doesn't have teeth that look like they belong to a great white.

"Oh, man. That's … a lot." I hand her the paper towel with a few ice cubes inside. She pushes one ice cube up to the edge so it's poking out and rubs it over his little mouth.

Louie François is not the same crazed lunatic he was just minutes ago. He has a faraway look in his eyes and he appears wounded.

He attacked me. But now I'm the bad guy?

"What are we going to tell Maman?" she says, swiping at the single tear running down her cheek.

"The truth? We didn't do anything wrong here. He lost his shit and knocked his own teeth out." I lean over to look at the pearly white one currently dangling from his gums like it is on its last thread.

Did Vivienne use whitening strips on her dog? For the few teeth he has, which is basically the one still in there and the one dangling, they are impressively white and shiny.

"We can't tell her we had sex in front of him." She shakes

her head and continues rubbing the cube against his gums as he lies there lifeless against her chest.

Louie would be the worst kind of criminal. He has zero follow-through. No conviction. He goes for the attack and then plays the victim card.

And it's fucking working like a charm.

Even I feel bad for the little bastard and he tried to rip my face off.

"Technically, there was no sex involved in this scandalous attack. We can tell her that we were getting ready for bed, and the little dude lost his shit. And he did, Cosette. This is on him," I say, and I'm not backing down on this one.

She smiles and a little chuckle escapes her perfect lips. "This is on him? He knocked his teeth out, Caden."

"Exactly. He clearly has a problem with foreplay. Or nudity. This is all your mother's fault."

Louie's dangling tooth drops into Cosette's hand and she shudders but continues stroking his head.

"How is this my mother's fault? She's not even here."

"Because she's been dressing him in these crazy outfits and therefore, he's not comfortable with nudity. Dogs were meant to be naked. He clearly has issues. And don't even get me started on the fact that his reaction makes it quite clear that no one has ever had sex in that house. Except him and Raffi."

Her head falls back in laughter and then she pulls herself together and studies me. "We said *I love you* for the first time tonight. This is not how I saw that going."

"Oh really? You didn't expect for us to finally say those three little words, only to be followed by a vicious attack by Louie François? Ending in blood and gnashing of teeth?"

"I did not." She shrugs and she looks a little sad, which

makes me want to move the sun and the moon to make her smile.

"It doesn't matter where or when we say it, or what happens around us. We love each other. Whether Louie knocks his teeth out, or Gus walks in on us, or your mother insults me. None of it matters. This." I motion between us. "This is all that matters. And I love you even more for icing that asshole's gums after he attacked me."

"I'd be icing your gums if you knocked your teeth out too," she says.

I offer my hand to Louie, who looks like he's survived a traumatic event, and he leans forward to lick it.

"You're all right, buddy. And I forgive you. God knows Gus has done worse than this."

Cosette leans forward and kisses me quickly, because clearly we're both still gun-shy about how Louie will respond.

"I love you, Caden."

"Love you too, lover."

The next few days go by without issue. Louie is down two teeth, and we put him in the guest room when we have sex so we don't risk another attack. Everything else is smooth sailing. Cosette had to tell her mother what happened because Vivienne FaceTimes her daily to see Louie. There was no hiding the two missing teeth. She toned down the story, saying that Louie must have been nervous to sleep in a different room.

We left out the fact that we were getting ready for a little bump and grind, because Cosette was mortified by the whole thing. Vivienne did not take it well and let us know that she was looking into veneers.

Yep, motherfucking doggy veneers.

The dude only had three teeth, so why does it matter if he is down to one now? She felt that his self-esteem would take a hit, and she was going to speak to some specialists about it.

I can't make this shit up.

I don't make it G-rated for my brothers. I tell them exactly what went down. Everyone else thinks it's hilarious, but Gus shivers and says he won't be coming by until the *cockblocker from hell* is gone. His words, not mine. The whole story traumatizes him. And he's avoided the dog at the hotel, because yes, we take the dude to work with us every day. Vivienne insists he not be left alone for more than twenty minutes. I can assure you, we spend a lot more than twenty minutes having sex every night, but what she doesn't know won't kill her.

This morning, I've taken Louie out on his walk and Cosette is making us breakfast when we return. We'll be headed to the hotel for a busy day soon.

There's a knock on the door. When I tug it open, Gus stands on the other side.

"Hey, what are you doing here? Since when do you knock?" I chuckled, opening the door and stepping back to let him in.

"Cosi texted me that she was making breakfast. She swears that CBLF will be on his best behavior."

Yes. My brother came up with the name. Cockblocking Louie François. Cosette's cheeks pink and I can't help but laugh.

"Stop being a baby and sit down," I say, as I lean over and kiss my girlfriend and Gus drops down at the dining room table.

"I'm the only one brave enough to come in here and face the tiger," he says.

"Spence, Emma, Jesse, and Mya were all here last night for dinner. None of them had a problem."

He gasps. "You had a party?"

"We had dinner," I say, rolling my eyes, because I'm in no mood for my brother's theatrics. I was hoping to come back and get a few minutes alone with my girl, because when it comes to Cosette, I can't get enough.

Who's the cockblocker now?

Maybe we could put Gus in the guest room with a few strips of bacon, and he'd leave us alone.

"And you didn't invite me?"

"We did invite you. You said you had a date," Cosette says with a laugh.

"That's right. Thanks, Cosi. At least one of you has my back." He looks down when Louie moves toward him.

"Dude. He's fine. Stop being ridiculous." I laugh as Louie checks Gus out.

Louie jumps up on two legs and wraps his little body around my brother's calf and ankle. He proceeds to hump him with the same passion he makes love to Raffi several times a day. I respect his passion, I just don't like him trying to cut mine short.

"What in the motherfuck is happening?" Gus quakes and his back straightens as if he's under attack.

I set a plate with eggs, bacon, cantaloupe, and an English muffin down in front of him. "Looks like someone's found a new lover."

Cosette covers her mouth and reaches for Louie's collar. "Sorry about that. He usually only humps Raffi. I've never seen him go to town quite like that with a human."

"It's the pheromones. This is why the ladies are all over

me. Apparently, it works on four-legged creatures too." He shrugs and takes a bite of bacon as if this is to be expected.

We all three laugh and Cosette sets Louie on the couch with Raffi.

I'm surprised by how normal our routine is now. We're one working unit.

And I wouldn't change a GD thing.

CHAPTER EIGHTEEN

Cosette

I can't believe the opening for the hotel is approaching so quickly. Caden and I are working more than ever and I'm thankful my mother returned from her trip to take Louie home. As much as I love him, he's a handful and I need to focus.

We're at the fun part of the project. I'm going floor by floor, making sure everything is hung and placed correctly in each room. I've never worked on a project of this magnitude and I'm really enjoying it.

My mother strolls through the door of the suite I'm currently working in. This is a boutique hotel, so the details matter. There is nothing cookie-cutter about this decor. We want it to be unique and inviting.

Simple elegance is the vibe I'm going for.

"Maman, I didn't expect to see you today." I walk toward her, kissing each side of her face. I pause to scratch Louie's head and he tries to wriggle free as he frantically licks my hand.

"I wanted to check on things. My name is on this building even if you've creatively done your own thing." She looks around the space and her nose is scrunched with disapproval. But that is her natural state most of the time, so I don't take it personally.

"We are hoping to finish up this floor today. I tried calling Dad yesterday again, but I haven't heard back from him," I say. I was surprised when my mother returned to the States alone. She insisted my Uncle Perry wasn't in good health and my father wanted to be there to support his brother.

"Darling, I told you he's at the hospital with Uncle Perry. Don't pester the man. He'll be back in a few weeks."

"Since when is speaking to him, pestering him?" I place my hands on my hips and raise a brow as I wait for her to respond.

"Since his brother had a heart attack. He needs to be there, darling. Don't be needy. You have a boyfriend for that nonsense. Or is that over? Jeremy is running the show at the restaurant in your father's absence and he keeps asking me about you."

"That's interesting, since the man calls me daily, so there shouldn't be anything to ask you. He never called me this much when we were together. It's ridiculous. And it's disrespectful to the man I am dating. I've asked him to stop several times. Maybe you could speak to him?"

"How can I say something?" she huffs as she strides through the suite studying every piece of art we've just hung.

"You could say, 'Hey Jeremy, seeing as you're like family, I'd like to ask you a favor. Stop stalking my daughter. You're making her uncomfortable.'"

"Nonsense. You've known him your entire life. You

aren't uncomfortable." She lifts the gold sculpture off the table and looks underneath for a name.

"It's not a name brand, Maman. All of the materials in the project come from local artists. The man who designed that piece is an up-and-coming artist in the city. He was just featured in *Manhattan Live Magazine*," I say proudly.

"Up-and-coming? What does that even mean? Until you've arrived, no one really cares."

I pull out the desk chair because she has managed to suck the life out of me in the few minutes we've been talking, and I sit down.

"Anyway, I'd appreciate it if you spoke to Jeremy."

"Cosi, you're being very selfish," she says, running her fingers along the wood on the tabletop and then turning her hand over to check for dust.

"How am I selfish?"

"Because I'm asking Jeremy a huge favor, and following that up with a request to stop contacting his longest and dearest friend seems cruel."

I am far from Jeremy's dearest friend, but I won't even go there.

"What is the favor?" She's piqued my curiosity.

"Your father and I want Jeremy to step up at the other restaurants. You know … in your father's absence." She pulls a beef stick from her purse and hands it to Louie.

"What? Dad will be home in two weeks. He has managers at each location. Why would he need Jeremy to step in?"

My mother rubs her temples. "You know you're exhausting, right? The endless questions are too much."

"I asked a few questions," I say, shaking my head as the woman is acting completely crazy lately.

"Well, it's far too many. Juliette just supports me. She

doesn't question everything," she snips. She loves to play my sister and me against one another.

"That's because she doesn't care about anyone but herself." It's not the kindest thing to say, but it is most definitely the truth. I've asked my sister to come see my new place multiple times, and she refuses to leave Manhattan. She's a snob through and through and my parents' business is of no interest to her. Unless it affects her trust fund, and then she will definitely get involved.

"Don't be petty. Your father wants to take on a partner. He's getting older and we want to travel more."

"He hates traveling. He loves work. And he's a complete control freak. He has the people in place that he wants to run everything." I was shocked he allowed Jeremy to get involved with one restaurant. "Now he's giving up part of his ownership in all of them? Why?"

And why Jeremy who has so little experience? I keep that one to myself.

She closes her eyes and takes a few breaths. "Cosette, I cannot do this with you today. Your brother has yet another appointment with the veterinary specialist about his implants, no thanks to you and your crazy shenanigans while I was gone. And have I brought it up once to you? Have I asked you what happened over and over?" She yanks her bag over her shoulder and stares at me.

"You've brought it up every day since you returned and you've made me replay the events leading up to the accident no less than a dozen times. You've grilled me about your dog losing two teeth and I'm not allowed to inquire about my father?"

Just then Caden walks through the door, and there's a shift in the air. The man has a way of calming me, and I move toward him instinctively.

Needing that comfort.

That warmth.

"Hey there, what's going on?" he asks, and he pulls me into his arms before reaching forward to scratch Louie's head. The two are thick as thieves once again. We've put the traumatic night completely behind us, aside from my mother insisting on seeking a veterinary dental specialist.

"What's going on? My own daughter is grilling me when I'm dealing with a lot right now. My darling boy needs implants, and Cosi doesn't even realize the impact this will have on him. They are going to insert a titanium screw into his gums, for goodness' sake. All because you two were frivolous with his care."

What in the actual hell is going on with her? Is this still about me breaking up with Jeremy?

"Mother, you've got a titanium screw loose yourself. What is going on with you? The dog has had three teeth for most of his life. Why in the world are you now insisting on getting him teeth? He's always been toothless. Now he just has one instead of three. Why is this such a big deal?"

"I see. So I must have a screw loose if I want to care for my baby?"

I let out a long breath. "I love you, Maman. Let's discuss this later. I'm at work, and this is just wrong for a multitude of reasons. If you talk to Dad, please let him know I'd like to speak to him."

"I see how it is. Good day." She storms out of the room and I shake my head with disbelief.

"You okay?" Caden asks.

"I'm fine. Just a little worried about my father, but that sent her sideways. What time do your parents arrive?" Caden's mom and dad are coming to town for the opening of the hotel. We're having dinner with them tonight and I'm looking forward to meeting them.

He wraps his arms around me and kisses the top of my head. "You know you're the most patient person I know. Don't let her get to you. It's difficult for me to see the way she treats you and keep my mouth closed."

I sigh. It's nice having someone that completely has my back. He's not on my parents' payroll, he doesn't care what my family thinks of him—he is in this for me.

And it only makes me love him more.

"Thanks for biting your tongue." The last thing I want is for Caden to get drawn into her craziness.

He leans down and nibbles on my ear. "The only thing I'm interested in biting is you."

His tone is all sexy as sin, and he chuckles against my skin as my heart starts to race. I swear every time this man touches me, he sets my soul on fire.

My head falls back as his lips move along my neck.

"Caden," I whisper. "We need to get back to work."

"I want you to relax, baby. You're all I give a shit about. This will all get done. You are all that matters."

I don't know why his words affect me so deeply, but a lump forms in my throat and tears start to move down my cheeks. I'm overwhelmed by how much he loves me, because it's such a foreign feeling.

Alarm bells are going off about my dad and I'm emotional … about *everything*.

"Thank you," my words break on a sob, and he hurries me over to the desk chair and pulls me onto his lap.

"Hey, hey, hey. What's going on?" He hugs me so tight and I burrow into him further.

Needing him in a way I didn't know I was capable of.

"I'm just tired. And I'm worried about my dad." I continue to sob. "My mom brings out the worst in me. I'm worried about the opening going well. And I want your parents to like me."

I pull back and swipe at my face and try to catch my breath.

"Baby. My parents already love you. The opening is going to exceed my expectations because of the work that you've done. And don't stop calling your dad. Trust your gut. But I don't think your mom would have left him there if he wasn't okay, right? But I understand that you're worried about him. And Cosette?" He tips my chin to look him in the eye. "Your worst is most people's best."

I sniff, not believing that in the slightest, but it touches me that he thinks so. "I'm sorry. I can't believe I'm being such a baby."

"You're the strongest woman I know. I've got you, okay?"

I nod. "I know you do. Thank you for that."

"Don't thank me. You do it for me every day."

I shake my head and chuckle. "I don't know what I did to deserve you, Caden Taylor."

"Just exist, baby. That's all you ever have to do."

There's a knock on the open door, and the contractor walks in. "Sorry to interrupt."

I stand up and Caden moves to his feet, wrapping his arms around me again. "Not a problem. What's up?"

"We need you on the fifth floor for a little electrical issue. Do you have a minute?" he asks.

Caden turns to look at me. "You all right?"

"Yes, go. I'm fine." I push up on my tiptoes to kiss him.

"I'll come grab you in an hour to head to dinner." He tugs me back against him and kisses me hard. I can feel my cheeks flame when we pull away.

"Okay. See you in a bit."

I bury myself in work again, which is easy to do.

"They can't wait to meet you," Caden says, as he pulls the door to the steakhouse open.

"I'm excited. It's just the four of us? Where is everyone else?" I was surprised when he'd told me on the walk over that it was just the four of us.

"My mom is big on making sure we all get equal time, and they want to get to know you without everyone talking at the same time."

I can't imagine that kind of thought process running through my mother's head. Nothing in our family is equal. It never has been. Juliette is Maman's favorite, and she doesn't try to hide it. I've always been Dad's favorite, up until these past few months when just trying to get him to sit down and talk to me is a challenge. My chest squeezes a bit, but I shake it off as the hostess leads us to the table.

I've seen pictures of Caden's parents all over his apartment, but their smiles are even brighter in person. Caden's mother, Melanie, exudes warmth. She pushes to her feet and pulls me in for a hug.

"Oh, my sweet Cosette. You are even more beautiful in person," she says and I lose my breath at her kindness.

"Nice to meet you, sweetheart," Garrett, Caden's dad, says as he pulls me in for a quick hug.

Caden hugs both of his parents and I watch the pure joy on their faces. I'm in awe of the love that this family has for one another. I wonder what it must have been like to grow up in a household with this kind of love and care.

Don't get me wrong. I have a life most people would

envy. I grew up in a sprawling estate. I've never wanted for anything.

Aside from this, right here.

This deep love and loyalty that pours out from every part of them.

Caden takes my hand beneath the table. We all order cocktails, and Caden selects a few appetizers. His parents watch him with such pride, and I watch them with such wonder.

I want to have a family just like this someday.

"We can't wait to see the hotel. Caden tells us your design for the property is unbelievable," Melanie says.

"I believe he said it was *cutting edge.* A notch above the rest." His father smiles at the server as she sets our drinks down and he raises his glass and waits for us to do the same. "To Cosette Dubois, the girl who stole our boy's heart."

I clink my glass with theirs and shake my head. "I'm the lucky one."

"I think you're both very lucky," Melanie says, with a wink.

And for the first time in my life, I realize what's always been missing.

A void.

A sort of loneliness that I wasn't even aware of.

Until this man came into my life.

And filled me up in a way I never knew imaginable.

CHAPTER NINETEEN

Caden

Opening day is everything I expected and then some. The lobby is booming, and the restaurant and bar are packed. This was an invite-only event, and I don't think one person declined the invitation to tour the new boutique hotel. *Manhattan Live Magazine* is here taking photos as they are doing a huge spread on hot new locations downtown. The publicity will only work to our favor. We have several possible buyers here to tour the facility and a few have already pulled me and the brothers aside offering top dollar to outbid the other.

It's a good day for the G.D. Taylors.

My family is here. Pen and her best friend, Beckham, flew in today. He's a part of the family, as the two of them have been thick as thieves since their first day of kindergarten.

Vivienne, Louie, Juliette, Beecham, and Jeremy all arrive together. Jeremy is not on the guest list, but I don't think that would ever stop Vivienne Dubois from doing what she wants. Cosette hurries over to them, and when our gaze meets across the room, I know she needs me. This is how we communicate now. We don't even have to speak. I know what this woman needs without her asking for it, and she knows me just as well. I never dreamed I'd have that with anyone but my family.

"Hey, thanks for coming," I say, as I lean forward and hug Vivienne. She stays completely still as I wrap my arms around her.

I could be hugging a lamp and it would have the same response.

I shake Beecham's hand and lean in to hug Juliette, but she puts her hand up to stop me. "I don't do contact."

My head tips back in laughter.

How the fuck did Cosette grow up in this household?

"I meant no offense. Where I come from, a hug is a hug."

"It's very American of you," she says, glancing around the room and making it clear with her resting bitch face that she's not impressed.

"You were born here. You grew up here. You are as American as it gets, Juliette," Cosette says defensively, before wrapping her arms around my middle. "I'll take your hugs all day long."

"Good. You're the only one I really want to hug anyway. You guys feel free to cruise around. There are appetizers and drinks that way." I point in the direction of the restaurant and bar.

I do a double take when Louie looks up at me from Vivienne's purse, and it takes all I have not to fall over in laughter.

The poor bastard looks like he's wearing an old man's set of falsies. They are oversized for his mouth, and he has a perma cheese smile, which doesn't fit his personality at all. The angst just does not come through with the Chiclets smile.

Gus walks over and pulls Vivienne in for a hug and does the same to Juliette and they both gasp in surprise. It's a mix of both annoyance and horror, and my brother doesn't miss a beat. He slaps Beecham on the back and stops to study Jeremy.

"Aren't you the ex? I'm quite certain you weren't on the guest list," Gus says, and Cosette uses her hand to cover her mouth to hide her smile.

My brother has zero etiquette when it comes to this stuff, and I can't say I mind it at the moment.

"I'm Vivienne Dubois' guest." Jeremy tips his nose up at Gus and smirks.

"This isn't Vivienne's party. So how about we don't be a dicksalami and treat me like I'm beneath you this time. You came uninvited. Just say *thank you* for allowing me in the door."

"He's my plus-one," Vivienne huffs.

"Bringing your daughter's ex-boyfriend to my family's opening, a night that's very important to my brother in particular, was a shitty move, Ms. Viv. But I'll give you a pass because you're Cosi's mom." He pauses and looks down before jumping back. "What the fuck happened to his mouth? He looks like a four-legged, furry Tom Cruise with that smile. That's not right."

Gus wraps his arms around himself as if he needs comfort, and Cosette and I burst out laughing, as Vivienne shoots daggers at us.

"Dr. Pussy happens to be the top veterinary dental specialist in the US. He's the best of the best." Vivienne frowns.

"With a name like that, he should have considered gynecology. Maybe he would have had more luck focusing on the actual pussy, because the dude has no business touching dog's teeth. Louie looks like he's wearing your husband's dentures."

I clasp Gus on the shoulder to get him to stop.

More gasps and disapproving looks from Cosette's mother and sister. Gus is on a rounder tonight. I don't know if he's been dipping in the alcohol early or just catching the bad vibes Cosette's family is putting down and not tolerating it. He's a good brother. However, discussing her father's dentures might be taking it too far.

"My father has veneers," Juliette says, as she glances down at her fingernails as if they are far more entertaining than my brother.

I personally find him to be one of the most entertaining people I've ever met. What he lacks in couth, he makes up for with his wicked sense of humor and endless loyalty. This guy has always had my back. He's more bothered that Jeremy's here than I am. I don't give a shit.

I've got the girl.

Jeremy can suck up to her parents all he wants.

"Okay, we're going to go look around. Louie needs to get home. It's been a big day for him," Vivienne says.

Cosette takes my hand and I don't miss the way her shoulders tense. They aren't staying and I'm sure that stings. She's worked her ass off on this project, and I know how much her mother's approval means to her.

"That was GD awesome," Cosette whispers to my brother.

Gus tugs her away from me and kisses the top of her head. "I see why you're drawn to my brother, Cosi."

"Why's that?"

"Because I've met corpses that were warmer than your

mother and sister. Damn. Those are some ice queens right there. How'd a little fairy like you manage to escape?"

She chuckles and I pull her back against me. "Doesn't matter how, just matters that she did. And I plan on keeping her." My voice is playful, but I mean every word I'm saying.

Cosette's the best thing that's ever happened to me.

Whether her family likes it or not, this is the real deal.

And there's nothing they can do about it.

We make our way over to my parents, and Penelope and Beckham walk over to join us. Pen is holding a cocktail and she holds it up when her gaze locks with mine.

"This place is just—it's amazing. You guys killed it. So proud of you." Everyone raises their glass to join in on the sentiment.

"Dude, this is really something. Nowhere else I'm staying when I'm in the city," Beckham says.

He flew here with Penelope on his family's plane so they could get back quicker, as they are both in their final year of college. The guy has more money than God, but you'd never know it. He's as down-to-earth as the rest of us.

"You'll be staying with me when I move here." Pen leans against him and laughs.

"You're not moving here. No fucking way. I can't survive without you, Penelope Layne. Not happening," Beck says, and we all chuckle. They've never not lived by one another, so I don't think he's kidding about this, but my sister laughs it off. We all want her to move to New York and work for the company after she graduates, but leaving Chicago will mean leaving Beckham, and I'm interested to see how that goes down.

"Oh, please. You'll be fine." She pats his cheek. There's always been an easiness between them. "So, I have news."

"What? Spill it," Emma says, as she walks up in the

middle of the conversation with Spence right on her heels, anxious to hear what my sister has to say.

"I met someone. He's amazing. He's going to be a freaking rocket scientist. And he's hot as hel—lo, is it me you're looking for. Sorry, Mom."

Even Mom laughs at that.

"A hot genius. That's a strong combo." Emma beams.

"That's exciting. How long have you been talking to him?" Cosette asks as her fingers intertwine with mine.

"Not long. It's new," my sister says.

Beckham groans and we all laugh.

"Have you met him?" I ask, because I want to see his reaction. These two have been inseparable for as long as I can remember. Pen claims it's never been more than friendship because Beck is a bit of a player. But I can't imagine either of them will ever find a partner that's okay with their arrangement.

"I have. I'm unimpressed. He's very clingy." He takes a sip of his beer and winks at my sister, but I don't miss the way his jaw clenches when he talks about him.

"Stop. You're far clingier than he is," Pen says, as she shakes her head and laughs.

"I'm allowed to be. I've got a history. He's—what? A genius? Big deal. And he has a stupid name." Beckham shrugs.

My mother's shoulders shake with her laugh. "I thought it was Peter?"

"It is," Pen says, as she slaps Beckham on the shoulder.

Beckham shoots me a look and I grin.

"It rhymes with cheater," Beck says with a smirk. "Enough said."

"For someone who has *ham* in their name, I don't think you can really talk."

If Beckham's offended, it doesn't show, their back and forth has been like this from the beginning of time.

"Well, he's a little boring, Pen. The dude could barely hold a conversation with me."

"Because you dominated the whole conversation. Well, when that hoochie you brought on the double date didn't have her tongue rammed down your throat," my sister says, and a pink hue covers her cheeks.

Is that jealousy?

"Caden, we have a potential buyer that has some specific questions for you and Cosette about the design inspiration. I said you'd meet him at the front desk," Jesse says as he walks over to the group with Mya beside him.

"Okay, let's go talk to him."

Cosette and I leave the group and she leans into me. "Penelope and Beckham have never dated?"

"Nope. They've just been best friends their entire life."

She stares straight ahead, but there's a ridiculous grin spreading across her pretty face.

"What? You're not buying it?" I ask.

"I'm not. They may not know it yet, but there is a sexy storm brewing there," she says over a laugh.

I shake my head and pretend to gag. "Do not use the word *sexy* in a sentence regarding my sister."

"I love your family," she says just as we turn the corner and see the man waiting at the front desk for us.

"Good. They love you too."

"I can't believe it's really done. What will I do now that I don't get to spend my days with my sexy boyfriend at the hotel?" Cosette says, as she turns to face me.

I love waking up with this woman. I know I want to do it for the rest of my life, but I'm not sure if it's too soon to think about those things. I never saw myself settling down before. And now it's all I think about.

"That's a good question. I guess it just means we'll have to spend more time in bed to make up for it." I roll her on her back and prop myself above her as she laughs.

"You can hold me prisoner here any time you want." She beams up at me, and my breath catches in my throat.

"Do you ever think about living together?" I ask, because I'm done holding back with this girl.

She runs her fingers through my hair and a beautiful pink blush covers her cheeks. "Who would I borrow eggs from if we weren't neighbors?"

"You've never borrowed eggs from me," I say, nipping at her bottom lip.

"Yes, Caden Taylor. I think about all the things with you." Her voice is just above a whisper, and her beautiful violet gaze locks with mine.

"What type of things do you think about, lover?" I graze my lips lightly against hers.

"I think about living together. A future together. You know, all of that."

"What does that look like?" I move my lips to her ear and tease her some more with my mouth. Her chest is rising and falling, and her breaths are coming hard and fast.

This is how it always is when we're together.

There's so much desire. So much love. I've never felt anything like it.

"I can't think straight when you're doing that," she whispers, and her voice is sexy and full of need.

I move my face back in front of hers. "Tell me."

"I don't know. I see us married someday. I see kids in our future. Does that make you want to run for the hills?"

"Nope. I see all of those things too."

And I do.

I just needed to make sure we're on the same page.

"You do?" she asks, as she tugs my mouth down to her.

"I do. I see it all."

"Does that scare you?" I ask.

"Nope." She shakes her head. "It just surprises me, that's all."

"Why?"

"Because I never knew I could be this happy, or feel this loved," she whispers, and my chest squeezes at her words.

"Buckle up, baby. I'm just getting started."

CHAPTER TWENTY

Cosette

We've had a new routine to settle into now that my job is done at the hotel. Caden and his brothers are deep into the negotiations with different buyers and it's been an exciting time for them.

But I miss going to work with him. Now that I'm back at my office most of the time, the environment seems more toxic than ever. I'm not prepared yet to branch out on my own, but it's definitely on my mind. Caden and I have talked about it a lot and he's encouraging me to go for it. I need to at least get one more year under my belt before I explore those options, but having the hotel design on my resume definitely puts my name on the map.

There's a knock on my door and I call out for them to come in. Jeremy and his father stroll through the door and I rack my brain trying to remember if we had a meeting scheduled that I've forgotten.

"Hey, Cosi. Hope it's okay that we stopped by. We just

spoke to your mother and she said you were available for a quick chat. I've been trying to reach you, but you haven't returned my calls," Jeremy says, and for the first time that I can recall he appears humble.

"Of course. Come in." I pause to give his father a hug and awkwardly hug Jeremy. I avoid the comment about returning his calls because I've asked him multiple times to stop with the excessive calling. He chooses to ignore my request and I don't want to embarrass him in front of his father.

"Sweetheart, you are looking as lovely as ever. May we?" Gerard motions to the two chairs across from my desk.

"Absolutely. What's going on?" I ask.

"Well, Aunt Sabine and I have been talking about redoing the lobby of our office building. We toured The Lux, and I have to admit we were both a bit taken by surprise with just how cutting edge the design was. Very impressed with you, which isn't a huge surprise." He chuckles. "So we spoke to your mother and though we are going to have her do the remodel to the townhome in the city, we'd like you to give the lobby a unique design. We have a lot of traffic in that building and I think it will be great exposure for you as well."

The Toussaints own one of the largest buildings in the city, and they occupy the top two floors with offices; the rest is leased out to some prestigious venture capitalists, one of the most successful finance companies, and the most popular bakery in New York resides on the ground floor beside the iconic lobby. It's in the heart of the city in one of the most well-known historic buildings out there. I place my hand on my chest to calm my breathing.

"I'd be honored. Thank you for thinking of me."

"You earned it. You've got a great eye, kiddo," Uncle Gerard says.

"Well, aside from your taste in men these days," Jeremy

teases and then holds his hands up. "I'm kidding. Dad, could you give us just a minute to talk alone?"

"Absolutely. How about you meet me first thing tomorrow morning in the lobby and we talk about some ideas? Sound good?"

"Of course," I say. "I'll be there."

"Great. I'll go fill your mother in," he says. I hug him goodbye, and Jeremy moves to shut the office door after his father steps out.

"I've been trying to reach you." Jeremy moves back to sit in the chair once again. I move back around my desk and drop down to face him. I want this job, and I don't want things to be awkward between Jeremy and me if I take it.

"I know. But I've explained to you that it's disrespectful to Caden that you keep calling me at all hours. I'm in a relationship, Jeremy. I'm really happy." I shrug. He needs to understand that this isn't a fling. This is the real deal.

He nods. "I know. Your mother filled me in that it's gotten pretty serious. I wanted to speak to you about Lydia."

"Who's Lydia?" I ask.

"I'm seeing someone, Cosi. That's all I wanted to tell you. I'm just sort of hoping that we can forget the way I've been behaving and go back to being friends."

The relief I feel is so strong that I jump to my feet and squeal. "Jeremy, that's wonderful. I'm so happy for you."

This will mean my mom will stop nagging me about Jeremy, Aunt Sabine will stop being distant, and we can all move forward.

He laughs. "All right, well, I thought you should know. We're going to be seeing a lot of one another with you working on the lobby project for my family. I still keep an office there, and that's where I spend most of my days."

I forgot he worked there, because when we were dating,

he rarely ever went to the office. Jeremy has always been a trust fund kid and he'd never displayed much of a work ethic. I thought for sure the restaurant would keep him more tied up than he was comfortable with … maybe he is finally growing up.

"Of course that's fine. I'll be busy working on the project and we'll probably barely see one another."

"I'd like to patch things up with you and with Caden. I know I've been terrible to him. Maybe the four of us could go on a double date sometime soon? You know, as a way of moving forward and showing you I'm good with everything."

I walk toward the door and he stands. "Sure. I'd like that."

"Me too. I'll talk to Lydia and shoot you a text later today to get something on the calendar. I want to make things right, Cosi."

I'm genuinely surprised by the gesture. I'd be thrilled to put all of this awkwardness behind us.

"That would be great. Thank you."

He leans forward and hugs me. "I'll see you soon." He winks before leaving the office, and I feel like things are finally coming together.

The design meeting with Uncle Gerard went as well as I could have hoped. My mother sat in the meeting just to observe, but she didn't interject even one time, which surprised me. She seems really thrilled that I've taken this project on, and she's busy redoing their residential space, so she shouldn't bother me too much when it comes to the lobby project.

I have a text from Caden asking me to meet him and his

brothers at Mean Mug when I get out of my meeting. He says it's important, and I message him right back to let him know I'm on my way.

As I walk down the sidewalk, I'm thankful that it's a quieter evening than usual. I check my messages to see if my father's called, and he still has yet to return my call. I dial my Aunt Chavon and get her voicemail.

Again.

So far I've just left messages letting her know I miss her and I'm thinking of her. I know she's got to be quite stressed with Uncle Perry being in the hospital, but I need her to call me back because I'm getting more and more concerned about my father.

"Hi, Aunt Chavon. It's me, and I'm sending all my love to you and Uncle Perry. I know you have a lot going on and I just wanted to see if you could possibly just give me a quick call back. I'm a little worried about Dad, and I know he's just there to be supportive, so I'm probably being selfish." I pause, feeling bad to be rambling with all she's going through. "Um, but if you could just give me a quick call to let me know he's okay, it would be so appreciated. I love you."

I end the call as I open the door to Mean Mug and see Caden, Gus, Spence, and Jesse sitting at a high-top table. I assumed Mya and Emma would be here, and I'm hoping they're on their way over. The three of us have grown really close, and I enjoy all the time I get to spend with them.

"Hey," I say, as I make my way to the table. Caden jumps up and wraps his arms around me and kisses me hard.

"Missed you, lover." He laughs when I tangle my fingers into his hair and hold him there.

"Lucky for you Louie François is not here right now. The cockblocker would not appreciate this"—Gus waves his hand in the air toward us—"public fornication. I feel like I'm watching a porno."

"Get your head out of the gutter," Spence hisses, and smiles at me.

Caden guides me to the chair beside his and I drop to sit. "Where's Mya and Emma?" I ask.

"Working late. They'll meet us here if they get out of there soon. But we wanted to talk to you about something."

"Okay," I say skeptically, and Caden finds my hand beneath the table.

"We're thinking of taking on multiple projects, you know, with the four of us and Penelope thinking about joining us after graduation. She can take on a lot of the finance stuff that Jesse's been doing, so he can take on more responsibility overseeing the projects," Spence says, as he holds his hand up for the server.

We all pause and order our cocktails and a few appetizers as I wait to find out where Spence is going with this.

When the server walks away, Jesse jumps in. "We want to have a full-time designer. Someone that has the same vision as we do."

"Jeez, spit it out, people. Cosi, we want you," Gus says with a wink. "Join the G.D. Taylors and help us grow this company."

I laugh because they all look so nervous and I'm absolutely honored that they want me to be part of the team.

"Way to put pressure on her, dickwanker. We were supposed to just introduce the idea. You shot your wad," Caden says as he rolls his eyes.

Gus smacks the table. "I did not shoot my wad, you douchecake. I'm a straight shooter. I'm not the one who had to start out fake dating my girlfriend before I finally made shit happen."

My head falls back in laughter as the server sets a plate of nachos and tater tots in the center of the table and places our cocktails in front of us. I reach for my Chardonnay as Gus gasps.

"Is that a motherfucking olive in my cocktail?" He jumps to his feet and shouts to the bartender. "James! You know how I feel about olives. What are you fucking thinking?"

James is laughing along with the rest of us now, well, aside from Gus.

"Sorry about that, Gussy. I have Sasha here training, and I must have forgotten to fill her in on your oddly dramatic fear of olives," James, the bartender, shouts back and waves for the waiter to bring the cocktail back.

"Must you always make such a scene?" Spence asks, as he piles some nachos on his plate. "Anyway, Cosi, Gus didn't quite stick to the plan, but what he said is true. We want to expand, and we'd love you to be part of the team."

"You're talented as hell, and we'd be lucky to have you work with us," Jesse says. "But Caden threatened our lives that we weren't supposed to pressure you in any way. We know you work with your mother, and you could still have other side jobs that you could take on."

"But we would keep you really busy, and we're a hell of a lot more fun than your mother," Gus says, as he searches the glass when the server places the fresh cocktail in front of him. He finally nods his approval.

"Dude, that's her mother. Be respectful. Cos, it's a lot to think about. Take as much time as you need. It's just another opportunity to consider, but if you aren't up for it, we will understand," Caden says.

He's so protective and thoughtful that my heart threatens to explode.

Working with the Taylor brothers would be an amazing

opportunity. They're creative and each talented in their own right. I'm excited at the thought.

I turn to face Caden. "Thank you for being you."

"Hey, what about me? Why does he get all the praise?" Gus whines and I turn to face him.

"I was getting to you next." I laugh.

"Thank God. I hate being second fiddle."

"You are such a needy little bastard sometimes," Spence says as he turns his attention to me.

"Honestly, I'm really flattered. I love the idea of working with you all as you build this company. Let me have some time to think this over and try to figure out how that would work with my mother."

"Sounds great. Totally fair," Jesse says, because he's the most agreeable.

"All right. How about you get back to us at the end of the week?" Spence says, because he's used to calling the shots. He's not about to leave the timeline wide open.

"Just say yes, Cosi. You know you want to," Gus says, because he's not used to anyone turning him down.

"You do whatever is best for you, lover," Caden whispers in my ear, because he loves me more than anyone ever has.

CHAPTER TWENTY-ONE

Caden

Going on a double date with Jeremy dicktrap Toussaint is the last thing I want to be doing tonight, but Cosette is so excited about the possibility that the bastard has moved on, I can't bear to put a damper on her hopes.

"Thank you for doing this," she says, kissing my cheek as we step out of the Uber in front of Dussaint Cafe.

I already don't trust Jeremy's intentions and knowing he chose his restaurant for this outing just makes me more suspicious. I'm being petty as fuck. Cosi looks up at me so hopefully, I feel guilty for my foul thoughts.

"Of course. This ought to be interesting." I try to hide the irritation from my tone.

"He seems to really be into this girl. I want that for him," she says, as I hold the door open for her.

I know that being here is bringing up the fact that Cosette has still not heard from her father. She intertwines her fingers with mine as we step inside.

"Cosette, so nice to see you," the hostess greets us and I nod my greeting. She leads us to the back of the restaurant and we follow. The place is packed and the cocktails are flowing. It smells like warm bread and honey and my stomach rumbles. I haven't been here since the opening, and I'm guessing Jeremy is running the show right now with Alban out of the country. I'm surprised he wants to meet here, as I'd assume that would make him very accessible to his employees. Doesn't seem like a relaxing situation for a date. Unless he's doing this intentionally to show Cosette just how important he is.

I wouldn't put anything past the dicksteak.

When we approach the table, Jeremy appears to be in deep conversation with his date. They both look up and push to their feet when they see us.

"Cosi, thank you for agreeing to have dinner with us. Caden, I'm hoping we can repair this little rift we've had between us. Let me introduce you both to my lovely lady, Lydia." He holds his hand out as if he's presenting us with a gift.

Douchesack.

"I've heard so much about you both. It's nice to finally meet you," she purrs, and her gaze locks with mine. I look away because her intense stare makes me instantly uncomfortable.

And how could he possibly have told her much about me? The dude doesn't even know me. My guard is up.

She reaches for Cosette's hand but then tugs her in for a hug instead. My girlfriend is beaming when they pull away because she's so pleased that this woman wants to be her friend. I'm not buying it. First off, who's this excited to meet the ex? They clearly haven't been together long, because

Jeremy has been calling Cosette incessantly up until this recent announcement about his sudden girlfriend.

Lydia turns to me and does the same thing. She wraps her arms around my neck while Jeremy pulls Cosette into his arms and hugs her. I'm watching, which he probably doesn't expect, because his so-called girlfriend is pressing her rock-hard tits against me, and she blows a breath into my ear.

And did she just lick my earlobe?

What the fuck?

I pull away quickly and shoot her a look of disapproval. She smirks as if we're playing some sort of fucking cat and mouse game.

We're not.

I'm not Jeremy. I don't fuck around on my girl, nor do I have any interest in anyone but Cosette. So the little temptress can play her cards all day long, but I won't be taking part.

I reach for Cosette's chair and pull it out for her as we sit beside one another at the table. Lydia takes the seat across from me, and Jeremy sits across from Cosette.

"I can't believe how packed it is here tonight. Business is good even with my father gone," my girlfriend says, as she gazes around the room.

"That's why I wanted to eat here. If they need me, I hope you'll all excuse me. But I'm basically running the show right now."

"I thought you hired a manager to run the place?" I ask before I can stop myself, and Cosette squeezes my hand beneath the table. It's not a nice question, but I know he's up to something and I'm not going to stand by while he plays games with us.

I find it ridiculous that he has no real job, yet he insisted that they hire someone to run the restaurant because he couldn't be bothered. Alban has given him this great opportunity, but he just wants to show up and walk around and look important. Not do any of the real work.

"Well, I'm only one man. And with me taking on a lot of the responsibility at the other restaurants in Alban's absence, I need to have someone I can trust to be my eyes and ears when I'm pulled away." He holds his hand up and snaps his finger for the server.

The dude has no class.

We all order cocktails, and I don't miss that Jeremy already has one drink in his hand and has ordered another double. I hope this isn't a replay of our last dinner together, because I'd hate for him to make a fool of himself at his place of work.

His date, Lydia, orders a shot of tequila and asks Cosette and me if we'd like one. We both decline and order a glass of wine. Lydia gets a whiskey as well, so I'm guessing this is going to be an interesting night.

We go ahead and place our orders for dinner, and the dickdong proceeds to order for my girlfriend.

"Cosi would like the seabass," he says. I let out a long slow breath, but before I can speak, she interrupts.

"Um, I can order for myself, Jeremy. That is not what I'll be having," she says to the waiter.

"Old habits." He shrugs.

"You never ordered for me," Cosi says as she scans the menu before settling on the filet.

"Sorry, darling, may I order for you?" he asks his date and she nods emphatically.

Every time I look up, Lydia is staring at me with this come-fuck-me look in her eyes, and it pisses me off. Cosette does not seem to notice, as she's just happy to be buying into the story that he's moved on to find his own happily ever after.

I get it. If Jeremy is happy, that takes the pressure off Cossette with her mother and Jeremy's mother. But the dude is clearly up to something, even if my girl doesn't want to see it.

A foot finds my shin and moves beneath my pant leg, and I jump just enough for Cosette to turn and look at me.

"Are you okay?" she asks as the waiter steps away.

"Yes, I think Lydia's foot found my leg," I say, and Jeremy glares at me before straightening his face.

"Darling, I'm right beside you." He nuzzles into her neck, and Cosette leans her head on my shoulder as she watches them happily.

"I'm so sorry about that. I thought I was finding Jeremy's leg. My man loves to play footsie," Lydia teases, and covers her face as if she's horrified by the whole thing.

Just wanted them both to know that I'd be calling this shit out right and left if needed.

"It happens," Cosi says. "So tell me. How did you two meet?"

Lydia's hand flies to her chest. "Let me tell them."

Jeremy beams and leans forward to kiss her. "Of course, my love."

I glance over at Cosette and she's so taken with their connection. She has a grin spread clear across her face, and I feel badly because she's fully buying this bullshit. I hate Jeremy a little more for fucking with her. The dude has an ulterior motive for everything that he does.

"So, I was leaving the soup kitchen, just as Jeremy was coming in," Lydia says, and she pauses to down her tequila shot and bite down on a lime wedge. Where did he even find her? Spring break at Daytona Beach?

"You're volunteering at the soup kitchen now?" Cosette claps her hands together. She volunteers there once a month. I know this because I've been going with her.

What a fucking coincidence that he's claiming to volunteer there now.

"I am. I know you tried to get me to go for so long, and it finally hit me. I have so much to be thankful for. I need to give back to those that aren't as fortunate," Jeremy says, and Lydia leans into him and reaches for his hand.

"So, our eyes locked, and I turned around and followed him inside," Lydia says, reaching for her whiskey and taking it down in one gulp. "I worked a double shift just so I could be close to him."

"I love that. And now that's something you two can share. Caden and I go once a month, and we really look forward to it." Cosette is so proud that we all share this great love for the community, and it pisses me off that this is a game to both of them.

"Maybe sometime we can all go together," Jeremy says as the waiter comes over and whispers something in his ear.

"Please have Javier handle that. I want to enjoy dinner with my lady and our friends," Jeremy announces loudly.

This is so staged I can barely stomach it. But Cosette beams at Lydia. "You're good for him."

"No. He's good for me. I'm such a lucky lady," Lydia says.

I groan and try to cover it with a cough, and Cosette shoots me a puzzled look.

Is she seriously buying this load of crap?

"I am so happy for you both," Cosi says.

I do everything in my power not to roll my eyes. Jeremy's gaze locks with mine and he fucking smirks. He knows I'm on to him, but he's loving that Cosette is buying his shit.

"So what do you do, Lydia? Are you in the hospitality business as well?" I ask, because I know how much this all means to Cosette, so I'm going to play along.

"I'm in commercial real estate. Jeremy told me that you and your brothers are developers. I may be able to help you with some properties in the future," she says, and she licks her lips as she watches me.

Cosette sips her wine and completely misses it. "Real estate is such an interesting business. Things are booming right now."

"Yes, business is good. Real good," she says slowly and wriggles her brow.

What is happening?

I lean down and whisper in my girlfriend's ear. "I need to use the restroom. Will you walk with me?"

She chuckles. "Of course. Excuse us. We'll be right back."

I pull out her chair and take her hand, as I lead us through the restaurant.

"Are you not seeing how flirtatious she's being?" I ask her as we stop outside the bathroom.

She chuckles. "Everyone's flirtatious with you, lover. I'm used to it. It doesn't bother me because I know you're mine."

"Damn straight. I think this is a game for them, Cos."

She rolls her eyes. "Baby, I know that you aren't a huge fan of his. I get it. But I think he's really happy with her, and that only helps us. He's practically family. I would love it if we could move forward and go back to being friends. Can you please try to be okay with this? For me?"

Fuck.

"Of course. Love you."

"I love you the most," she says, before she pushes up on her tiptoes and kisses me.

Who's the dickhead now?

Who cares if Jeremy is full of shit? It has no bearing on my relationship with Cosette. I need to suck it up. This is important to her.

"Let's go back and join the lovebirds," I tease.

She leads me back to the table and we find Jeremy and Lydia in a hot and heavy make-out session. Maybe I've been misreading the whole damn thing. Wanting to see the worst in the guy because I don't like him.

Lydia pulls away and giggles. "Oops, we forgot we had company."

Cosette's entire face lights up. She's so fucking happy that the guy has moved on, and I'm getting on board. Whether it's bullshit or not really doesn't matter.

I kick back and enjoy the ridiculous conversation with Jeremy overselling the relationship and I don't even fucking care. Cosette's happy, and that's enough for me.

We laugh, make a few jokes, and enjoy a delicious dinner. I still don't trust the dude as far as I can throw him. But Jeremy is not a threat to me.

Thankfully, we call it a night, and we all make our way out to the street. No one has called on Jeremy again at the restaurant which is strange to me, considering he's the boss. I don't get the feeling he spends a lot of time here, because the servers are friendlier to Cosette than they are to Jeremy. It's almost like he's a silent partner.

He shakes my hand and claps me on the arm. "We good?"

"Sure," I say, hoping he really is ready to let this go.

He pulls Cosette in for a hug and I turn to say goodbye to Lydia. She thrusts her body into mine and her hand settles between us, gripping my cock.

There is no mistaking this one.

I wrap my fingers around her wrist and step back before dropping her hand and shaking my head.

What kind of fucking game are you playing?

She just smiles and hands me a card. "This is my business card. Keep me in mind on your next project."

Not a chance.

I ignore her and Cosette steps into my arms. I definitely didn't misread any of this. Lydia was here for a reason, and it was not as Jeremy's date. She was here to come between Cosette and me. If only this dickho knew that nothing could come between us.

CHAPTER TWENTY-TWO

Cosette

It feels strange to kiss Caden goodbye and go to work at the Toussaint building. I'm feeling so much better about things now that Lydia is in the picture. And my mom has been quiet for a few days, so she must know about Lydia and is choosing to suffer in silence. Thank goodness.

Caden has been very supportive of me taking this job, and I appreciate the fact that he trusts me completely. When I enter the lobby, I'm surprised to see my mother standing there with a sketch pad. She is working on the residential property while I was hired to design the lobby.

"Maman? What are you doing here?"

"I have a few tweaks to your design that I'd like to discuss," she says, and Louie's head pops out of her purse to greet me.

"A few tweaks? Uncle Gerard already approved the design." I cross my arms over my chest and study her.

"Cosette, this is my company. You work for me. If I want

to make tweaks, I will make tweaks." Her tone is harsh. When my mother wants something, she can be uncomfortably direct.

"I thought we were partners?" I say, and I cringe because my voice sounds small and timid.

"You thought wrong. Maybe someday I will pass the baton, but today is not that day. It's my name on that door, not yours." She crosses her arms and stares at me with no expression.

Sometimes I wonder if my mother even has a heart. She can be awfully cruel when she wants to be.

"Technically, it's both of our names." I just want to stick it to her where I can. Dubois Designs is not Vivienne Dubois Designs.

"That company is mine. You are just an employee. And you will do your job. I may not be able to control your personal life, and the ridiculous choices that you've made, but I can control this. And I intend to."

My mouth goes dry. Her words cut me deeply.

"I see. This is good to know."

"Glad we cleared that up. Here are the changes. I'll be stopping by daily to make sure that you uphold the correct design. I've already met with Gerard and he's signed off."

The lump in my throat is thick. I nod. "Okay."

Jeremy walks over and he studies me before speaking. "Everyone okay?"

"Yes. Just a few changes to the design." Maman hands him the new drawings to look over.

"Did my father see these?" he asks.

"He did. We both agree this design has more longevity. My daughter is fickle and so are her designs. She'll grow out of it with more experience," she says, as she adjusts the purse strap on her shoulder and raises a brow at me.

I'm not going to fight her, because this is her company after all. It's just more of a reason for me to break out on my own. I think about the offer from Caden and his brothers and the freedom it would provide.

"Thanks for stopping by, Maman. Have you heard from Dad?" I change the subject to a topic I know she will want to avoid, which will mean she'll be leaving sooner rather than later.

"Yes. He's fine. He sends his love."

I snort and she shudders at the sound. "He sends his love? I still haven't heard from him. I've left a couple dozen messages."

"The world does not revolve around you, my dear," she hisses, and turns on her heels to leave.

I feel like a wounded bird, but I hold my shoulders high and refuse to let my emotions get the best of me.

"You all right?" Jeremy asks.

"Yes, of course. This is nothing new."

"I don't know. She seems a bit harsher than usual. Maybe she's stressed with your father gone."

"Maybe. Have you spoken to him?" I hold my breath because if he tells me that he speaks to my father daily, my heart just might shatter. I'm feeling a bit fragile after the encounter with my mother, and I've been so worried about my father, that the thought of him being fine and chatting with Jeremy would really sting.

"Nope. He hasn't returned my calls. Your mother said that he's busy in the hospital and that I should work directly with her. She wants me to start taking over even more of the responsibilities at the other restaurants, but I would like to talk to him about that before we move forward with that plan."

I nod. "It's weird that we can't reach him, right?"

"Well, hospitals are exhausting. He's not the best with technology either, so I'm not totally surprised. His phone is probably dead and he won't be good about charging it."

"That's true. I'm probably worrying for nothing."

"He'll be fine, Cosi. Thanks again for doing dinner the other night. Lydia really liked you," he says, and I'm thankful that we don't have that awkwardness between us anymore.

"Yeah. She's great. I'm really happy for you."

"Thanks. How about you and Calden?" he asks.

I roll my eyes and shake my head. "Caden."

"I'm just teasing. How are you two doing?"

"We're doing great. He makes me really happy," I say, and I can't stop smiling.

Thoughts of Caden turn my sour mood around immediately.

"Good to hear. You deserve only the best," Jeremy says, and it's probably the kindest thing he's ever said to me. "And between you and me … I liked your design better than your mother's."

I chuckle and he winks before walking toward the elevators. I wave goodbye just as the contractor arrives. I lead him to the office that the Toussaints are allowing me to work out of during the renovation. There are a lot of changes to be made.

And not only on the design of this project.

The changes in my life are going to continue to take place long after this job is done.

———

I am so thankful for a night out with Mya and Emma, especially after the day that I've just had. My mother popped back over a few hours after she pulled the plug on my design to make sure that I followed through with the changes.

I did.

I'm not going to fight her any longer.

It is her company after all, and I am just an employee there. That's what I've been telling myself all day.

What that means for my future is still to be determined. But because of the Taylors, I now know I have options.

Emma is hosting a *Real Housewives* night at her place, and Caden and his brothers all went to Mean Mug for dinner and drinks.

Mya and I both step off the elevator at the same time and laugh.

"I'm so glad we are having a girls' night. Work was hell today," she says.

"You and me both." I knock on the door.

"Are you ready to get housewife-baptized?" Emma asks as she opens the door.

I've watched a few episodes, but apparently Mya and Emma are pros when it comes to all things *Housewives*. I am ready to get lost in someone else's drama.

Their apartment smells like lavender, and she's always burning candles. She and Spence have a cozy place, and Emma has an amazing eye for design. The white sofa with the black throw blanket, the velvet pillows bring in a lot of texture and a splash of color, and the long modern silk curtain panels warm up the space.

She sets down a charcuterie board on the coffee table, hands us each a glass of wine, and we make our way to the couch.

"How did day one at the douchenoodle's place of work go?" Emma asks, and Mya spews wine across the table at her choice of words. "What? I'm engaged to a Taylor. Douchenoodle comes with the territory."

"That's definitely a new one," Mya says, wiping up her mess with a napkin as she continues laughing. "I've been conditioned with the dicks but not the douches."

Emma wiggles her eyebrows. "And what a way to be conditioned."

We all laugh and sigh collectively into our glasses. The Taylor boys know how to please their women.

"It was actually not a bad day as far as things with Jeremy. I told you guys that Caden and I went out with him and his new girlfriend, right?"

"Yeah, how did that go?"

"It went really well. She's nice and they seem happy. I can't ask for more. But that certainly didn't get my mother off the warpath like I hoped it would," I say, before taking a sip of wine.

"What do you mean?" Mya asked.

"She changed the entire design for the lobby project. She reminded me that it's her company, and I'm just an employee. She thinks my designs are fickle." I shrug, trying to push away the hurt.

"Fickle? How dare she! Cosette, forgive my French, but your mother is a mother*fucker*." Emma claps her hands back and forth as if she's getting rid of crumbs and raises a brow.

Mya and I both fall back on the couch.

"That's not French," Mya says over her laughter.

"Pardon, ladies. Motherfucker is universal. My bad."

I'm trying to pull myself together before I speak. "I don't know what is going on with her lately. She seems to be more tense than usual."

"Any word from your dad yet?" Mya asks.

"Nope. I'm going to reach out to my aunt again next.

We've texted and she says Dad's fine, but it's been very short and to the point, which is not like her."

"Definitely call her," Emma insists.

"So fill me in on what I'm signing onto tonight. I want to be in the *Real Housewives* Club." I lean forward and pile some crackers and cheese on my plate. The board is almost too pretty to eat, but I'm starving and I can't resist.

"Tonight is my favorite. Beverly Hills." Mya pops a cracker with some cheese on top in her mouth and groans. "Damn, girl, this is so good."

"It's from the shop up the street. I swear they have the best cheeses and meats ever."

"Well, they carry more than that. Isn't that where your grandmother got her nipples?" I ask, and they both burst out in a fit of giggles.

"Sure is. Meats. Cheeses. Nipples. How can anyone compete?" Emma says before reaching for the remote. "So here's what you need to know. This will be a baptism by fire. We'll fill you in as we go. You've got your big players, Kyle is married to Mauricio, the king of Beverly Hills real estate, and they have a bunch of gorgeous daughters. We would most definitely be friends with her."

"Definitely," Mya says. "And my favorite, Erika Jayne. She's an icon. A powerhouse in the fashion world. She was on Broadway, she sings, she dances."

"She was married to a rich old dude, and apparently there are some legal issues there, but power to the woman. She left him and is finding her way on her own and we are here for it," Emma says.

"Kathy is a new fave housewife. She's Kyle's sister and funny as hell. Lisa Rinna is on the show," Mya says, covering her mouth as she chews.

"The lady from *Melrose Place*?" I ask, absolutely fascinated.

"Or *Days of our Lives* if you're talking to Yaya or Estella. Hells to the yes. The woman doesn't age," Mya says.

"Ooohh … who is she?" I ask, pointing at the screen as each woman reads their taglines and I'm already captivated.

"That's Dorit. She's quite the fashion icon herself. The woman knows how to dress, that's for sure," Emma says, shoving a loaded-up cracker in her mouth. "And she takes a selfie like a pro."

"Holy mother of dragons, is that Garcelle from *NYPD Blue*? I love her!"

"Yes, ma'am. Buckle up, girl. We're just getting started."

We spend the next hour entranced in all things Beverly Hills. There is some sort of catfight going on over the use of the word *violated.* There are tears and arguments, fabulous clothing, a few low blow digs, a gourmet meal prepared by the sexy Harry Hamlin. I mean, you can't make this stuff up. This cast is as good as it gets.

But most importantly, I laugh through the entire show. The commentating from Emma and Mya is as entertaining as the show. They choose sides, they give me the backstories, share their favorites—and I'm all in.

I feel a closeness to Emma and Mya and a comfort I'm not used to. I love it.

"Thanks for getting me up to speed. You're stuck with me now, because I only want more," I say, shaking my head after we watch the previews for next week.

"Right? I told you. You're the missing piece to this trio," Emma says.

"I'm so glad you and Caden are together. You two just fit, you know?" Mya refills our glasses with wine.

"He's the best. I never knew I could be this happy," I admit, feeling a little vulnerable with my words.

"You deserve it, Cosi. I'm so happy for you." Mya leans over and wraps an arm around my shoulder.

"I get what you're saying though. I had a hard time believing I could be as happy as I am. But once you let yourself just enjoy it and stop worrying about the other foot dropping, you realize that you really can just be that happy. You found one of the good ones. And he's lucky to have you too," Emma says, dabbing at her eyes.

"Ever since this one got engaged, she's all sappy." Mya laughs and hugs me a little tighter.

"What can I say? Old Solemn makes me sappy."

"Sappy looks good on you." I stand up and help them clear all the food to the kitchen just as the door flies open.

"Honey, I'm home," Gus sings out as he bursts through the door.

Spence, Jesse, and Caden stroll in behind him. Caden wraps his arms around my middle, his chest to my back, and rests his chin on my shoulder.

"How was the show? Did you have fun?"

"So much fun."

"Good. Missed you, lover," he whispers against my ear and I melt into him.

"Missed you too," I say.

"Good Lord. Get a room, people," Gus shouts out.

My head falls back in laughter, and I hug everyone goodbye. Because even a few hours away from Caden is too long.

"You ready?" he asks, as he pulls the door open.

"Yes."

The answer means so much more than what he's asking. Because when it comes to Caden Taylor, I'm ready for all the things.

CHAPTER TWENTY-THREE

Caden

"What are we doing tonight? Jesse said Mya invited all of us over for dinner?" I kiss Cosi hello, putting my arms around her waist and pulling her as close as I can get her. "Mmm, you smell so good."

"Yeah, her mom is in town. I'm so excited to meet her!"

"Oh, have mercy on us all. Why couldn't we have gone to a restaurant?"

She giggles. She doesn't realize. We've tried to tell her about Estella's cooking, but no one ever thinks it's as bad as it is until they've sampled it firsthand.

"I'm going a little bit early to help Mya. I thought you'd want the extra time to shower and get ready."

"You sure you wouldn't rather help me get ready in the shower?" I nuzzle into her neck and love the way she trembles into me, like my words and closeness cause her to shiver.

"I'd love nothing more than that, however, I'm having a

good hair night and don't want to have to redo it." She pulls back, grinning and I kiss her on the forehead.

"Your hair always looks good. I always want to sink my hands into it and give it a good yank."

She laughs and skirts around my wandering hands. "Later you can have your way with my hair." She blows a kiss and backs out of the room. "I'll see you in half an hour."

I watch as her sweet cheeks walk away, her sway reeling me in. When she glances back once more and sees where my eyes have been, her cheeks turn that rosy shade I love and she laughs.

"I'll make it worth your while, I promise," she says, her voice husky.

"You always do," I whisper, adjusting myself. My regular state of being when it comes to her.

When I get to Jesse and Mya's, Jesse opens the door and there's explosive laughter inside.

"Sounds like the party is well underway." I glance at my watch and I'm a couple minutes early.

"Oh, that's just Estella and the girls. Estella has been telling us about being sent a sample to try." He leans in closer. "For women and camping."

I frown, not getting the picture he's laying out. "Women and camping?"

"You know, so they can pee in the woods and not make a mess." He chuckles under his breath. "Estella thought it was a cooking gadget."

I snort and we both crack up when we hear a roar of laughter in the other room. I walk into the living room and Cosette's head is thrown back and she's holding her stomach. When she sees me, she fans her face.

Estella turns and jumps up. "There you are. I've been getting to know your beauty queen here. She is just beautiful." She smiles back at Cosi. "I hope you never let her walk outside alone. With looks like that—the last *Dateline* I saw was a beauty pageant girl. On her way to a blind date. She walked, the poor thing. You can just imagine what happened to her." Estella clicks her tongue against her teeth and gives me a huge hug. "So good to see you!"

I laugh. Never a dull moment with Mya's mom around. Spence comes in and Estella squeals.

"So proud of you for making our Emma an honest woman … well, almost!"

"Mama!" Mya says. "What does that make me?"

Estella lifts one eyebrow and purses her lips. "Well, I just hope you're saying your prayers at night. I know I'm sayin' them for you." She cackles then and we all laugh with her.

She looks a little different, but I haven't put my finger on it yet.

"What have you done with Estella?" Spence asks, when she hugs him.

She beams up at him. "Forty pounds gone, just like that." She snaps her fingers.

Shit. I just thought my observation skills were on point. Turns out, not so much. I didn't think she had any weight to lose, but she does look tinier than ever.

"Gus said he's on his way," Jesse said. "We could go ahead and sit down at the table. Mya made pulled pork and Emma made the mac and cheese." He gives Spence and me pointed looks, so we know if we veer from those dishes, it's our own damn fault.

"And I made my special punch! It's all I had time to make since my flight got in so late," Estella says, clapping her hands together.

The rest of us avoid looking at each other and my sweet Cosette speaks up.

"Oh, I can't wait to try it."

I squeeze her hand. She glances over at me and my eyes plead with her to not ingest the poison. Jesse starts laughing and tries to cover it with a cough, but he can't.

"You look great, Estella," Emma speaks up.

"This is part of my news," Estella says. "I wanted to wait until Gus is here since he was so vital in helping me figure it out!"

"What's going on, Mama? Tell us," Mya says. She gives Jesse a stern look for laughing but looks like she might start laughing herself. Too many memories of past holidays with Estella's cooking has us gun-shy and on the verge of hysterical laughter.

We hear a yell from the door. "The party has arrived!" And there's Gus.

He walks through the kitchen and glances at the table where we've all taken our places. It's more formal here than usual and he grins when he sees us sitting down.

"Estella, my lady! Good to see you." He points at the punch bowl and whistles. "Yes. My kind of party." He fills a glass with it and then finds his place at the table. "Sorry, I'm late. Had a hot date that wouldn't let me go."

He takes a long pull of the punch and it goes spewing across the table. "What the fuck is that?"

Estella cackles. "Now that we're all here, I can tell you my news! Because of everyone's love for my recipes, I got to thinking I needed to expand my reach. I'm being published!" She whips a book out from under the table and it's a cookbook—*Estella's Electrolytes, Lose 20 Pounds in 10 Days!*

I don't even know what to fucking say.

She stands up and passes a cookbook to everyone. I glance under the table and she has a box stashed under there and we're all the lucky recipients. I just watch her and try my best not to glance at anyone else or I will never get it back together.

She smooths down her blouse. "I've lost forty pounds and it just keeps dropping."

Wow.

"Juniper fucking Holloway, the gift that just keeps on giving," Gus mutters. He wipes his mouth and lets out a huge burp. "Pardon me. I'm about to go lose five right now," he says, heading to the bathroom.

"Take that to your condo," Jesse yells. "We don't want that here."

"Better steer clear of the punch then," I say under my breath.

"A good gut is like a working garbage disposal," Estella says. She's the happiest woman I know. And we all adore her. Just never ever want to eat anything she touches. And would rather not talk about a good gut and garbage disposals at the table, not after what happened to Gus last Christmas.

"So you've got a book deal?" Mya says, her voice quiet. I think she's in shock.

"This is the mockup, but yes! The real thing will be even more beautiful. They are saying I will be the next face of weight loss programs with these recipes, I will be taking the diet industry by storm." Estella's proud smile hasn't left her face once.

"That's … amazing," I say.

"Can't believe it," Spence speaks up.

"What an … unbelievable thing," Emma finishes.

"Congratulations, Estella!" Cosette says.

"So, I think we should all start the night with a toast." Estella moves from the table and goes to the punch bowl. "Fill your plates and I'll pass out the punch. Gus got ahead of himself, but what else is new?" She laughs and we all join in, relieved to let some of it out.

Cosette feels the tension in the room and I want to save her, God help me, I do, but Estella hands her the punch first. Cosette waits for everyone to get theirs and looks at me like *what is going on with everyone?*

I lean over and whisper in her ear, "Try to drink as little as possible."

"What?" she asks, turning to face me.

I shake my head. "*Try to drink as little as possible,*" I mouth.

"Try to drink responsibly?" she whispers.

I shake my head frantically, but we're running out of time.

"*Don't drink,*" I try again.

"Grocery?"

I lift my eyes to the ceiling and pray for deliverance. We all have our glasses now and Estella lifts hers as she stands at the head of the table.

"To classy gas and trim waistlines around the world!"

We lose it on *classy gas* and I have to work to not spill the punch as I laugh my head off. But then Estella is still watching expectantly for us to take a drink, so I hold mine out to clink and everyone else joins in. There's a collective breath as we all gather our nerve and then we all go in.

I know immediately why Gus ran. It has an overwhelming olive juice taste, which would send him sideways. But it's also mixed with something fruity and as usual with Estella, fire from the demons.

I get a sip down and feel the fire travel down my intestines like a wildfire just getting started. Cosette starts coughing and I see to her even though my stomach is making me want to double over. Mya runs out of the room and Emma lets out a long groan.

"I'm so sorry," I whisper to Cosette. "Here, can you try some water?" She coughs and coughs and coughs until tears are streaming down her face, and then she clutches her stomach.

"I'm so sorry, baby," I repeat.

She looks at me with pain.

"Let's get you home."

She nods frantically and we rush out of there.

"Always so good to see you, Estella!" I yell before we make our escape. "Congratulations on your book deal! The world isn't gonna know what hit 'em!"

Cosette spends the rest of the night in the bathroom.

Through our group text the next morning, the fam reports a collected weight loss of ten pounds. Pretty good results from just one sip.

I think Estella is onto something.

CHAPTER TWENTY-FOUR

Cosette

Caden encourages me to reach out to my Aunt Chavon again. My mother has been so strange about everything with my father, and he still isn't taking my calls. This is a whole new level of distant. We've never gone more than three days without speaking, and I don't like it.

"Hell, Cosi, it's nice to hear from you," my aunt says. "I'm sorry I haven't called you back before now." Her French accent only makes her more beautiful. She helped me with my French and I helped her with her English when I lived there. We've always been close, but I'm surprised that she sounds so chipper, considering her husband is in such a dire situation.

"It's nice to hear your voice too."

"I hear you and Jeremy are going strong? Your mother says an engagement is in the near future?" she asks, and I push up from my desk chair and to my feet in frustration.

"I'm not with Jeremy. It's been over for quite some time. I actually met someone and he makes me really happy."

"Oh my darling, that is wonderful news. You know I wasn't a huge fan of Jeremy," she says, and we both chuckle. He'd behaved like a pompous ass when he met my aunt and uncle, and they'd never forgotten it. "It doesn't surprise me that your mother refuses to acknowledge your choices. Not much has changed."

I nod even though she can't see me. "Yeah. That's sort of why I'm calling."

"You want me to speak to her? I do believe she's a bit afraid of me," Aunt Chavon says, and I can picture the smile on her face. Very few people intimidate my mother, but my aunt is a straight shooter and she says what she thinks, which I've always loved and admired.

"I might consider that at some point, but for now, I'm more concerned about Uncle Perry. I haven't heard from my father, and I've left so many messages. It's so unlike him."

"Don't you worry one bit about Uncle Perry. He's fine. He's happy to be spending time with his brother right now," she says.

"You don't need to be with him?" I ask, because I can't fathom her being at home while he's in the hospital. They are the most in-love couple I've ever known. Even all these years later. I've always hoped to find what they have. And for the first time in my life, I feel like I *have* found it.

"I see him every day, darling. And he's been at the facility with your father every day and they are running a ton of tests. A lot of this stuff is cutting edge, you know, trial stuff."

For a heart attack?

"I didn't realize that. Maman didn't mention it. I wonder why my father can't sneak away for just a few minutes to call me back."

"I think he's exhausted from all the tests they've been running, and truthfully, my love … I think he's a bit shaken at the moment. Maybe even a little insecure about where he stands with his wife."

"Insecure about his wife? Why would he be exhausted from the tests they are running on Uncle Perry?"

There is a long silence on the other end of the phone.

"Auntie? Did I lose you?"

"I'm here, darling. I think there's a bit of a misunderstanding. You know it's your father who's having tests run? Not Perry."

My heart starts to race and I move back to my chair to sit. My legs feel a little wobbly and I want to prepare myself for the blow that I can feel coming.

"I thought my father was sitting bedside as Uncle Perry recovers from a heart attack. That's why I kept sending you the texts that I was thinking of you," I say, rubbing my temples to push away the oncoming headache.

"Oh my darling, I thought you were just being sweet, Cosette. No, Perry has not had a heart attack, and I won't let my anger get the best of me that your mother would tell you that. Your father is the one that is staying with us as he goes through all of these bouts of tests."

I shake my head in disbelief. "What does he need tests for?"

"He's okay, Cosi, I promise he is. I mean, physically, he's okay. It's, ummm, it's all part of the aging process. Everything doesn't work the same, you know? Your mother married a man twenty-two years her senior, and some of this is to be expected."

"I don't know what we're talking about? What is going on?" My words are shaky as panic courses through my veins.

"I thought he was just being distant because of my breakup with Jeremy. He's sick?"

"He's not sick per se. He has some issues with his hearing, and they've been running tests. They want him to use a hearing aid, which the doctor back in the States also recommended. Your mother didn't want him to do that. She feels it will make him appear old and not be good for business. But that's not the major issue going on with them at the moment."

"That sounds like such an easy fix. I've noticed him not joining in on conversations lately, and that must be why. That actually breaks my heart. What is the major issue if it's not his hearing?"

"Oh, darling. This is slightly uncomfortable, but I'm just going to say it."

"Please do."

"Your father is having some issues in the, er, the bedroom. It's normal for a man his age. But your mother thinks it's a much bigger deal than it really is, so she demanded that he see a specialist here in Paris."

My ears threaten to catch on fire. This is not a conversation that I want to have. It certainly explains Louie's reaction to sex.

"Um. Wow. I did not expect that. What kind of specialist is he seeing?"

"Well, he spent ten days seeing multiple doctors looking for anyone that said they could repair his hearing without needing the assistance of a hearing aid. It's ridiculous, really, darling, a hearing aid is not a big deal. And this past week, he's been seeing a sex therapist."

I choke on the sip of water I've just taken. "This is madness. I cannot believe my mother sent him away—for what? Because he's aging?" I ask, as I push to my feet and reach for my purse. "I'm catching the next flight out. Can you pick me up? I need to see him. He needs to know that he's loved and that this is not a big deal."

"Of course, my love. But be prepared. He's pretty down at the moment."

Of course he is. His wife has all but rejected him. "Okay. I'll text you my flight information."

I yank my office door open and try to calm my breathing as I march to my mother's office. Her door is open and Juliette is inside sitting in the chair across from Maman. She is going to blow her top when she hears what my mother's been keeping from us.

"Cosi, what's wrong?" Maman hurries to stand and rushes over to me. "Did Caden end things?"

A maniacal laugh leaves my mouth. One I've never heard before. "No. This has nothing to do with Caden. Would you like to tell Juliette about the secret you've been keeping about our father? About the fact that you claimed Uncle Perry had a heart attack? Mother, you've always been controlling, but this is a new low, even for you." I step back, needing to put space between us.

"It was a necessary lie until your father gets better."

"Gets better? Are you aware, Juliette, that our mother sent Dad away because he's getting old? Because he can't hear as well as he used to and apparently isn't rocking her world in the bedroom. So what did she do? She flew him to France and left him there." Anger is radiating from me, and I don't think I've ever been this upset with her before.

"Stop making a scene. People will hear." Maman rushes to the door and closes it.

"I don't care who hears. You lied to me. You can't be okay with this, Juliette," I say, watching my sister who seems notably calm considering what our mother has done.

"I'm aware of the situation. We knew you would overreact. We are trying to keep this under wraps. We don't want people to know he's … unfit," Juliette says, and she shows zero emotion.

Of course she knew.

"He's getting older. It's part of life," I shout, and my mother's bottom lip starts to tremble, which surprises me.

"I was afraid to tell you," Maman quakes, and she grips her desk like she needs the support. "He's not the same man lately."

"Would you not have a problem if Jeremy couldn't hold a conversation with you and was unable to perform his husbandly duties?" Juliette rolls her eyes and it takes all I have not to pummel her.

Her lack of compassion and empathy is criminal.

"Well, I don't think that would be a problem seeing as I am not with Jeremy anymore. But no, if *Caden* had physical limitations, it would certainly not make me love him less. What is wrong with both of you? Do you not have hearts?" Frustration takes over. I don't relate to them, and they're my family. I've always felt disconnected, but this is just unbelievable.

"My heart is fine, thank you very much. I just don't behave like a blubbering fool over trivial things." She pushes to her feet and grabs her Chanel bag and storms to the door.

"If it's trivial, why was he flown to another country and left there?" I shout.

"He's old, Cosette. It's part of life. Maman wants to fix him," she says. "There's no shame in that."

Um, really? I think there's actually a lot of shame in that. My jaw is on the ground as she storms out of the office.

"I'm getting on the next flight. I can't believe you aren't with him." I shake my head at my mother.

"I sent him to the best doctor in France. They will fix him and he'll come home."

"We're his family. We're supposed to stick together, not return someone when they aren't up to par."

"Oh no. Is this about boarding school again?" She pinches the bridge of her nose as if she can't listen to one more word that I have to say.

"No, Maman. This is about a hell of a lot more than you sending me away to school at such a young age. I got over it. But turning your back on your husband, *our father* ... it's inexcusable. Shame on you." I point my finger at her and back away to the door. "I'll see you when I get back. I'll be taking a leave from work to do what you should have been doing all along."

She stares out the window as if she can't even stand to look at me.

It doesn't bother me this time.

Because I can't stand the sight of her.

I call Lilith, the woman who handles all of our travel, and ask her to schedule me on the next flight out to Paris and to text me the information. I hurry back to my apartment to throw a few things in a bag.

I dial Caden as I walk toward our building.

"Where have you been? I've been trying to reach you. You okay?" he says, and his voice soothes all the hard edges that have formed over the past hour.

For the first time since I spoke to my aunt, I break down. Because this man has become my safe place.

"Baby. What's going on?" I don't miss the concern in his voice, as I continue walking. I don't care that a few people turn to look at me, as the tears stream down my face.

"My family is so messed up. My mother sent my father away. She left him in Paris because he's having hearing issues and he apparently can't, you know," I whisper as a sob leaves my throat. It's not only disappointing, but it's embarrassing admitting just how cold my mother is.

I look up to see my gorgeous man running my way. Because he knew I needed him. He weaves through a few people, and when he reaches me, he just wraps his arms around me and holds me close. "I've got you, Cosi."

And he does.

He has all of me.

CHAPTER TWENTY-FIVE

Caden

Cosette has been gone for almost a week, and I may as well have cut off a fucking limb. I'm miserable without her. I'd offered to go with her, but she said this was something she needed to do on her own.

It stung a little bit, but I understand her desire to be independent. This is a sensitive situation with her father, and I'm proud of her for going and facing it all head-on. We talk a few times a day, but my mood is sour and my patience has run thin.

I miss her.

I feel a distance there and I worry it's more than just the miles currently between us. I am not that dude. I don't get worked up over this shit. But Cosette is different in every way. Talking to her isn't the same as being with her. Hearing her laugh. Touching her. Kissing her. Knowing that we are okay.

"Oh no. I can't do another day of doom and gloom.

Brother, get it together," Gus says as he strolls into the office.

I hold up my middle finger, no expression on my face, and flash him the bird as I return my attention to my computer screen.

"Well, that's pleasant." He oozes sarcasm. "How do you expect to have a good day when you start out with this kind of greeting?"

"Don't start with me. I'm not in the mood for it."

"She'll be back before you know it. Stop moping around like a big ole baby."

"Takes one to know one," I grumble, making no attempt to snap out of it.

"Hey," Jesse knocks on the open door, because he's the only Taylor with any goddamn manners. "Vivienne Dubois is here to see you."

"She is? All right. I wasn't expecting her. Send her back," I say, straightening my top and thrusting my thumb at Gus to get out. "Go."

"Fine. Can we please go to Mean Mug and get a drink after? It's been a long week," he whines, and I roll my eyes. Is the love of his life in another country at the moment?

"Maybe. I'll find you after Vivienne leaves."

He steps out of my office, and I hear him make small talk with Cosette's mother as I push to my feet. She strolls in, with Louie and his oversized chompers panting inside her purse.

"How are you? This is unexpected," I say, leaning forward to give her a hug, though she doesn't reciprocate much. Louie all but lunges from the bag to get to me, and I scratch the top of his little head.

"Well, there is something I need to discuss with you. And

seeing as my daughter can't take the time to return my calls, I thought I'd come here myself and speak to you."

I hold my hand out, inviting her to take the seat across from me and I move back around my desk.

"All right."

"Have you spoken to Cosette?"

"Of course I have," I say, intertwining my fingers and setting my hands on my desk. I'm not happy with the way she's treated my girlfriend, but she's still her mother, and I'll bite my tongue. For now.

"I didn't know if you two were still a thing?"

"Of course we are. She went to see her father, she didn't leave me." My tone comes out with more of an edge than I mean it to.

She nods. "I see. I just thought with Jeremy being in France with her, maybe you two had parted ways. You don't strike me as a man who shares, but who am I to judge?"

My hands form into two fists, and I move them to my lap to try to control the anger that is currently taking over every inch of my body.

"I don't share."

She raises a brow. "Oh. I'm sorry. I thought you knew, but it's obvious that this is a surprise for you. Caden, you need to understand that Jeremy is very much a part of Cosette's life. He wanted to be there with her, and I think spending all this time together away from here has been good for them."

I push to my feet and walk to the bar area and grab two bottles of water. I set one in front of her because I don't want her to know I'm fighting the urge to throw it against the wall. She wants to get a rise out of me, and she is certainly succeeding. I spoke to Cosette this morning and she never said a word about Jeremy.

"Did you come here to tell me that? Or are you here for an actual reason?"

"I wanted to ask if you would mind if a local magazine wants to shoot some photos of the hotel before the sale goes through. *New York Life* is doing a spread on my Dubois Designs, and apparently they were very impressed by Cosi's work on that particular project."

"Of course, that's fine." I don't take my seat, I stand over her, waiting for her to leave. "Are we done?"

I'm seeing red and I need to speak to Cosette.

Would she fucking lie to me?

Her mother came here for one reason only, and if she's telling the truth, this just might work in her favor.

Would Cosette play me that way?

"Oh, yes. All right then. I'll be on my way." She pats me on the shoulder and I yank the door open.

She turns around to say something and I let the door shut in her face. She didn't come here for any other reason than to get in my head.

I try calling Cosette and she sends me to voicemail.

Not a good start to calming me down.

I send her a text.

Is Jeremy in Paris with you?

The three little dots move across the screen, and my motherfucking stomach wrenches with nerves. She didn't take my call. Is she sharing a fucking baguette with her cocksucking ex-boyfriend? I offered to go and she insisted she wanted to go talk to her father alone. But Jeremy is there with her?

My head is fucking spinning.

The doctor is just on his way in to go over the plan for my dad to return to the States. Can I call you when we leave the hospital? I want to explain what's going on.

Holy shit. This is really happening.

Answer the question, Cosette. Is Jeremy there?

The three dots are moving again. What is there to think about? It's a one-word motherfucking answer.

Yes, but I want to explain. I will call you in a few minutes.

I shut off my phone. I've been fucking played.

I whip my door open and find Gus walking toward me.

"Everything okay?" he asks, and I don't miss the concern on his face as he takes me in.

"That cocksucker Jeremy is in France with Cosette." I intertwine my fingers and press them behind my head as I close my eyes and try to compose myself.

I want to hit something.

Hit someone.

Preferably Jeremy.

"Let's go. Time to get a drink," Gus says, and he shouts for Spence and Jesse to meet us at Mean Mug.

And that's exactly where I plan to spend the next several hours.

Numbing myself so I don't have to deal with the ache that has settled in my chest.

Except Mya and Emma show up too, and while the brothers are playing darts and I'm nursing a beer and sulking, they swoop in. And their piercing eyes and female wiles get the truth right out of me, damn it all to hell.

"What's going on, Caden?" Emma asks. "Why the angry vibes?"

I sigh. "No angry vibes here. What are you talking about? No. Angry. Vibes." Except at Jeremy's face.

Emma looks at Mya and snorts. "Yeah, and I'm not a she-devil."

Mya laughs and then looks at me with concern. "Are you okay?"

I run my hands through my hair and then lower my head, suddenly feeling like all the energy has been zapped out of my body.

"Vivienne paid me a visit today … she wanted me to know that Jeremy is in Paris with Cosette."

"No!" Mya says. "That's—"

"*Crazy* talk. There has to be an explanation," Emma says.

"Cosette didn't tell me. I don't need more of an explanation than that to know that she was trying to hide it from me."

"So why aren't you there right now?" Emma asks.

"Ooo, yeah." Mya perks up, taking my hand in hers. "You need to go see her. Find out what's going on. In Paris." She looks at Emma, grinning. "Can you imagine how romantic it would be if they—"

"I'm sorry if I'm not feeling the romance of it all right at the moment," I interrupt before they get all swoony. "Did you not hear the part where I said she kept it from me?"

"But she can't stand Jeremy. You know that. She loves *you*," Emma says. "Give her a chance to explain." She lowers her voice. "You're the smart one in the family, don't start being a dipshit now."

"Emma!" Mya laughs. But she leans in. "It's true. You're not using your head right now. Come on, Caden. Hear her out. Cosette wouldn't lie to you."

"She already did." I tip my head back and finish my beer before holding up my glass to ask for another.

I'm not going to Paris to chase her down. She should have told me. I had to hear it from her goddamn mother.

"She didn't lie. She withheld the truth and she deserves the chance to explain herself." Emma's tone is somber now. She knows I'm not budging on this one.

"I had to hear it from her mother, who was thrilled to tell me, by the way. And then I had to ask my girlfriend if it was true. I'm done talking about it."

Mya nods. "Okay. Sleep on it. You just need to cool down."

I nod and force a smile. My head is spinning. I didn't see this coming. Cosette blindsided me, and I'm pissed.

I spend the next two hours drinking until I don't feel the anger anymore. Not the best coping strategy, but it is what it is.

I've never loved anyone the way I love Cosette and this one is going to hurt for a while.

The next morning my head is spinning. My mouth is dry. I pat the bed beside me and it's empty. No Cosette.

Memories flood back and I squeeze my eyes closed, wishing I could go back to sleep. Forget everything that happened yesterday.

I fumble around on the nightstand and find my phone. When I turn it on, messages flash across my screen. I'd turned it off after I'd spoken to Cosette and it remained off until this morning.

There are forty-two missed calls from my girlfriend. There are just as many texts.

Caden, please pick up the phone.

It's not what you think.

Please talk to me.

I can explain everything.

I love you. I love you so much. Please don't shut me out.

CADEN!

The texts continue to flood my screen and I push to sit up in bed and scrub a hand down my face.

I didn't give her a chance to explain. I shut down the minute I heard he was there.

But she should have told me, right? I deserved to know. Hell, I am all in on this girl, and she kept a pretty big secret from me. Her ex-boyfriend is in Paris with her. Isn't that the motherfucking romance capital of the world?

No. I am not going to be played.

I reach in my nightstand drawer and pull out the ring box and lift the top. I study the princess-cut diamond that I've chosen for Cosette. I don't know if she's ready to spend her life with me, but I sure as shit am.

Or was.

Until yesterday.

And it hurts like hell.

I picked out diamonds because once she left, I realized just how lost I am without her. She is exactly what's been missing from my life. And she's been canoodling with her ex in Paris? How could I be so fucking stupid?

I drop the ring back in the nightstand drawer and slam it.

The calls and texts stopped coming during the middle of the night. That's probably because she was with Jeremy then.

I groan.

I need to shower and eat something greasy and pull my shit together. I am not this guy. I do not fall apart.

I push to my feet and head for the shower.

Fuck Jeremy.

Fuck everyone.

The hot water pours down my back and I rest my pounding head on the wall beneath the stream.

I know this girl. Hell, I know her better than anyone. She isn't a liar. She isn't sneaky.

Could there be an explanation?

Did I jump to conclusions?

Fuck. I'll call her back when I get out of the shower. She deserves to at least explain what happened. I was ready to propose to her just yesterday. Am I really going to throw in the towel that easily?

Damn my wounded ego.

I've let it get the best of me.

I need to fix this.

CHAPTER TWENTY-SIX

Cosette

I search my purse for the key and make my way into Caden's apartment. I can hear the water running in the bathroom, and I drop my bags at the front door and hurry down the hallway.

I caught the first flight out, after not being able to reach Caden. I know he's angry, and I need to speak to him in person.

So, here I am.

Exactly where I want to be.

I've missed him so much.

I'm not happy with him for not letting me explain what happened, and I don't know how he knew that Jeremy had showed up in Paris, but either way—we need to talk.

The bathroom door is open and I walk through. Steam surrounds me and there stands my gorgeous boyfriend with his head pressed against the wall, letting the water rage against his beautiful body.

"Tough night?" I ask, and he whips around to face me.

His dark eyes are pained, but he doesn't hide how happy he is to see me.

I move toward him, not caring that the water is running and I am fully clothed, but he puts his hand up to stop me. He turns off the water and reaches for a towel before wrapping it around his waist.

"I can't think clearly if you step in this shower with me and you know that. I've missed you so fucking much, Cos. How could you keep this from me?"

His words sting. The hurt. The disappointment. A large lump forms in my throat.

"Do you want to go sit down?" I ask. "I'd like to explain."

"So explain," he says, and he doesn't move. He leans against the double vanity and crosses his arms over his chest.

I fight the urge to walk toward him. Caden is my safe place. My happy place.

I nod. "Jeremy showed up yesterday at my father's doctor's office, of all things. It was after you and I had spoken. I was going to tell you immediately, but you literally called me two minutes after I saw him. He claimed he had business to discuss with my father. Of course I didn't buy it, I mean he could have just called. But when you phoned me, Dr. Fury had just called us back and he was signing off on all the paperwork for my father's hearing aids. I had to finish up with him and then I called you immediately. I told Jeremy he'd wasted his time being there when he finally admitted that he came to try to win me back. How did you even know he was there?"

His eyes soften. "Your mom came to see me yesterday. She told me he was with you. I thought you were keeping it from me."

"Caden." I move into him. Needing to know we're okay.

To feel his warmth. To show him how much I love him. "I'm so sorry she did that. I wondered how he knew where the doctor's office was."

"I'm sorry I overreacted. I was just missing you so damn much. More than I ever thought I could miss someone."

"I missed you too," I say. "So much."

"And hearing that he was with you, it just sent me sideways. I thought you'd lied to me, but I knew better. I swear I was about to call you when I got out of the shower."

I pull back to look at him. "My mother did that just to mess with you. I should have known. I'm so sorry that you had to feel that. Being away from you … well, I had a lot of time to think and sort out my feelings. There's so much I need to tell you."

"I'm listening."

"I'm done living my life for other people, Caden. You are everything that I want. Everything that I need. That's the most important. Also, I want to work with you and your family, where I'd have the freedom to be creative and use my own designs. My mother doesn't want that for me. And I can't spend my life trying to make her happy. I'll never fit into her perfect little mold like Juliette does. She should've known that when even boarding school couldn't 'fix' me. And after seeing what she did to my father," I say, as all the emotion overflows and it's difficult to speak without crying.

"Baby, you're okay. I'm right here," he whispers as he wraps his arms around me.

"She sent him away because he isn't able to have sex as often as he used to? Who does that? And she didn't want him to wear a hearing aid because it makes him look old. It's horrible. She had him undergoing all of these ridiculous tests, and guess what the conclusion is?"

"What?" he asks.

"He's freaking eighty. He's actually in pretty good health considering his age. The hearing aids are an easy solution. The sex stuff, oh my gosh, I wanted someone to set my ears on fire after hearing in-depth about his struggles. But that is also an easy solution. He will take some medication. But I think there is a lot more to repair between them than their sex life. I think he's been depressed for a long time. Even the fact that he put up with her foolishness is so unlike him. The time away was really good for him. I feel like I got my dad back."

"Yeah. I'm guessing the way she treats him doesn't give him a lot of motivation in that department."

"It made me realize how lucky we are, Caden. To have found what we have together. To know that I want to wake up with you every single day for the rest of my life. To know that we love each other. We desire each other. We have one another's backs. That's all I've ever wanted. And you are all I'll ever want." I put it all out there, and I sound like a blubbering fool.

"You are all I want too, Cosi."

Before I can stop myself, I drop down on one knee and swipe at my face. "You are my forever, Caden Taylor. I don't want a big fancy party, I just want to make it official. You and me."

His eyes are wet with emotion as he stares down at me, stroking my cheek with the pad of his thumb.

"Hold that thought."

He hurries out of the bathroom, and I'm down on one knee feeling a bit foolish and wondering what the hell just happened. He returns before I can move to my feet, and he drops down to face me. "You and me, lover."

He holds a ring in his hand, and my breath gets caught in my throat.

"What is this?" I cry.

"It's an engagement ring. Of course I planned to do a whole thing, you know, the candles and the flowers and the whole bit. But this feels right. Real. And that's all I've ever wanted. There was a long time that I just didn't think I'd ever find someone that I'd want to spend my life with, and then you showed up. Lavender eyes, white-blonde hair, and a smile that lights up my entire world. You are everything I want, Cosette Dubois. Will you marry me?"

I'm sobbing now, as he slips the stunning ring onto my finger. I'm nodding furiously, and it takes a minute before I can get the words out. "Yes. But on one condition."

"Name it." He's so close that his warm breath tickles my cheek.

"I don't want the fancy dress and the big showy event. I want you and me. Standing near the ocean. Our closest friends and family, and only those who truly wish us well. No fuss. My whole life has been about the fuss. This is about us. You and me. Forever."

His lips crash into mine.

I push his towel off and he has my shirt and pants off within seconds. I'm greedy for him, loving the way his skin feels under my fingertips, wishing I could crawl right inside of him. I've missed him with a constant ache that only now is beginning to ease. I'm relieved we're okay, relieved we're together again, relieved that he wants to be my forever as much as I want to be his.

"I love you so much," I whisper, as he lifts me up and wraps my legs around his waist.

"I love you, baby." He drops me on the bed and prowls over me like a tiger ready to pounce. "I can't wait to be inside you," he says with a grin. "I'm going to fuck the jet lag right out of you."

I giggle. "I can't wait."

He doesn't waste any time either. He bottoms out in me with one deep dive and I'm breathless. I was ready for him, and when we start moving, our rhythm is frantic.

"I can't get enough of you," he says. "I'll never get enough of you."

"Let's do this every day for the rest of our lives, okay?"

He puts his fingers between us and teases me there. Except his eyes are as serious as they get.

"You're really gonna be my wife?" he asks, driving harder and harder and so deep I feel like I'm going underground.

"First chance I get."

"Next week?" he sounds winded now, and I'm meeting him with every thrust.

"Next. Week," I whimper.

"Come with me, Cosette."

I cry out and he's right behind me, searing me with a kiss that causes time to stand still.

I shake and shudder, whisper his name over and over again, the aftershocks coming hard even after we've kissed.

"I want to shake your world each and every time," he says. "The way you shake mine. How about we put that in the wedding vows?"

I laugh into his chest and run my fingers lightly over his skin. "Absolutely. Were you serious about next week?"

"Serious as I can be. Were you?"

"I would marry you yesterday if I could."

He grins down at me and kisses the tip of my nose. "I just need to get my parents and Pen here. The brothers and their girls will make it work."

I squeal. "My dad will be happy to walk me down the

aisle or grass or wherever it ends up happening. I can't believe we're doing this. I'm so *excited*!"

"Oh, you know who will want to be in on this? She wouldn't go too over the top or make it feel stressful … Alice."

"Who's Alice again?"

"The one who created your fairy garden magic."

"Ohhhh, yes. I would love that. Oh my God, Caden. I can't believe we're doing it. I cannot wait!"

He turns to face me and pushes my hair back. "Welcome home, Cosi."

I sigh and lean into him, kissing him until we heat up to combustible levels. He pulls me on top of him and this time, we take it slow.

I fall asleep afterward and a little later, I feel him kiss my shoulder as he pulls the covers around me. "Sleep, my beauty. And when you wake up, we'll start planning all the things for a non-wedding wedding."

I drift back off still smiling.

"You sure you're ready for this?" Caden asks as we walk up the steps at my parents' home.

"I am. I spoke to my father this morning and he and Maman have been working on things since he returned from France. He is taking control of his life, and it's time I do the same." I type in the code and we step inside.

My parents are both sitting beside one another on the couch in the formal living room as if they are waiting for us. I didn't tell my mother I was coming over to talk to them, I only shared this with my father.

I haven't talked to my mother since she tried to hurt

Caden by making it look like Jeremy and I were together in France and the fact that she sent my father off to another country to "fix himself" … I'm still not over either one. It's appalling and I wanted to cool down before we spoke.

It's time.

No more avoiding confrontation.

I've found my voice and I'm ready to use it on the one woman who has managed to silence me most of my life.

"I've missed you, darling," Maman says, as she hurries over and hugs me. "Caden."

He chuckles at how cool she is toward him and hugs her in spite of her rudeness.

I kiss my father on each cheek when he stands. Caden extends an arm and my father ignores it and pulls him in for a hug instead. We talked about my relationship with Caden a lot while I was in France with my father. He shared that he never thought Jeremy was good enough for me. He had pulled away from me because he was struggling with depression about his flailing marriage, the fact that he wasn't hearing well, as well as all of the other limitations he'd been experiencing. He admitted he'd had a late in life identity crisis. He laughed when saying that, like he never thought it would happen to him, and it surprised me too—just goes to show that it can happen to anyone. He didn't regret going into business with Jeremy because he thought he had good business sense. But he didn't think he made me happy and he was fine with us going our separate ways. He loved the way that I lit up when I spoke about Caden. He said that's how he's always felt about Maman, which made my heart ache a little bit because of the way she'd treated him. He reminded me that marriage was a journey, with many highs and lows, and they were currently in a low. But that didn't mean they couldn't turn things around.

Caden and I drop to sit down on the lush blue velvet loveseat across from them. My mother has a silver tray with a tea set out for us. I hand Caden a teacup and then make one for myself.

"I just wanted to come over here to speak to you both. I don't want to focus on the past and the recent events that have upset me," I say, my gaze locking with my mother's. She looks away quickly, but I see the shame there, and I'm happy to see she feels *something* about her despicable actions. Dad told me on the phone the other day that she'd agreed to counseling, which is a huge step for her. "I'm here today to discuss the future."

"I think moving forward is a good thing. Your mother and I are doing the same. It doesn't excuse the hurtful things that have taken place," my father pauses and sets down his tea and looks at my mother, "but hopefully we learn from our mistakes and we do better."

I nod. "Agreed. Moving forward, I would ask for your blessing with what I'm about to tell you. But I also need to make it clear that I don't need it. It would make me happy, but it won't determine what I choose to do for my own happiness."

"What does that mean?" Maman asks as she zeroes in on the large spectacular diamond setting up residence on my ring finger.

"It means that Caden and I are getting married. I've never been happier. The only thing that would make it more perfect would be for you to be happy for me." I lean into my boyfriend for comfort almost instinctively. He wraps an arm around my shoulder.

"I love your daughter more than I ever knew possible. I will spend the rest of my life showing her how important she is to me," Caden says, before leaning down and kissing my forehead.

"I don't think we could ask for more," my father says. "Thank you for coming to speak to us." He winks at Caden. "And for our little one-on-one chat already. You absolutely have my blessing."

All eyes turn to my mother.

She looks away, eyes wet with emotion. "What about Jeremy?"

"Maman, you have to let that go. I was never happy with him. I care about him and I wish him the best, but he is not the man I want to spend my life with."

She nods. "I can see that. And apparently, this wedding is going to take place with or without my blessing."

"It is," I say, and I have no emotion in my voice. I'm not allowing her to make this about her.

I'm happy to say that this time with Caden has helped me find myself—working on the hotel project has too. My mom only wants the best for Juliette and me, it's just that her best isn't what I want ... God knows what Juliette thinks, if she even does—she's so brainwashed. Even though my mother and I don't see eye to eye, she is my mom, her own person, and I will always love her. But I need to be who I'm meant to be now and hope that she'll come to understand that. Opening my own business is going to be another step on the ladder of life.

I can feel Caden tense up beside me. The whole thing is offensive. She doesn't even know why she doesn't like him for me. He isn't Jeremy. A man who cheated on me repeatedly and whom I had nothing in common with. And no, he isn't obscenely wealthy. But with my trust, I have enough to never need another thing, and Caden is actually rapidly working his way up the ladder. It's damn impressive to see him building his company with his brothers.

"I'm happy for you both," my father says, and he pulls his hand away from my mother, and she stiffens. She suddenly gets very busy with tucking the blanket tighter around Louie, and he bounds out of the blanket and jumps on my lap before moving to Caden's and settling in.

"Thank you. So the other thing we wanted to discuss is the wedding."

"Oh, do we have a date? Shall we book the club?" she asks. Juliette and Beecham got married at the country club and it was very fitting for them. It was formal attire, elegant, and cold as hell. No laughter. No sentiment.

But it was exactly what they wanted. That is not what Caden and I want for our special day.

"We're getting married two weeks from today. We've booked a lovely resort on the Hudson River for both the ceremony and the reception. It will be family only. No fuss. Just a special day with the people we love most."

My mother's eyes bulge out of her head. "Two weeks? A resort? On the river? Why not at the club?"

"Because it isn't what we want, Maman. Our wedding should be about us. This isn't about putting on a show, it's about celebrating the fact that we want to spend the rest of our lives together, and we want to start right now."

"I think it sounds wonderful," my father says, and he winks at me.

"Thank you," I say, before turning to look at my mother.

"Well, I guess I better get on board then."

"I guess so," I say.

I'll tell her about my job decision another day.

CHAPTER TWENTY-SEVEN

Caden

"I'm so looking forward to meeting your parents," my mother says to Cosette as we make our way into PLUSH, one of the restaurants in Manhattan that her family owns. My parents flew out here for the weekend specifically to meet the Dubois before the wedding.

I can feel Cosette's shoulders stiffen at my mother's words. I squeeze her hand and lean down to kiss her cheek, wanting her to know that everything will be fine. My parents will love her parents because they love her. It's just who they are.

Alban Dubois is standing in the bar pointing to a few tables, and he has a smile spread clear across his face. He's back in his element, and Cosette said that he seems more like himself now than he has in a long time. I'm guessing that his hearing aids have a lot to do with getting his confidence back. His wife is the only person who cares that he wears them, but the good news is that her opinion doesn't appear to matter to him when it comes to being able to hear.

News flash—hearing is not something that one should give up if they don't have to. The man simply wears a device which allows him to engage with others. Her lack of empathy is difficult to relate to, but she's Cosette's mother and therefore she gets a pass from me.

He sees us and hurries over. He introduces himself and my parents beam as they all embrace right there by the hostess stand.

It's a very Taylor thing to do, but not a typical Dubois response. Maybe the tides are changing. Cosette standing up to her mother was the first step.

Alban guides us all to the private room in the back, where we find Vivienne placing an oversized arrangement in the center of the round table. Louie has somehow earned himself a seat at the table tonight and it's a rare sight to see him outside of her handbag. He's sitting on a booster seat wearing a tuxedo top with a bow tie. My mother giggles and my father stares with complete amusement.

"This must be the infamous ring bearer," Mom says, and she uses her hand to cover her mouth, most likely to hide the fact that she's gaping.

Vivienne turns to face my parents and she smiles. "This is Louie François Dubois."

"This is the dog that haunts Gus' nightmares, right?" my father whispers in my ear and I fight the urge to laugh when I give him a single nod.

We share a few more introductions before we all take our seats. Things are going better than I expected, if I'm being honest. Vivienne hasn't insulted anyone, not that my parents let stuff like that bother them. The only time there will be a problem is if she says something unkind to me or Cosette in front of my parents. They won't stay silent for that.

"We are just thrilled for the kids. And I have to say, Mel and I like the idea of an intimate wedding. Focusing on what it's all really about, right?" my father says, as he reaches for his wine glass and takes a sip.

"Agreed." Alban raises his glass and we all clink them together. With the exception of one person.

Cosette's mother.

"Well, I still prefer a big celebration. My daughter Juliette had the most amazing wedding. It was featured on page six in the local paper because we spared no expense," Vivienne says, swirling her wine in her glass as if it isn't quite up to par just yet. I cringe at her words. The woman is such a snob. I've heard about the page six bullshit more times than I can count. Who cares? Juliette and Beecham are two of the most miserable people I've ever met. I'd skip page six and head to couples therapy if I were them.

Cosette stiffens beside me at her mother's words and I wrap an arm around her. "Well, a lifetime of happiness with my girl is all I care about. Page six would be lucky to feature us, baby."

My mother beams at us before turning her attention back to Vivienne. "We're looking forward to meeting Juliette and Beecham. I know you've met Caden's siblings, and we can't wait to do the same."

Watching Vivienne and my mother interact is sort of like watching a kitten play with a scorpion.

"I'm not sure you will meet Juliette," Vivienne says as she sets the menu aside.

"They aren't attending the wedding?" Cosette asks, completely caught off guard. Her sister has made a few snide remarks about the wedding being too small, but she hasn't mentioned not attending as far as I know.

"She and Beecham have a wine tasting event that same night," Vivienne says as if Cosette should have known, and my father spews the wine in his mouth across the table. Now I can't help myself and I bark out a laugh.

"A wine tasting?" Mom uses her napkin to help Dad clean up the mess. "Her sister is getting married."

"Cosette knows that Juliette and Beecham plan their social calendar months in advance."

My dad turns to Cosette and winks. "Well, I can't imagine any event that would be better than celebrating Cosette and Caden. It will be the social event of the year."

"Pfffft, the social event of the year is the fourth of July in the Hamptons. A small event at an unknown resort will not be newsworthy," Vivienne says.

Appetizers are brought out to the table, and a small plate is set in front of Louie. My parents stare at him as if they are watching a freak circus show.

They kind of are.

"I've never seen teeth like that on a dog before," Dad says and Alban chuckles. The dude is completely engaged now that he can actually hear the fucking conversation.

"Those aren't his, my wife had them made." He shrugs as if he thinks she's as crazy as the rest of us do.

"Louie went to a well-known specialist, Dr. Pussy." Vivienne dabs her mouth and Cosette squeezes my hand beneath the table.

"They are something. Dr. Pussy must be very talented," Mom says, and I close my eyes for a few seconds to keep from laughing at the ridiculous conversation.

"Yes, he really is."

"There won't be a ring bearer in town with a better set of chops than yours," Dad says, grinning at Louie.

Louie proceeds to dry heave at the table ferociously, and Vivienne pats his back as he coughs up an oversized piece of filet mignon. Everyone gasps.

"I'm so sorry," Cosette whispers to my mother as Vivienne is in a frenzy making sure he's okay.

"Are you kidding? This is the most fun we've had in a long time. We love you, Cosette. And that means we love your family."

Cosette relaxes against me. It's exactly what she needs to hear. The girl was born to be a Taylor.

I'm at dinner with the brothers, on the countdown as a single man.

"Don't mistake my attitude with not being happy for you," Jesse says, as he runs a hand through his outrageously tall hair. "But you guys are making me look fucking bad. Each one of you keeps proposing and planning weddings faster than the next."

I snort. "I promise you we aren't doing it to make you look bad."

"Stop being a pussy and just propose then," Spence barks at him.

"Don't say pussy. Vivienne ruined the word for me because now all I see is Louie's set of chompers when I hear the word." Gus snorts. "But listen, I am down with all of this. I love weddings. Good food. Hot chicks. Free cocktails. I would like to request that you'll all be hosting an olive-free bar. You know, out of respect for me and all," Gus says, as he reaches into the center of the table for a few tater tots.

"Oh, for God's sake. An olive-free bar?" Spence hisses and shakes his head.

"It's a respect thing, brother. I will not be attending if it is not an olive-free zone. Because I'll be whooping it up in the cocktail department, you know, drinking on your dimes … and I don't want to have to concentrate on making sure the bartender doesn't fuck up with the wrong garnish," Gus says over a mouth full of tots.

"Are you drunk right now?" I ask because he's acting crazy.

"I am not. I just have to draw the line somewhere. We all have our things. You don't like Cosette's dicklicker ex, Jesse doesn't like confined spaces, Spence doesn't like people … aside from Emma. *And I don't like olives.* I'm hardly the most concerning one in the group."

"You're definitely the most concerning one in the group for more reasons than you even know." Spence rolls his eyes and tips his head back to down his beer. "I think it's great that you and Cosi are doing this quick. I'm guessing her ice queen mother doesn't like how fast this is happening?"

"She's not happy about it, but we don't really care. I think Mom and Dad were pretty entertained by the Dubois when they met them last week. Her dad's on board, but her mom isn't quite there. We made it clear that this is our day. We aren't about the big party, we just want to start our lives together."

"I like the sound of that. I've had a ring for Mya for a while, but after fucking things up with Tiffany, I don't want Mya to think I don't take this shit seriously. I want to find the perfect way to propose," Jesse finally says. My baby brother escaped a lifetime of hell when he left his last fiancée at the altar before he met Mya.

"Don't let that concern you. What you had with Tiffany is nothing like what you have with Mya. We all see how happy you are. If you're ready, pull the trigger. When you know, you know." I hold my glass up and he clinks his against mine.

"Exactly. Like I fucking know how I feel about olives." Gus shakes his head and clinks his glass to ours.

"That has nothing to do with the fucking conversation, dickdog. But we love you anyway." Spence holds his glass up now as well.

"I can't believe I'm getting married in a week." We found a little resort on the Hudson River to accommodate our group. It's exactly what Cosette and I want.

"I'll drink to that," Spence says. "Emma's planning a wedding fit for fucking royalty. I just saw an email with information for a horse and carriage ride."

He tries to act irritated, but we all know he's as involved in it as she is.

"Don't try to act like you aren't part of every detail. You want the Hallmark movie wedding too, dickpube," Gus says, barking out a laugh. "You're a sentimental bastard whether you want to admit it or not."

Spence laughs. "Whatever. So, are we doing a bachelor party for you?"

"I think we can count this as the bachelor party. I've had plenty of wild times. I'm ready to start my life with Cosette. We've got the fitting for our tuxes in two days. The timeline's pretty tight."

"And what did Cosette decide to do about the ex-boyfriend and his family?" Jesse asks, because Vivienne Dubois is adamant about the Toussaints attending the wedding.

"She went to speak to them. Jeremy's parents were actually really supportive. They said they were happy for her, and that they really want to be there. She met with Jeremy afterward and she told him that she'd like to move forward as friends but after all that he'd done to try to come between us, she just didn't feel comfortable having him there. He actually agreed and apologized. So there you go."

"Good for her," Spence says.

My parents decided to stay out here until after the wedding. Penelope and Beckham are flying in two days before the wedding, and everything is coming together.

Cosette and I have decided to keep both of our condos and knock the wall down between our two homes and do some major renovations. We'll be doubling our space. We want to put in a large home office, since Cosette will soon be branching out on her own, and she's agreed to work with us on all of our future projects.

"Is that weird-ass dog still going to be the ring bearer?" Gus asks as he shivers at the thought.

"Yes. Cosette knew it would mean a lot to her mother."

"That woman is fucking crazy. I can't imagine what it was like to grow up in that household." Jesse says. "Cosette is meant to be a Taylor."

"I think that all the time."

She's most definitely meant to be mine.

I knew it the first time I met her.

Most people have all sorts of anxiety leading up to their wedding day, but Cosi and I aren't experiencing any of that. We've been working on the layout for our new home, and she drew up the plans, which we handed over to Spence a few days ago. My brothers and the team are going to get to work while we're on our honeymoon in the South of France. I'm looking forward to two weeks alone with my wife.

Tonight is the rehearsal dinner, and Alban and Vivienne are hosting the event at their lavish home. I'm sure it will be far more extravagant than our wedding day, but her parents wanted to do something for us and I was fine with it as long as Cosette was.

The meeting between the parents went better than I thought it would. I'm sure my parents found them to be a bit overwhelming, but they'd never say a negative word about Cosette's family. That's the way my parents roll. They are loyal as hell, and Cosi is a part of the family now. She has been since the day I fell for her.

My mom and Cosette have been spending a lot of time together. They've stayed up late every night talking, and my mom is honored that she's seen my bride's dress ahead of time.

Cosette and I knock on my brother's door, as Gus is going to drive over with us to her parents' house. The rest of my family will be in two other cars.

"You excited, baby?" I ask, as I graze her ear with my lips as she knocks on the door.

"I'm excited to officially be Mrs. Caden Taylor. Tonight is about giving my parents the chance to throw a party for us, but I'm just excited to spend my life with you."

"Damn, I'm a lucky man," I say as the door flies open.

"Sorry I'm running late," Gus hurries out to the hall with his shoes in hand, and his hair is disheveled.

"What the fuck happened to you?" I ask as I link my fingers with Cosette's as we make our way back to the elevator.

"Whoever bought that condo next door moved in today,

and they've been banging and pounding nails in the wall all fucking day. I was trying to take a nap, you know, get my beauty sleep before tonight, but that did not happen. It's like a pack of animals moved in there. I am not okay if my neighbors are going to be out of control fraternity boys, do you understand me, brother?" He shakes his head like this is the most inconvenient thing he's ever experienced.

The door flies open and the tiniest human I've ever seen pokes her head out. She's got her light brown hair tied up in some sort of messy knot on top of her head, gigantic brown eyes, and a little cherub face.

Fucking adorable.

Nothing like the pack of wild animals I expected to see behind that door.

She holds her little hand up and smiles and Gus comes to a stop and stares at her, as if he's never seen a child before.

"Hi there, cutie pie," Cosette says, and Gus studies her.

"Olive, you better not be opening that door, baby girl. Come help Mama in your room," a voice calls out from the distance.

She waves before pushing the door closed and Gus gasps. "She did not fucking call her daughter Olive, did she? No, no, no. It must be a nickname, right?"

Cosette's head falls back in laughter as we start walking again. "Olive is an adorable name."

"I would name my nemesis Olive. Not a cute little thing like that. I can't live next door to someone named Olive," he says, and he steps on the elevator and falls back against the wall.

"She's quite possibly the cutest human I've ever seen next to my gorgeous fiancée," I say, nuzzling Cosette's neck.

Gus claps his hand together. "You two need to take this seriously. Who the hell bought that condo?"

"I'm not positive, but I'm pretty sure the realtor told me it was a single mom with a little girl. A far cry from wild animals and fraternity boys, you dickwick." I shake my head and laugh.

"I feel like the universe is messing with me, giving me a neighbor named Olive." He crosses his arms over his chest. "But I'll drop it for tonight because it's your day."

"Damn straight, brother."

"Maybe the mom will be as adorable as the little girl." Cosette wriggles her brows at Gus.

"I don't mess around with single moms. I have rules." Gus pinches the bridge of his nose as if he can barely handle the thought.

We arrive at the Dubois home, and twinkle lights line the drive and walkway up to the front door. When Cosette steps inside, she gasps. There are floral arrangements on every surface within view. Floral archways lead to the formal living area, and pink and white blooms fill the space.

"Um, wow," Cosette whispers. "So much for subtle."

Louie comes flying around the corner with his full set of veneers leading the way, and he's wearing a black velvet jacket and a pink corsage on his chest.

"The dude has a better wardrobe than me, which is saying a lot. Aside from the weird set of falsies, he almost looks like he has swagger."

My parents walk in just then, and Cosette's parents come around the corner to greet us.

My mother swoons over the flowers, Penelope, Emma, and Mya whisk Cosette away asking for a tour of the home, and Alban leads us into the living room for cocktails.

They have a bartender on staff and Gus beelines over there, most likely to go over his pretend allergy to olives, and Jesse and Spence both flank each side of me.

"You ready for all of this?" Spence asks.

"More ready than I've ever been in my life."

"Happy for you, Caden," Jesse says, and he pulls me into a hug.

Our families may be completely different, but Cosette and I were made for each other.

CHAPTER TWENTY-EIGHT

Wedding Day

Cosette

When I was a little girl I used to play this game with my friend next door, and we'd both take turns being the wedding planner and the bride. I always enjoyed being the bride. I loved fairy tales and happily ever afters as a kid. Somewhere along the way, I lost sight that life could really be that magical, but here I am living my very own fairy tale.

I've found my real life prince, and I've never been happier. I've never felt more complete, more loved, more cherished.

I glance in the mirror at the satin strapless princess-style dress that I'm wearing, and I swoosh the full tulle skirt from side to side. I may have wanted to pass on the over-the-top wedding, but I certainly didn't skimp on the gown. It's everything I've ever dreamed of. The satin bodice works as a corset and hugs me from my chest to my waist. It also makes it appear that I have a little more going on upstairs than I really do, which is a bonus.

I spin in a circle and the tulle skirt sparkles where the light hits it. My hair is slicked back in an elegant chignon, and my teardrop earrings add just the sparkle that I want. Aunt Chavon brought them for me, as they were my great grandmother's, and she and Uncle Perry thought this was the perfect day to give them to me. My mother thought they were old and dated, and pushed her Harry Winston earrings on me, and as gorgeous as they are, I like the idea of adding a little history to my look.

There is a knock on the door and I hurry over to let Mya, Emma, and Penelope in.

"Oh wow, Cosi," Mya says, covering her mouth with her hands as her eyes are wet with emotion.

"Girl, there are no words. You look like a real live princess," Emma says as she pours us each a glass of champagne and hands the flutes to each of us.

"You could be on the cover of a bridal magazine. In fact, page six is going to be very mad they missed this event," Penelope teases, as they've all heard from my mother about my sister's grand wedding and all the attention that it garnered.

Emma groans. "I don't know how anyone interviewed your sister. No offense, Cosi, but she's a real piece of work. She just told Gus that he was invading her personal space and he was sitting one row away from her."

My head falls back in laughter. "Why is she saying anything to poor Gus?"

"Because apparently she has a cocktail with an olive in the glass and he asked her to please eat it quickly because it was giving him hives," Penelope cracks up. "My brother is such a drama queen sometimes."

"Yeah, Juliette whipped around and shot daggers at him. I thought Gus was going to rip the glass from her hands. She told him to mind his business and stop invading her personal boundaries." Mya shakes her head and shrugs.

"I'd like to knock that girl into a boundary of her own," Emma huffs.

"That's her sister," Mya whisper-hisses at her best friend.

"I'm quite aware how tough Juliette can be. I'm just shocked that they passed on going to the wine tasting to be here tonight. It's very out of character." I laugh and apply one final coat of light pink lipstick and rub my lips together before reaching for my veil.

The girls help me attach the veil to the back of my head, and there's a knock on the door.

My father stands there looking very regal in his black tuxedo. "Are you ready, darling?"

"Looking good, Mr. D," Emma says before she kisses me on the cheek and Mya and Penelope follow suit.

The three girls wish me luck and make their way out to the chairs. We have the gorgeous ceremony set up out on the water with enough twinkle lights to brighten a small country.

"You look gorgeous, Cosi," my father says, and he swipes at the single tear rolling down his cheek. He's not normally an emotional man, but he is full of surprises lately. After all that has happened over the past few months, I feel closer to him than ever.

"Thank you. You look very handsome yourself." I kiss his cheek.

"Are you ready?"

"I'm so ready. Let's do this," I say, linking my arm through his.

There are no wedding planners for this event, it was all put together by me and Caden in an unbelievably short period of time, and I'm thrilled to see how gorgeous it looks.

When we open the door and walk out through the lobby of the resort, we make our way outside. There is a light breeze and the sun is just starting to descend. The sky looks like someone painted it just for us. Pinks and oranges and yellows blend together like watercolors on a canvas.

My breath catches in my throat when my father stops to allow me to take it all in. We have a tented area to the right, with two long tables on each side.

The ceremony is taking place right on the water. Twenty or so white chairs flank the grassy area with an aisle running down the center. Blush, rose, and cream flowers flank each row with delicate blooms of roses, hydrangeas, and peonies. Sprigs of greens are mixed in the colorful bouquets to give them a natural feel as well. My bouquet is a grander version and I close my eyes and breathe it in before the music starts to play.

The sweet sounds of Mya with her cello and her violinist friend play the traditional wedding song, and my father leads the way. My eyes lock with Caden's as he waits for me at the end of the aisle. Gus is standing beside him now, as he begged and pleaded to officiate the wedding. Because of course Gus Taylor has been ordained on the internet to perform weddings.

We didn't want a wedding party, as everyone here is important to us. They are all here because we love them and we want to share the most special moment of our lives with them.

My gaze never leaves Caden's. He's all I see. He's been all I see since the first day I met him. My father kisses my cheek when we come to a stop and he shakes Caden's hand.

"Be good to her. You've got a good one. The best girl around," my father says and I hear my sister gasp, which leads to Gus barking out a laugh and Caden shooting him a warning look.

I can't help but chuckle as my father steps away. I hand my bouquet to Penelope who is already weepy.

I glance around and see both of our families, the most important people in our lives. They all played a role in helping us get here, one way or another.

Okay, maybe not Juliette and Beecham, but they're here and that means they must care because God knows they have a social calendar that rivals the royals.

I turn my attention to my handsome groom. The man who owns my heart. The man who saved my life in ways he can't begin to imagine.

Gus clears his throat in the most theatrical way which makes the small audience laugh. Even my mother is smiling at this point which is saying a lot, because the woman never smiles.

"Ladies and gentlemen ... *and Juliette*," Gus says, and everyone covers their mouths to contain their laughter. I glance over at my sister and she's rolling her eyes so hard I fear they might stick up in her head. "I'd like to take a moment to tell you a little about myself before I marry these two beautiful people off. My name is Gus Taylor. I'm Caden's brother and I'm fairly certain I would have been Cosette's second choice if this union hadn't worked out." He smirks and there's more laughter, even Caden can't help but chuckle. "Which leads me to the most important part of the ceremony. There are a few of you who I haven't met and I'd like to make it known that I am currently single. I'm a Virgo. I like long walks on the beach. I like piña coladas and making love in the rain."

Laughter erupts around us before Spence shouts out, "And you're afraid of Juniper Holloway and olives. Get on with it, fool. Marry these two so we can have dinner. We're starving."

More laughter. My gaze locks with Caden and he smiles. My heart rate speeds up just like it always does around him.

He mouths the words, *you're beautiful*, and I bite down on my bottom lip to keep from lunging into his arms.

Gus turns off the comedy routine and focuses on the reason we're here.

"These two amazing humans fell in love right in front of our eyes. They pretended they were in love in the beginning. Then they fell madly in love. Then they tried to pretend they weren't in love when we all knew they were." More laughter from everyone.

"They finally admitted to themselves that they were in love, and by then we were all exhausted, and then they surprised us all and said they were getting hitched. *In two weeks!* Does it get any better than that? It's the dream, right? Finding that special someone that loves you for everything you are. These two right here have the kind of love that you can't fake. It's the real deal, and I'm honored to witness this amazing union."

Our wedding is the perfect mix of charming and comfortable and warm all at the same time.

This is us.

This is the life I never knew I could have.

Gus goes through the traditional wedding rituals and we both say our vows. We've written our own vows that we have agreed to read to one another tonight after the wedding. Some things are meant to be private, and my deep feelings for this man that I want to spend my life with mean something to me. And they mean something to him.

"And now, for the highlight of the evening. I'd like to invite the ever dapper Louie François over to present the rings." Gus holds his hand out to my mother, and I watch her swipe at her cheeks.

Vivienne Dubois does not cry.

She did not shed a tear at Juliette's wedding.

Could she have allergies?

She meets my gaze as she sets Louie down on the ground and I realize in that moment that my mother *is* crying. She smiles and mouths the words, *I love you,* and I nearly lose it.

I'm overcome with emotion by all of it. The way my groom looks at me like I hung the moon. The way my father has come back into my life just when I needed him most. Even the way my sister shows no emotion, but I know deep down she cares because she's here. I glance around at the Taylors and my heart is so full I think it might explode. This new family of mine has helped me find my way here. Jesse blows me a kiss, Spence winks at me, Melanie and Garrett are huddled together and she's crying as she watches us and he keeps blinking, which tells me he's trying his best not to fall apart. Mya, Emma, and Penelope have tears streaming down their faces and they wave at me.

Gus snaps his fingers together. "Cosi, work with me. I'm trying to make this godda--"

"GD!" Penelope shouts from the audience.

"This GD, big-toothed, well-dressed, four-legged, ring bearer, stay put to give Caden the rings."

My head falls back in laughter and Caden leans down and takes off the little velvet bag that's tied to his collar. Louie runs over to Gus and proceeds to jump up on two legs and wrap his body around his calf, and as if he's making mad love to Raffi, he starts gyrating against my new brother-in-law.

The laughter rings out all around us as Gus tries to shake his leg, but Louie's not having it.

"I'm a lover, little buddy, but you're definitely not my type."

Caden's laughing as he takes my hand and slides the ring on my finger.

"You're mine forever, lover," he whispers against my ear, and I reach for the other ring.

I slide the ring onto his finger. "And you're mine forever."

"I now pronounce you husband and wife. Let's get on our feet and make some noise for the new Mr. and Mrs. Taylor," Gus shouts, and everyone is hooting and hollering around us.

Even my mother is joining in the cheering and my dad looks at her and shakes his head at me before joining right in.

We have danced the night away. And laughed our heads off. For as proper as Maman is, she sure does love to dance. But I've never seen her let loose the way she does tonight.

When she starts dirty dancing with my dad, it is a shock to us all. Turns out a few drinks and a party with the Taylors is what it takes to get the girl to loosen up.

I know I've loosened up a lot since I let Caden into my life. My whole body feels free, my mind too … true happiness and love are the cure.

I put my arms around him and get as close as I can get, burrowing my face into his neck. I can feel his chin lift with his smile and love the sound of him laughing too.

"You've made me the happiest girl in the world, Caden," I tell him. "And look, you've even won over my sister."

We look over and Juliette is dancing like Elaine from

Seinfeld. We both lose it again then and he kisses me mid-laugh.

"I love you with all my heart, Mrs. Cosette Taylor."

I will never get tired of hearing him say that.

"Forever," I whisper back. "I love you."

AFTERWORD

Thank you for reading Another Motherfaker, book 3 in The G.D. Taylors Series. We hope you enjoyed your journey with Caden and Cosette! Please consider leaving a review on Amazon/Goodreads!! They help authors SO MUCH!!

Would you like to read Caden and Cosette's vows? Click here to sign up for our newsletter and to download the bonus scene:

https://bookhip.com/PPCCJNV

Do you want to know what happens next with Gus and Susannah in Book 4, Don't Cry Over Spilled MILF...

Pre-Order Here: http://mybook.to/DCOSM

Bloggers: Sign up here to continue reading the series!
https://forms.gle/6PXf9DTcvJE7J5vs6

Other books by Willow Aster & Laura Pavlov
The G.D. Taylors Series
Add to your Goodreads TBR:

Wanted Wed or Alive: https://bit.ly/3jTsCtM
The Bold and the Bullheaded: https://bit.ly/3vS1UqC
Another Motherfaker: https://bit.ly/3dHcfyS
Don't Cry Over Spilled MILF: http://bit.ly/3sbakHv
Friends with Benefactors: https://bit.ly/3bw53mC

ACKNOWLEDGMENTS

Thank you to everyone who has been part of this G.D. Taylor experience!

Every reader and blogger, thank you so much for taking the time to read this series! If you've left a review, thank you EXTRA!

Sue Grimshaw, Christine Estevez, Jena Brignola, and Give Me Books, we're so grateful for the time you've put toward making our books better and for making our writing life go more smoothly. THANK YOU!

Thank you to our author friends who are so kind and generous with passing on the book love.

And thank you to our family and friends who love us even when we're distracted. We love you!

OTHER BOOKS BY WILLOW ASTER

Standalones
  True Love Story
  Fade to Red
  In the Fields
  Maybe Maby
  Lilith

The La Jolla Series
  5,331 Miles
  Miles Ahead

Kingdoms of Sin Series
  Downfall
  Exposed
  Ruin
  Pride

The End of Men Series with Tarryn Fisher:
  Folsom
  Jackal

JOIN MY MASTER LIST…
  https://bit.ly/396CFqT

FOLLOW ME…
  Website: https://bit.ly/3faYdWY.

Newsletter: https://bit.ly/31geVvW
Facebook: https://bit.ly/3tSAxLs
Twitter: https://bit.ly/3fc0QI3
Instagram: https://bit.ly/39dJtTx
Bookbub: https://bit.ly/3sjRHkG
Amazon: http://amzn.to/2AJu5uo
Goodreads: https://bit.ly/31dNQcT
Join the Asters group: https://bit.ly/3cjg4ZW

OTHER BOOKS BY LAURA PAVLOV

KEEP UP ON NEW RELEASES...
Linktree: https://bit.ly/2L4M2ON

FOLLOW ME...
Website: https://bit.ly/3hoxrIL
Newsletter: http://bit.ly/2M3MzRv
Goodreads: https://bit.ly/3g4jroa
Instagram: https://bit.ly/2TKf5Zs
Facebook: https://bit.ly/3kVyWjk
Join Pav-Loves Readers: https://bit.ly/2XAK9vF
Amazon: https://amzn.to/2NSnGcK
BookBub: https://bit.ly/3ii8Vdp

Made in the USA
Coppell, TX
22 October 2022